# HUNTED

## *DS Hunter Kerr Thrillers*
## *Book Six*

# Michael Fowler

SAPERE
BOOKS

# HUNTED

Published by Sapere Books.

20 Windermere Drive, Leeds, England, LS17 7UZ,
United Kingdom

**saperebooks.com**

ISBN: 978-1-80055-115-2

# ACKNOWLEDGEMENTS

I would like to express my gratitude to all those who have given their time to help me complete this book, especially to Sark Island Cop 'Budgie' Burgess, who gave me great insight into the policing of the island, how its Parliament works, and for his tour of the Emergency Services HQ. The joint working practices of the Police, Fire and Ambulance services are something the UK Government should be looking to.

I also thank beta-readers Claire Knight and my wife Liz for their experienced sharp-eyed comments.

Finally, thanks to everyone at Sapere Books. What a great bunch of guys.

# CHAPTER ONE

On Glasgow's Castle Street, rain fell in sheets, making driving conditions slow and precarious. The driver of the black cab crawling in nose-to-tail traffic was extremely nervous. It wasn't the weather or the slow-moving traffic making him anxious. Seated in the back of his cab was a serial-killer, Billy Wallace, clamped between two prison guards. His left eye was badly swollen, and he had a nasty gash above it that had been temporarily Steri-Stripped. Dried blood streaked most of the left side of his face, making it look a lot worse than it was, though the prison nurse had determined he needed an X-ray because it was a head injury, hence this morning's journey across the city to the hospital.

As the taxi crept towards the rear entrance of Glasgow Royal Infirmary, the driver released a heavy but grateful sigh. He couldn't wait to offload his passengers. The fifteen-minute drive here had felt like an eternity. He pulled up sharply in the yellow hatched area, directly outside the automatic double-doors, quickly releasing the rear passenger door to let out one of the guards.

The courtyard was one huge puddle and as the prison officer jumped out, his boots sploshed down into two inches of standing water, forcing a curse from his tightened lips. In a fit of temper, he reached in, grabbed the sleeve of Billy's sweat top and pulled him out of the warm cab to join him in the cold and damp.

As the second guard paid and waited for his receipt, Billy Wallace straightened his back, lifting his face to the sky. It had been eighteen months since he had last experienced the rain, and it felt good. Billy lowered his head and held out his cuffed hands. "These cuffs are too tight, boss. Can't you slacken them?" he asked.

"Another hour and you'll be back in your nice warm cell, and they'll be off, Billy," replied the burly prison officer, tightening his hold and guiding him towards the automatic doors.

As the doors swished open, the sudden squeal of tyres grabbed their attention, and they snapped their heads back in the direction of the gated entrance. Speeding through the gatehouse towards them was a black Range Rover, its engine screaming. It skidded sideways to a halt yards away, throwing up a wall of water and soaking them. Before the prison guards had any time to react, the back doors flew open and two men in ski-masks jumped out. They were dressed in black fatigues and sweatshirts, and both were pointing guns directly at the heads of the two officers. Within a split-second, the armed men were in the guards' faces. One of them drew back his gun and side-swiped the guard holding Billy across the face. He instantly released his grip and slumped to the floor, letting out a cry as his head smacked the wet concrete.

The masked man immediately switched his attention to the other guard, jamming the barrel into his forehead. "Keys, now," he growled in a broad Glaswegian accent.

The sight of the two men in ski masks was menacing enough, but the burning hatred in the eyes of the one pressing the gun momentarily froze the standing prison officer.

"I said fucking keys, now. I won't say it again," the masked man yelled.

This jolted the guard out of his hypnotic state and he grabbed at the long chain fastened to his belt, fumbling out his bunch of keys from a pocket. He offered them up, his hand shaking.

The masked man lowered his gun and prodded the guard in his chest. "Unlock the cuffs," he said, flicking his head at Billy.

Billy Wallace thrust his hands forward.

After a couple of seconds of nervous juggling, the officer inserted one of the keys into Billy's handcuffs and released them. They fell to the floor with a metallic splash.

Billy and his two accomplices exchanged quick glances, upon which the one threatening the guard lunged forward, whipping the prison officer across the face with the gun's butt and dumping him on the ground to join his unconscious colleague.

Free from his shackles, Billy spurred into action. He sprinted around the front of the Range Rover and threw himself into the passenger seat. The two masked men leapt into the back. Seconds later, the car was fish-tailing its way back out through the gates, tearing away from Glasgow city centre.

# CHAPTER TWO

A large throng of mourners had gathered outside Barnwell Crematorium for the funeral of Barry Newstead. Many were talking, but in hushed voices. Hunter Kerr was among them, waiting to pay his respects and say his final goodbye, and he allowed his gaze to drift among the gathering. He knew the vast majority, either by name or sight. Many of them had been his colleagues as well as Barry's. He noticed that some had put on a few pounds since he'd last seen them, and for some the years hadn't been kind. He knew it was this job that had been responsible for that. It aged many. He had seen a statistic somewhere that many cops didn't get to see beyond five years after they had retired. Barry hadn't even seen that. Though his death hadn't been natural; Barry had been murdered two weeks ago, and his killer was currently in prison awaiting trial.

Hunter felt his chest tighten as images of that night once again visited him. The sight of Barry being tossed into the air by the speeding car — deliberately mown down — and then immediately after, when Hunter had dashed to his aid and seen his crumpled form, knowing he was dying, had re-run itself inside his head perpetually. The doctor at the hospital had told him that there had been nothing anyone could have done for him — he had been too badly injured. A well-meaning sympathetic gesture, no doubt, but it hadn't been any consolation. That night, he had not only lost a close colleague but a good friend as well.

Taking a deep breath, Hunter held it for several seconds and then released it slowly, pulling back his composure while continuing to scan the line. The sadness was palpable. Many of them met Hunter's gaze and exchanged a sorrowful nod of recognition before dragging away their eyes. Hunter hated funerals at the best of times, but police funerals he always found sadder than most. A series of murmurs grabbed his attention, and he followed turned heads to see the funeral cortege coming towards them. It was led by four mounted officers in full regalia. Hunter felt his chest lurch and he fought to suppress a sob. He caught the same look in a couple of faces nearby — people he knew, hardened by experience, who normally wouldn't bat an eyelid at the thought of death, had watering eyes. He dropped his look to the ground. He was finding it difficult to hold himself together, and he took a series of breaths and watched the shadow of the procession pass across him.

The shuffling of feet forced Hunter to raise his head — a signal the mourners were starting to head into the chapel. Into the corner of his eye ambled his working partner, Grace Marshall. He turned and exchanged a pained smile with her.

It was a good gathering. Hunter managed to find standing space against the back wall with Grace and several others. Those following behind were shown into a side room where a large screen had been set up to allow them to follow the service. Hunter wasn't surprised by the crowd. Barry's reputation had gone before him. *Now it's over.* Sure, he would be talked about for a while, and the coverage of the forthcoming trial for his murder would be a reminder of what had happened, but then the memory of him would be forgotten by many — until the next police funeral.

'Over the Rainbow', the version sung by Eva Cassidy, struck up and the congregation took their seats. Hunter again found himself fighting back his sorrow as the song washed through his thoughts. He distracted himself by searching the aisles. To his right he spotted his boss, Detective Superintendent Dawn Leggate. She, like Grace, looked elegant. Her auburn hair was arranged in a chignon, and she was wearing an expensive-looking black coat with a velvet collar. Her sombre gaze was glued to Barry's casket. Hunter wasn't surprised. It had been her ex-husband who had killed Barry, though he hadn't been the intended target. She had. It had been Hunter who had first heard and seen the speeding car coming towards them as they had exited the pub that night, and he had managed to throw himself out of its path and shout a warning. Barry had been the one who had reacted the fastest, leaping at Dawn, bundling her to safety. But in doing so, he had taken the full impact and it had ended his life. That act of courage had been his swan-song. Hunter knew from brief conversation with Dawn since that she still bore the brunt of the guilt for what had happened a fortnight ago, even though she wasn't to blame.

Sudden movement at the periphery of Hunter's vision made him refocus his gaze, and he caught sight of a dark suited man with iron-grey hair taking to the pulpit.

It was a Celebration of Life Service, the first that Hunter had been to. The Celebrant delivered Barry's life story in such upbeat fashion and with such humour that it was as if he was regaling Barry's living years in a pub environment. Everyone laughed at the anecdotes — even Hunter, who had heard them many times before — and everyone shed a tear at his passing. As the Celebrant said goodbye to Barry, and Frank Sinatra started singing 'My Way', the pain of grief detonated through Hunter and he started to weep.

# CHAPTER THREE

In his car Hunter slackened his tie and undid the top button of his shirt collar, tugging it away from his neck. His airway was constricted and the invisible band around his chest still felt tight. He had dealt with a lot of death over the years, even personally, with the loss of his first girlfriend who had been murdered, but none had affected him like this. He took a deep breath and turned on the engine, his concentration diverted by Grace adjusting the passenger seat to her required position. Then he watched her pulling down the visor to check her image in its mirror.

Running her fingers through her dark curls, she appeared pleased with what she saw and pushed the visor back into place. "Good to go?" she said, fastening her seatbelt.

"Not really." Hunter took another deep breath. "To be honest, Grace, I'm not really feeling up to this one bit. If it had been for any person other than Barry, I would've made an excuse not to go to his wake."

Grace reached across and gently clasped his wrist. "I understand what you're saying, but people will expect you to be there. Everyone knows how close you two were. You were his buddy as well as his sergeant."

Hunter sighed. "That's what's especially hard. It was bad enough back in the chapel. Now I'm going to have to go through it all again."

"Barry would want you to be there." Grace gave his wrist a squeeze. "I know this is hurting, but you need to make an appearance. There'll be enough people around for cover if you want to disappear early."

Hunter nodded. "I've already thought of that. If you don't mind, I'm going to show my face, have a shandy and a bit of food, and then leave. Are you okay with that?"

She let go of his wrist. "That's fine by me. I've got to finish off sorting out my desk anyway."

"Yeah, me too." Two months ago, the Force had opened its new multi-million-pound training centre on a nearby industrial estate, and the state-of-the-art building was now going to house Barnwell's Major Incident Team. Five weeks ago, Hunter had been given responsibility for overseeing the move to the new incident room, but that had been postponed because of the last investigation. That had been recently wrapped up, and yesterday afternoon Detective Superintendent Leggate had called Hunter into her office and, apologising because of the circumstances, she had told him that she had just taken a call from the Assistant Chief Constable (Crime), who had insisted that she make the move to the new facility happen as soon as possible. Hunter had seen the anxiety in her face as she had told him and had felt for her. He had wanted to take a snipe at the ACC but refrained, because he knew the reality was that in spite of the tragic death of a colleague, the job had to move on. Biting his tongue, he had left Dawn's office reassuring her he would make a start on it once Barry's funeral was over. And although he hadn't meant that it would be immediately *today*, he had already decided that morning that throwing himself into the move would be a timely distraction from the sadness of the day.

Barry's wake was being held in the centuries-old George and Dragon pub in the quaint village of Wentworth. It had been his favourite watering-hole; Hunter had spent many a happy hour with him there over the years, laughing and joking at things that had gone on at work, listening to his anecdotes, discussing cases, and, most importantly, counselling one another, like cops did over a beer after a shit day. Ironically and sadly, it had been in the rear car park of this pub where Barry had met his demise. Yet in spite of that, Sue, his partner, had determined it should be the venue for Barry's final farewell because she knew he would have wanted that.

The car park was full by the time Hunter and Grace got there. Hunter saw the last available place being taken as he finished his circuit, but he recognised the car pulling into the slot. It belonged to Tony Bullars. He was driving and Mike Sampson was his passenger. Both detectives were part of his syndicate.

Hunter pulled in tightly behind and double-parked, jumping out to greet them. "I'm not staying long, guys. I'm only having one and then I'm going. I've got to go back to the office to move my stuff to the new place."

"We're not staying long ourselves, so we'll follow you out," Tony replied, fob-locking his car.

As the four of them made their way to the side door, Hunter felt his chest tightening again. It was right *here* where Barry had been killed.

As if sensing his anxiety, Grace slipped an arm through his and said, "Let me buy my favourite Sergeant a drink."

Her light-hearted gesture was instantly soothing, and Hunter opened the door for them all.

They entered the small snug. The place was heaving — customers were spilling out into a corridor. It looked as if everyone who had been to the crematorium was here.

"We've no chance of getting a drink here," Hunter said, looking at the swamped bar. "Come on, let's go through to the main bar."

They had to squeeze their way past the drinkers, nodding to a few as they pressed forward. Finally pushing their way through into the front bar, Hunter saw it was just as busy as the snug. People waiting to be served were at least four deep, and the few staff behind the bar seemed overwhelmed. Over the sea of recognisable heads, Hunter spotted Sue Siddons at the far end where the buffet was, a glass of wine in her hand. She was huddled between two larger-than-life retired detectives Hunter knew, whose jaws were going ten-to-the-dozen. He guessed they would be spewing out their exploits from their working days with Barry, and although Sue's face wore an interested expression, he somehow knew it was false.

Hunter nudged Grace. "It looks as if Sue needs rescuing. Get me a Bitter Shandy, will you, and then come and join us?" He weaved his way between those waiting to be served and stepped up to where Sue was. The two retired detectives were still jabbering away, but it was more between themselves than with Sue. He stepped into the middle, separating the guys from her. Following a quick 'Hello' and 'long time, no see,' Hunter said, "Do you mind if I have a brief word with Sue, guys?"

His request did the trick, and the two pensioners offered their condolences, said their goodbyes, and sidled away, picking up their conversation before melding into the throng.

Hunter met Sue's red-rimmed eyes. "They're lovely guys, but I'm guessing it's not what you want right now? Am I right?"

Sue nodded. "You're right, they are lovely, and I know they're only trying to make me feel better, but all I want to do is hide away in a corner and drown my sorrows. I'm not in the mood to chat with anyone at the moment. Maybe in a few weeks I'll feel different." She stroked his arm. "Present company excluded, of course." Pulling away her hand, she took a slurp of her wine.

Hunter gazed down at her, recalling the first time he had clapped eyes on Sue. It was a little over eighteen months ago, during the 'Demon' investigation. A body had been discovered on the old Manvers Colliery site, and Sue had contacted Barry and told him that she believed it was her fifteen-year-old daughter, Carol, who had gone missing in 1993. Barry had been retired from the job then, but he had contacted Hunter and requested that Hunter go and see her. He had explained to Hunter that he had investigated Carol Siddons' disappearance back then, but because she had been a difficult child in care, at the time of her going missing, no one among the hierarchy had taken her disappearance seriously and he had been pulled off the enquiry. Carol was still on the missing list when Hunter and Grace had followed up Barry's request.

The moment Sue had opened the door to them, Hunter could remember thinking that she was the most youthful fifty-year-old woman he had ever seen: barely five-foot tall and petite, with short blonde hair. He couldn't help but notice that except for a few laughter lines around her eyes, she hardly had a blemish to her complexion. And, as he looked at her now, almost two years since that visit, she still didn't appear to have aged, despite what she had gone through: after talking with her, it had sadly transpired that the body they had found was that of her daughter Carol. It was also during this stage of the investigation that Barry had dropped his bombshell: Carol had also been *his* daughter. He revealed to Hunter that he'd had a fling with Sue during his early days as a detective, and because he'd been married they had kept it their secret.

"Why does it happen to me? I finally get the man of my dreams and then he's gone," Sue said, taking another sip of her wine.

Unsure how to respond, Hunter shrugged his shoulders and offered a wan smile. He knew what she was alluding to; the fling — as Barry had put it — had happened after she had been hospitalised, following a brutal beating by her boyfriend. Barry had dealt with the case, and following that meeting they had engaged in their brief liaison that had brought about Carol. Although Barry had taken responsibility for Carol, because he was married, he had secretly dipped in and out of Sue and Carol's life. When the 'Demon' case had come along, Barry had been retired almost three years and he was no longer married — he had lost his wife to a stroke. That phone call from Sue had been the catalyst for them rekindling their relationship. They had only just started living together when this tragedy occurred.

"He thought the world of you, Hunter," she said, lowering her glass. "He told me on numerous occasions how you'd saved his arse a few times."

Hunter met Sue's eyes, studying her features. After Barry had disclosed that he was the father of a victim of the 'Dearne Valley Demon', he had sworn him to secrecy. It had caused Hunter much angst at the time, but fortunately it had never been necessary to reveal the secret during that enquiry. Since it had ended, he had told no one. He had not even divulged to Sue what he knew about Carol, and as he tried to read the look she was giving him, he wondered if Barry had ever revealed to her that he had told him. Pulling back his gaze, he decided now wasn't the time to check it out. As far as he was concerned, Barry had taken it to his grave.

Issuing a weak smile, Hunter responded, "He was a nightmare at times, especially where authority was concerned, but he was such a massive help to me in my early years, it was the least I could do."

Sue let out a little laugh. "A nightmare is an understatement; he could be a damn pain in the backside sometimes, but I'll certainly miss him." She fell silent for a moment, locking eyes with him. She added, "I'm so glad you were with him when he died."

Hunter saw her eyes well up, raising a lump in his throat. Before he had time to respond, Grace joined them, pushing a pint of bitter shandy into his hand. Inwardly he heaved a sigh of relief. Grace's timing couldn't have been better; his eyes had been about to water, and he turned his head sharply to blink away the film of tears.

"God, that was a trawl. Don't you dare ask me to go to the bar again, Hunter Kerr." Grace also had a glass of wine for Sue. "I thought you might need another," she said, handing it over.

Sue took the glass, finished the drink she had and set down the empty glass on one of the buffet tables. "You must have heard me tell Hunter that all I wanted to do is drown my sorrows."

"If that's what you feel the need to do, Sue, you do it," Grace replied, taking a sip of Chardonnay. "If I hadn't got to go back into work, I'd join you."

Hunter took the top off his shandy. He said, "It was a lovely service, Sue."

She removed the wine glass from her lips. "Wasn't it just? Barry would have loved it if he'd have been there." For a moment, they locked eyes. Then, simultaneously, they all let out a laugh.

# CHAPTER FOUR

Hunter stood before his new desk, admiring it. It had a curved extension with side panels, and he had his own desktop computer, which meant no more sharing. Grace's desk abutted his. All the desks in the MIT Suite had been arranged in twos so that detectives could sit opposite their partners. The room was huge in comparison to the one they were vacating, and bright, with high-glow lighting and cream coloured, freshly painted walls. Lots of boards filled wall space — he and Grace had one to share — and these were currently void of notices and newspaper cuttings. Hunter knew that wouldn't last. The next incident would change all that.

He dumped the large box on his desk, pushing it alongside the other two he'd brought from the old office. In them was everything he had collected from his eighteen years of police work. Looking at their contents, he knew it was going to take at least an hour to sort his workspace. He had already decided, as he had packed the boxes, that some of it was no longer needed, but he just wanted to double-check some of the files' contents before disposal.

The first thing Hunter took out was the framed photo of Beth sandwiched between Jonathan and Daniel. He had taken the family pose on holiday in Minorca two years ago. As he set it beside his computer screen, he couldn't help but notice how out of date it was. The boys, especially, had changed — Jonathan in particular; he was still skinny, but this last year he had rocketed in height and he was starting to grow his hair long. Lining it straight, he vowed to update the frame with a more recent snap over the next few days. The next thing he took out was his football mug. Hunter took some stick for supporting Sheffield United, especially from Tony Bullars, who was a rival Sheffield Wednesday supporter. He had just set it next to his bundle of pens when his phone rang. It took him by surprise, because he hadn't given out his new number to anyone yet. In fact, he didn't know it himself. He answered. He instantly recognised the soft yet firm Scottish voice of his boss Superintendent Dawn Leggate. She told him that she was in her office along the corridor and she wanted to see him.

Hunter left the room and walked the thirty metres to where her new office was. The entire frontage was floor-to-ceiling frosted glass. He could just make out her silhouette sitting behind her desk as he approached. He rapped on the glass door and she called him in. Like the new MIT Suite, her room was bright and airy and smelt of fresh paint. To the right, one wall had light oak bookcases and cupboards, and there was a round table with four chairs. The long desk was of the same honey-coloured wood as in the MIT Suite.

"Afternoon, boss," said Hunter.

"Good afternoon, Hunter."

He saw Dawn's hair was still up in a chignon, and she hadn't changed out of the fitted black dress she'd worn at Barry's service.

"How did the wake go?" she asked.

"So, so, boss. To be honest, I wasn't in the mood. I had a shandy and dipped out of it. I had a quick word with Sue, but what do you say to her? I'll go and see her in a couple of weeks."

"That's one of the reasons I didn't go. It wasn't that I was being disrespectful."

"You shouldn't feel guilty, boss. It wasn't your fault what happened."

She held up a hand. "Nevertheless, I do. Maybe when Jack gets his just desserts in court, I can move on." She was silent for a moment, then she said, "Anyway, it's not that I want to talk to you about, it's this." She beckoned him forward, turning her computer screen as far as it would go.

Hunter couldn't see the screen from where he was standing and so slipped around the side of her desk to get a better view. Filling the screen was the front page of the digital version of *The Daily Record* — Scotland's main newspaper.

Dawn said, "My ex-DS sent me this ten minutes ago."

Hunter knew she was alluding to Detective Sergeant John Reed, a former colleague she'd worked with in Stirling CID. He had met him just over a year ago during a joint investigation, hunting two dangerous thugs who had murdered three former detectives up in Scotland. Hunter felt his stomach knot. It had been that case that had rocked his world. He had discovered things about his dad during that enquiry that he had found difficult to believe. In fact, he was still coming to terms with the things he had learned about his father's past; their relationship still hadn't returned to what it had been.

Hunter shook himself out of his reverie and focused on the screen. The headlines caused him to catch his breath. As his eyes leapt to the paragraph below, his heart accelerated. By the time his gaze had drifted to the photograph beside the article, it was pummelling his chest.

# CHAPTER FIVE

Hunter held his breath for a few seconds before slowly letting it go. He read the article again, this time at a steadier pace.

## MANHUNT UNDERWAY FOR ESCAPED GANGLAND KILLER

*This morning, police in Glasgow are searching for serial-killer Billy Wallace who was sprung from custody by two armed men after they attacked the prison officers escorting him.*

*The two masked men sped away from the scene in a black Range Rover after both the prison guards were knocked unconscious. Police have confirmed that Wallace was being escorted to Glasgow Royal Infirmary for treatment of a head injury following an assault by a fellow inmate. The public have been warned not to approach Wallace, who is described as extremely dangerous. Billy 'Braveheart' Wallace, 59, was serving a whole life sentence at Barlinnie prison for the murder of five people and the attempted murder of another committed eighteen months ago.*

Hunter felt his heart lurch. He had seen the Scenes of Crimes photographs of Billy's handiwork. They were horrendous. His victims had been tortured before being killed. His father could have been one of them had it not been for extreme luck and his dad's boxing skills. Without warning — not for the first time — the spectre of that event eighteen months ago leapt inside his head. Hunter had raced to his father's gym following his dad's frantic phone call alerting him that Billy had turned up armed with a knife. He had got there just as the fight was finishing and been faced with his dad throttling the very life out of Billy. It had been he who had dragged his father off and saved Billy from certain death, though that never came out in court. Instead, Billy had been charged with attempted murder, because it had been he who had attacked his father, wounding him. Hunter took another deep breath and finished the article:

*Wallace was the son of Glasgow Gangland Boss, Gordon Wallace, who ran a black-market, protection and drug empire across the city during the 1950s, 60s and 70s, and Billy, who was known for his psychopathic tendencies, took a leading role in the family's criminal empire. In 1971, he shot dead a young woman and her 5-year-old daughter over a drug debt and was sentenced to life, together with an accomplice.*

*Following his release in 2008, he embarked upon a campaign of revenge against those who brought about that conviction; three retired detectives, the wife of one of them, and a police informer met a horrible death at Billy's hands. A former gang member, who gave evidence against him at his trial, was injured in a knife attack before he was finally captured. In court, the judge described Billy Wallace as 'a danger to the public who should never be released.' Wallace is described as 6'4" tall, of broad build with dark greying hair, grey eyes and a noticeable 6" scar to the left side of his face.*

The article ended with a request for information as to his whereabouts and a telephone number. Hunter's eyes drifted across to the photograph of Billy Wallace. It was the one taken after his arrest, the ugly healing knife wound snaking across the bridge of his nose onto the left side of his craggy face, enhancing the menacing look he gave.

Hunter lifted his gaze from the screen and locked eyes with his boss. The knot forming in his stomach was tightening. "Jesus," he said.

"Jesus exactly," Dawn replied, twisting the screen back to face her.

"That was yesterday?" he asked, pointing at the monitor.

She nodded. "He was supposedly found unconscious in his cell during morning unlocking. He had a nasty gash above his eye, and it looked as though he'd been in a fight. He was being taken to hospital in a taxi, and had just got there when this Range Rover with armed men appeared and sprang him."

"A taxi!" Hunter interjected.

Dawn threw up a hand. "I know! I've not long had this same conversation with John. You wouldn't believe it, would you? A dangerous criminal like Billy Wallace and they arrange for him to go to hospital in a bloody taxi. Standard practice now, I understand. What is this world coming to?"

Hunter shook his head in disbelief. He said, "But the guards were attacked before they got into hospital?"

She gave a brief nod. "It looks like a well-planned operation. John tells me they've found footage of the Range Rover used in the attack parked up in the hospital's main car park a good half hour before Billy arrived. They must have also had someone inside the hospital keeping watch, because the moment he arrived at the rear entrance the Range Rover set off. It was all over and done with in a little under two minutes. An enquiry has already started, but that's too bloody late now. Billy Wallace is free, and given that it was two armed men who freed him, he's more than likely armed himself now."

Hunter pulled up a seat, placed it in front of Dawn's desk and dropped down onto it. "Any clues who's behind it and where he might be?"

She shook her head. "As you know, Billy had lots of criminal connections. Many of them were old, like him, but nevertheless they had the links to make this happen, and these days it wouldn't need that much cash. So far, I'm told, they have no idea who is behind it. The men who freed him were wearing ski masks. The CCTV footage of the hospital car park just shows the vehicle parked up, not who was in it. And the Range Rover was found burnt out on wasteland just outside Glasgow less than an hour after his escape. They're trawling CCTV along the route the vehicle took to see if they can get any glimpses of who was driving, but there's nothing yet. They've also tried speaking to the prisoner who supposedly assaulted Billy, but he's refusing to talk." She paused, holding his gaze. "Guess who it is?"

Hunter pursed his lips, throwing her a questioning look.

"Rab Geddes!"

Hunter's mouth dropped open. "Rab Geddes!"

"I thought that'd be your reaction."

"Rab attacked Billy!" Hunter shook his head. "I don't believe that for one minute. Rab's been Billy's right-hand man since they were teenagers. He was with him when they shot that woman and her kid back in the seventies, and also when they tortured and killed those retired detectives and attacked my dad eighteen months ago." Setting his mouth tight, he studied Dawn's face a moment before saying, "There's more to this, isn't there?"

She nodded. "Pair of them set this up without doubt. John says he's spoken to the Prison Governor on the phone, and he's told him that a few weeks ago there was a falling out between the pair that came to blows, and there's been a couple of incidents recently where there's been violent outbursts between them. It's been recorded that Billy accused Rab of selling him out at the trial. We can now guess that was all staged for yesterday's big performance. I've asked John if he can fix up a visit to speak with Rab as a matter of urgency, but

I don't hold up much hope of us getting anything out of him. Like Billy he's on a whole-life-term, so he's nothing to gain."

"Bloody hell!"

"There's a full search going on up in Glasgow, but if his escape is anything to go by, I'm guessing he'll be holed up in a pretty good hiding place right now."

For a few seconds Hunter sat looking at his Detective Superintendent, studying her closely. Then he said, "Does my dad know about this?"

"No. I only got this twenty minutes ago. John's told me it's only just hit the news up there, but given what happened to your dad eighteen months ago and the publicity it got, I'm guessing it won't be long before it's on the local news. And, although the press don't know the exact full story about your dad's involvement in Billy's past because of his identity change, I'm sure the least they'll do is make the connection to the attack on him. Sooner or later I'm guessing there'll be questions from the media, and I want to not only protect you and your family from that intrusion but the Force as well. I also need to think about the immediate safety of your family, and that's why we're having this conversation."

Hunter let out a heavy sigh. "Wow!"

"Wow indeed. You know our security measures are pretty inadequate for this kind of thing, Hunter. Especially given how dangerous Billy Wallace is. Sure, we can put in CCTV and fit a personal alarm, but it won't stop Billy breaking into your parents' home. I could probably budget for someone to stand outside their house for a couple of days, but that's all, and I certainly couldn't afford for someone to be at his gym as well. Sadly, I'm afraid this comes down to pounds and pence. We need to come up with a plan that I can afford and which is going to protect your family until Billy Wallace is re-captured. I say we, because I want to include you in this."

Hunter eased back in his seat. Suddenly, it felt as if a great weight was pushing down on him. His chest tightened. "Christ, boss, I can't believe this is happening."

"Neither can I, Hunter. But it is, and I need to put something in place fast. And by fast, I mean in the next few hours. We know Billy knows where your mum and dad live, from when he was down here before he was captured, and it's now over twenty-four hours since his escape. He could even be down here right now for all we know. I've already got a patrol going over to their place. The ideal scenario is that they leave as soon as and stay somewhere else for now."

"You mean like come and stay with us?"

Dawn pursed her lips. "To be honest, Hunter, I don't even think that's a good idea. We can't be certain he doesn't know where you live as well. We don't know what he's been up to while he's been inside. He's obviously planned his escape well, so we can't take any chances."

Hunter thought for a moment. "There's Beth's parents', but they live on Sark, and I know for sure their house isn't big enough for all of us. In fact, it'll probably not even take me, Beth, and the boys, never mind Mum and Dad. It's only a two-bedroom cottage."

"Okay, Hunter, until I can get a handle on what's happening up in Scotland, I'm going to have to make some decisions you're not going to like. Firstly, I'm going to arrange for you all to go to a hotel. I know this is going to be a real disruption for you, and if there was any way around this, believe me, I would take it, but right now I have no room for manoeuvre. So, I need you to put in a phone call to your mum and dad and tell them what's happening and get them to pack a bag for a couple of days. Then go home and speak with Beth. I'm going to arrange for someone to help your parents while you sort things out with her. In the meantime, I'm going to have security measures put in both your homes and sort out a hotel for you all." Dawn Leggate took a deep breath. "I'm sorry about this, Hunter, but I don't want to be the person held responsible for anything happening to your family. Billy Wallace has already tried to kill your dad once and failed. I want to keep it at that."

# CHAPTER SIX

At the Doncaster Car-Hire place, Billy Wallace took back his forged driving licence, scribbled an indecipherable signature on the hire agreement form and then handed over £180 in twenties to the pretty sales assistant in exchange for a set of keys. The car he had hired was a Vauxhall Astra: nothing too ostentatious and something which would easily merge with traffic.

Following the young lady sashaying across the forecourt to where his car was waiting, Billy fought to hide the lustful stare breaking out across his face; as his gaze fell upon the blonde-haired girl's pert bottom, clad in a pair of tight dark blue trousers, he could feel himself starting to get hard, and he patted the bundle of notes in his pocket, knowing he had enough money to be able to afford something like it later. It had been almost eighteen months since he had last felt a woman's body against his.

*First, though*, he told himself as he unlocked the car, *you've got something more pressing.*

It had taken him almost twenty hours to make it to Doncaster. Following his escape, he hadn't stayed long at the flat where they had taken him. Within a matter of hours, he had decided it wasn't a safe place for him to remain. The woman whose place it was was a right mouthy bitch, and as a jumpy as a frog, and he'd only stayed the night, doing what he needed to yesterday morning and then high-tailing it out of there. He'd caught the bus to Edinburgh and then the train to Berwick-upon-Tweed, leaving the station to get a change of clothing and some stuff to change his appearance, before returning back to the station and catching a train to Doncaster. It had left him knackered, and right now, as desperate as he was to catch some much-needed shut-eye, before he got his head down, he needed to check something out before finding a motel.

It was a long, straight street, and although there were a few parked cars, and trees at regular intervals to hide among, he was worried that staying here for any length of time might expose him. Lowering the peak of his baseball cap to hide more of his face, Billy Wallace took out his mobile and pinned it to his ear; anyone passing his parked car would merely think he had pulled over to take a call.

It had taken him a good ten minutes of driving around the estate before he had located what he had been searching for. The last time he had been here was eighteen months ago, and had it not been for the police car parked outside he might never have found the house. He had driven past at first, with his heart racing, but seeing the police car empty had reduced his anxiety and he had driven to the next street, pulling up to think about his next move: he had not done all this planning to be thwarted at this stage. After a moment's deliberation he had the bones of a strategy, and he returned to the street, coasting past the semi to get a closer look. Eyeing the front, he confirmed to himself that this was definitely the right house and let out a chortle: the last time he had been here he had thrown the dead body of a police informant through the lounge window and scared the shit out of his target.

The police car was still unoccupied as he passed. He parked up a hundred metres from his target's house, behind a small car, where he still had a good view. All that had been twenty minutes ago. Now he was watching the uniformed cop loading a large suitcase into the boot of his car, as Jock Kerr — as he now called himself — and his wife appeared at the top of their drive. He saw Jock casually look his way and he instinctively ducked down in his seat. Seconds later, as he lifted his head, the back doors of the police car were closing and the cop was just climbing into the driver's side. Starting the engine of his hired vehicle, Billy watched the marked car drive off. When it had gone thirty yards, he pulled away from the kerb and followed.

# CHAPTER SEVEN

Hunter heaved the second of their cases onto the king-size bed and ran his eyes around the family room they had been given. His initial thought was that the suite wasn't bad for a budget hotel — it looked as though it had been recently refurbished — but at the same time he was hoping their stay here wasn't going to be for too long; no matter how nice or comfortable any hotel is, there is nothing better than being in your own home, he thought.

He rested his roaming eyes on Jonathan and Daniel, who were grappling one another for control of the TV remote, and he was about to tell them to pack it in when Beth piped up, "There're not enough hangers." He turned to see her stood by the fitted wardrobe, its door wide open. Her face was set tight. The look she gave him was one of exasperation. Just one of many similar looks she had thrown his way since he had broken the news. During the last three hours, he had repeatedly apologised for the inconvenience, adding, on several occasions, that "it wouldn't be for long," but it hadn't appeased her. All Beth had returned was, "But why is this affecting us? This is to do with your dad." He had done his best to explain his gaffer's concern about the safety of them all, but from her reign of silence during packing he knew she wasn't impressed.

To add to matters, her enforced absence had not gone down well with her Practice Manager when she had rung him. Even as she had explained to him the circumstances, his only concern had been how they were going to manage her patients.

She had almost slammed the phone down after ending the call, swearing under her breath. Beth very rarely swore.

Hunter knew this was going to need some emergency repair to their relationship once it was over. Meeting her eyes and offering up a placatory smile, he responded, "I'll nip down to reception and ask for more."

"Don't bother. I'll manage," she huffed, pushing the wardrobe door to.

Pulling back his gaze, Hunter unzipped the suitcase. It contained Jonathan and Daniel's clothing, and he lifted out a couple of folded T-shirts.

Beth stomped up to him and nudged him aside. She pulled the T-shirts out of his hand. "Why don't you go and see how your mum and dad are getting on?" She picked out more of their sons' clothes from the suitcase without looking up. "Take the boys with you while I sort these out."

Closing the door, Hunter watched the boys bolt down the corridor to his parents' room. Suddenly, frustration and sorrow overwhelmed him. This was one of the lowest points in his family's life.


Jock sat on the edge of the bed staring at his reflection in the wardrobe mirror, unhappy with what was staring back and trying to remember when everything had changed. He'd once had strong facial features and thick dark hair. Now his face was losing its definition, the flesh starting to drop, and his hair was almost white and thinning back to a widow's peak. *I look old.*

He lifted his head, casting his gaze upon the scar over his right eye, and reached up to touch the jagged leathery mark. Picking up that injury had been the catalyst that had changed his life. It had been caused by a punch thrown after the bell during his sixth professional fight, ruining his career and his ambitions, and it had been the primary cause of the mess he now found himself in. Had it not been for that, he wouldn't have been forced to do door work and get mixed up with villains. More so, he wouldn't have met Billy Wallace, and therefore wouldn't have been with him that fateful night when Billy had murdered a young mum and her five-year-old bairn, shooting them at point-blank range over a drug deal that hadn't been of their causing. Jock had fled the scene as a wanted man, albeit an unwilling accomplice, but it hadn't taken detectives long to track him down, and they had forced him to make a statement against Billy and his criminal accomplice, Rab Geddes, and go into the witness box.

The jury had found Billy and Rab guilty, and the judge had given them life. Following that, Jock had had to leave his birthplace, dragging his wife from their home in the middle of the night to make a new life in Yorkshire. For a long time, they had been strangers in a strange land. It had been especially hard for Fiona, because she had been closer to her family. And then Hunter had been born, and the changes in their lives took on new meaning and a fresh purpose. Jock had used his boxing skills to advantage, setting up his own gym and making a good reputation for himself. He produced some good young fighters, like he had once been.

But then two years ago, all that had changed. Billy Wallace had been released after 36 years behind bars with a score to settle, his focus to exact revenge on the man who had turned Queen's evidence. Billy had eventually tracked Jock down, after torturing and murdering the detectives who had provided him with his new identity, but in a fight to survive he had beaten Billy, returning him to prison for the rest of his life. Or so he thought. Billy's recent escape was now bringing fresh jeopardy, dragging Hunter into Billy's firing line. It was a mess. A mess of his causing. Jock knew it and he felt totally useless.

The sudden opening of the bathroom door made Jock jump, and turning his head he saw Fiona appearing in the doorway with a towel wrapped around her.

"The shower's warm," she said, dragging fingers through her limp, damp hair.

He pushed himself up from the bed, taking one last look in the mirror. Staring back was the face of someone feeling sorry for himself.

After showering, changing into fresh clothes and unpacking, Jock tapped on Hunter and Beth's door and asked if they would like to go out for their evening meal, stating in jocular fashion it was a 'peace proposal'. His offer melted the iciness in Beth's look, easing some of Hunter's tension, and as they drove towards the pub recommended by Beth, he felt his mood lifting.

The place they pulled into was an old stone pub in a small village twenty minutes from the hotel. Once upon a time the building had been the 'family seat' of the local landowner. It had become a pub in the 1950s. Hunter and Beth had been before with the boys, but it was a first for his parents. Hunter parked up round the back, out of sight of the main road, his parents following behind in their car. As he got out and locked up, he paused for a second to check if anyone had followed them. When no car appeared, he chased after his family, heading into the pub.

Approaching the bar, Hunter spotted Black Sheep on draught and ordered a pint. His dad chose the same. Beth and Fiona had a glass of white wine and the boys wanted Coke.

Beth was already warning Daniel not to spill it before his glass had even been poured.

"I'll get these," Jock said, before Hunter could put his hands in his pockets. His dad handed over a £20 note and grabbed a handful of menus. Tucking them under his arm, he collected his change, picked up his beer and they all made their way to a table.

Hunter chose two tables near a window, dragged them together and picked a seat that gave him a view across the car park. Easing himself down, he took a long gulp of his beer, set down his glass, and opened one of the menus. It didn't take him long to select what he wanted — the homemade pie was steak and ale, accompanied with real chips and mushy peas. He put down the menu with a smile, picked his beer back up and, one eye keeping lookout over the car park, settled back to wait for his meal.

# CHAPTER EIGHT

After following Jock and his family to the hotel where they were now holed up, Billy Wallace returned to the street where Jock and his wife lived, drove slowly past the house, and seeing no police guard, pulled up a hundred yards beyond. Listening to the tick of the engine as it cooled, he scoured the street. There were more cars parked than earlier, but all of them appeared empty, and he guessed they belonged to the residents who had returned from work. The only people he saw were a couple with their dog fifty yards ahead, walking away from him.

Opening the car door, Billy eased himself out, once more casting his eyes around. The couple with the dog were just disappearing behind a hedge, turning the corner into the next road. *Good.* He shut the door with his hip, making as little noise as possible, and stayed there for a few seconds, listening. The only sound was a dog barking in the distance, and he thought about the couple who were now out of view. Zipping up, and pulling up the hood of his top, he went to the boot, popped it, reached inside and lifted out a plastic canister of petrol and a couple of rags. In another half an hour, Jock's house would be up in smoke. And this was just the start of what he had planned for him.

Slipping the canister and rags into a carrier bag, he locked the car and set off towards the semi, keeping his head down. As he approached the driveway, he dropped his already slow pace and viewed the house. The first thing he looked for was an alarm. There was none. The blinds to the lounge were half-shut, and upstairs the bedroom curtains were closed, he guessed to make it look like someone was in, though he knew different. He scanned around him again. The street was still quiet. Dipping his head to obscure his face, he strolled down the drive to the side of the house and made his way around to the rear. Stopping by the back door, he gazed around the garden and listened. He was pleased to see that chest-high fencing ran around the entire garden and that several mature trees prevented prying eyes. He couldn't have wished for better.

Setting down the plastic bag, Billy picked up an edging stone from the flower border, took out the largest of the rags from the bag, and placing it over the bottom corner of the kitchen window, he threw the stone. The first blow cracked the double glazing with only the slightest of noise. The second smashed both panels, and after making a quick check that the sound had not brought out the neighbours, Billy dropped the stone and began picking out the largest shards of the broken glass. A minute later, happy with the size of the hole, he lifted the plastic canister out of the bag, pulled up the funnel and began pouring petrol into the house. Jock was going to regret he'd ever spoken out against him.

PC Richard Flynn sat in his patrol car jotting down a few notes, cursing under his breath. For the last half-hour, he had been subjected to the moans of a couple who were complaining that their neighbour was spraying water over their drive every time he cleaned his car. Richard had initially wanted to ask them if they were being serious, but such was the graveness of their look and the anger in their voices he could tell they were. It hadn't helped when he had told them there was nothing he could do other than have a word with their neighbour. They had almost escorted him out of their house, hissing after him, "We don't know why we bother paying our taxes if that's the service we get," before slamming the door.

When Richard had gone around to have a word with their neighbour, the man had merely laughed, believing it was a joke himself. Then, when he'd seen Richard's serious look, he had launched into his own tirade, calling his neighbours 'knobheads' and 'troublemakers', telling him that the couple had already reported him to the council for allowing clippings to go into their garden after he had cut his hedge, and for having a noisy washing machine. Finishing his rant, he told Richard he wanted to make a complaint of harassment against them. When Richard explained it wasn't harassment, the man had also rebuked him and slammed the door. Richard had walked back to the car, shaking his head in frustration, knowing full well that in a week or two he would be back at these addresses, doing his level best to mediate, despite knowing he was wasting his breath and valuable time. Ending his notes, he set aside his pen and gazed at his watch. Another two hours and his shift would be over. He couldn't wait. It had been one of those days. When he got home, he was going to have a shower and a couple of beers, and unwind on the sofa, cuddled up with his wife, watching some catch-up TV.

Starting the engine, he was about to engage gear when his radio activated; a report had just come in that a hooded man had been seen going down the drive of a house a few streets away and the neighbours calling it in had just heard the sound of breaking glass at the rear. Richard took the call, slammed into first and screeched away from the kerb. It took him a little over a minute to get to the address, and he jumped out of the car, running his eyes over the front of the semi. The upstairs curtains were closed, there was no light on downstairs, despite dusk approaching, and there was no car on the drive. He bolted down the path, slipping out his baton and racking it out to its full length.

As he turned the corner, Richard caught sight of the burglar. He was wearing a black top with the hood up and looked to be a big man — well over six feet in height and broad across the shoulders. It looked to Richard as if he was holding a petrol container, and he could see he was tipping its contents in through the broken kitchen window. The burglar turned quickly, and Richard got his first look at his face. The villain wasn't young by any means; he looked to be in his sixties, was unshaven and had an ugly-looking scar that snaked across his nose onto his right cheek. Richard's initial thought was that despite this man being a senior citizen, he looked a hard bastard, and he instantly activated his status-zero button on his radio, requesting immediate backup.

As Richard drew back his baton — about to tell him to drop the canister — the man twisted swiftly, dragging the plastic container out of the broken window and flinging it in his direction. It hit him in the chest, some of its contents emptying over his stab vest, splashing onto his neck and face. The liquid went into his eyes, instantly causing a stinging sensation, blinding him. Within a split-second, the smell of petrol caught the back of his throat and panic overcame him. As he staggered back he heard a click, which reminded him of a zippo-lighter being struck, and then it felt as if his face was melting.

The day was giving way to dusk by the time the Kerrs returned to the hotel. The entire journey Hunter had repeatedly checked his rear-view mirror to ensure they weren't being followed. He tucked his car behind the hotel and ushered everyone through the rear doors. Taking the back stairs instead of the lift, he said goodnight to his parents and watched them enter their room five doors along, before entering his own room. He turned on the light, quickly taking in the surroundings as Beth and the boys followed. Nothing appeared to have been disturbed. It was only then he relaxed.

Jonathan instantly grabbed the TV remote, threw himself onto the king-size bed and activated the TV. Daniel joined him, stacking the pillows against the headboard and making himself comfy. Hunter grinned and turned to Beth. "Still angry with me?"

Beth held his eyes for a few seconds. Hunter could see that the spark in hers had returned, intensifying their blueness.

She answered, "Not mad with you. Peed off with what's happening, but not mad."

"Good, and I'm really sorry that you've been dragged into this."

"Your dad should be saying this, not you."

"Well, I'm speaking on his behalf."

Beth shook her head, releasing shimmering locks of honey-blonde hair, and broke into a smile.

"I love you, Beth Kerr." He was about to reach out and embrace her when the bedside phone rang.

Beth was nearest and picked it up. Following a short conversation, she removed the handset and held it out to him. "It's the receptionist downstairs; someone's asking for you."

Hunter threw her a puzzled look and took the handset. "Hello?"

"I'm guessing I'm speaking with Jock's son… Hunter, isn't it?"

It had been over eighteen months since he had last heard the man speak, but Hunter instantly recognised the harsh, gravelly Scottish voice. He glanced quickly at Beth and the boys and then made for the bathroom. "How have you got this number, Billy?" he hissed, back-heeling the bathroom door shut.

A short laugh came down the line. "I'm very resourceful. You should know that from last time. I found your dad once and I've found him again."

"Billy, you need to hand yourself in. This is only making it worse."

"Me and your dad have some unfinished business. You know that. I'm telling you this because I've no reason to hurt you, and I don't want to. But if you get in my way, then I will. Do I make myself clear?"

"I'm ending this conversation, Billy."

"Okay, but before you do, I have to say that wife of yours is a fine bonnie lassie, and your boys look like they're going to be fine young men. You wouldn't want anything bad to happen to them as well, would you?"

Before Hunter had time to answer, the line went dead. For several seconds he stared at the handset, listening to the strident burr. Then his hand started to shake.

# CHAPTER NINE

Hunter immediately put in a phone call to Detective Superintendent Leggate while Beth re-packed the cases. Ten minutes later, two armed-response-vehicles screeched into the hotel car park, and four officers wearing Kevlar vests and carrying Hecklar & Cock MP5s jumped out and secured the premises. The manager wondered what the hell was happening. His face was still a picture as he watched Hunter and his family being rushed through reception under armed guard to their vehicles at the back.

Within twenty minutes, Hunter and Jock were flooring their cars down the M1 under escort to Sheffield police headquarters, where the Chief's top floor flat had been made available for them. This week, he was out of town at a conference.

Halfway there, Hunter's mobile rang. It was Dawn Leggate. He hit the hands free button. "Hello, boss…" He was about to update her when she interjected.

"I know you're on the way to Headquarters, and I've made sure there's a parking spot allocated for both you and your dad. When you get there, I want you to go straight up to the flat, and all of you stay there until you hear from me. Understand?"

Hunter could tell from the tone of her voice that something was wrong. He grabbed the phone from the hands free set and stuck it to his ear — he didn't want Beth or the boys to hear any more of the conversation. "Is something up, boss?"

"You could say that. I've currently got half your dad's street on lockdown. Half an hour ago, one of the duty group officers was attacked at your dad's house. One of the neighbours reported a prowler, and the cop who turned out had petrol poured over him and was set alight. He was found by other officers responding. He's been rushed to hospital, and I'm waiting for an update to see how he is. I've got Grace and Mike Sampson on their way there as we speak."

"What?"

"I've got the entire area cordoned off, and it's swarming with officers, but there's no sign of the person who did this, and to be honest we've only got a very vague description from your dad's neighbours who saw the prowler."

Hunter's thoughts spiralled back eighteen months. Billy had used petrol and set a husband and wife on fire then — after first torturing the husband, a retired detective, by chopping off each of his fingers on his right hand — forcing him to reveal Jock's new identity and address. He responded sharply, "Billy Wallace?"

"He's certainly at the top of my list."

"Who's the cop?"

Dawn revealed his name. Hunter knew him; Richard was an experienced cop in service, but at thirty-two, still relatively young. He and Beth had been to his wedding reception three years ago. He had an eighteen-month-old daughter. Hunter felt his stomach empty.

"There's something else as well. It looks as though the prowler was about to fire your mum and dad's place. That's how Richard Flynn got doused in petrol and set on fire." Dawn paused a moment and continued, "I want you to keep that to yourself. Your parents will be worried enough. I'm arranging for extra security for both your places as we speak, so I don't want you worrying. Besides, with the boots I've put out on the ground, if it is Billy Wallace, he's going to be keeping his head down. When I find out anything else, I'll ring you. You stay put until I get back to you. I've got my hands full, as you can imagine, but I will get back to you sometime this evening. Until then, I don't want any of you wandering off." With that, she ended the call.

For a brief moment, Hunter's thoughts went into a spin. Beth's voice quickly dragged him back.

"Something happened?" she asked.

Hunter removed the phone from his ear and put it back in the hands free. He jerked a nod to the back seat where Jonathan and Daniel were belted up. "I'll tell you later," he replied, his thoughts still getting to grips with the news that he'd just been given.

From the underground car park at Headquarters, Hunter and his family were ushered up a back stairwell to the top floor by two of the armed contingent. Jonathan and Daniel were enjoying every moment, but Hunter could see that Beth looked scared. They were shown into the flat by one of the leading armed officers, who did a quick eye-sweep of the place.

He said, "I understand there's tea and coffee in the cupboards and some fresh milk in the fridge. If you want food, you're to contact reception downstairs and they'll order it for you. Other than that, the Chief says to make yourself comfortable." The armed officer winked. "It's not every day you get to use the Chief Constable's place, is it? I'd make the best of it." Handing over a key, he tipped Hunter a quick nod and left.

Closing the door and placing the key in the lock, Hunter first looked to Beth and then to Fiona and Jock. They all looked bewildered. "My boss says she'll ring me tonight. Until then, it's as the officer just said: we're to make ourselves comfortable."

For the next hour, they made drinks and freshened up in the one bathroom the flat had. Jonathan and Daniel took up the sofa, and after channel-surfing the TV, they found it had Sky movies and selected the new Iron Man film. Hunter saw that they at least had made themselves at home.

In the bedroom Beth opened up the cases, and while she selected a change of clothes for herself and for the boys, Hunter told her in a hushed voice what had happened.

She clasped a hand to her mouth. "Oh God, Hunter, that's terrible. His poor wife. His daughter."

"I know."

"And do they think it's this Billy Wallace guy?"

Hunter shrugged his shoulders. "I don't think it could be anyone else. It certainly has all his hallmarks, especially with this happening at Mum and Dad's house."

"So, what's going to happen now?"

Hunter again shrugged his shoulders. "The boss says she'll ring me this evening and update me, but other than that we have to hang on here."

"You mean in this flat?"

"Well, given what's just happened, and that phone call I got from Billy back at the hotel, it's too dangerous to go back home or anywhere else at the moment. No one knows where he is."

Holding out open hands, Beth aimed a look of frustration at him. "We can't stay in this place for more than a couple of days — it's not big enough for us all. You can see for yourself."

"What else can we do? What do you suggest?" Hunter tried his best to hide the irritation in his voice.

Beth sucked in a deep breath, turning her head away. "Jesus! I can't believe this is happening to us."

Hunter ordered a Chinese takeaway for them all over the phone and went down to reception to collect it when it came. As they laid out the table, which was only big enough for four, Hunter broke the news to his mum and dad about the attack on the young cop. They were as shocked as Beth, and initially they sat around the table eating in silence. The only sound in the room came from the TV; Jonathan and Daniel were back on the sofa watching another movie, eating from plates resting on their knees. It was one big adventure for them. For the grown-ups, it was different. There was a feeling of tension around the table, especially coming from Beth. Hunter had found a bottle of red wine in the fridge and he decided to open it, hoping it might relax her. He poured out four glasses.

"I don't want to speak out of turn here…" Beth said on a soft note, spooning out another portion of egg fried rice from its container, "but I think this place is far too small for all of us. Living like this for longer than a couple of days is going to get me down."

"I agree," said Fiona.

Hunter's mouth stretched taut. Shifting his gaze between Beth and his mum, he said, "I guess I have to agree as well. I'll speak with the boss tonight — see if she can come up with anywhere else more suitable."

Jock took a sip of his wine, lowered the glass and hopped his gaze from one to the other. "Can I make a suggestion?"

Everyone looked at him.

"I'm really sorry this has happened." Jock paused, casting a look around the table. "Look, I've got a bit of money put by. Why don't I book us a holiday somewhere abroad?" He paused again, then added, "When your boss rings up, son, just tell her we appreciate what she's done, but we've decided we want to go away. I'm sure something can be fixed up without Billy

48

finding out. He's not like one of them drug cartel guys, who can afford to have everyone in their pocket. Billy's just a vicious thug. We could book something on the internet for a couple of weeks and get some of your cop friends to take us to the airport. What do you think?"

Hunter looked from his dad to Beth.

She nodded. "I totally agree, and that's just given me an idea. Why don't I speak with my mum and dad and see if they can get us a cottage on Sark? It's off-peak there now. I'm sure with their contacts they'll be able to find us a nice place for a couple of weeks." She looked around the table. "What do you say?"

Jock reacted first. "That sounds a great idea, Beth." Letting out a light laugh, he added, "Not only will it be a nice family gathering, but it won't hurt my pocket as much."

With the briefest exchange of nods the holiday was agreed.

# CHAPTER TEN

Beth secured flights and ferry tickets via the internet — their flight to Guernsey from Manchester was scheduled for 8.50 a.m. the next day. Hunter hardly slept — his head was so crowded with the day's events. At 4.30 he gave up trying and got up, made himself a cup of tea and had a shave. At 5 a.m. the alarm woke everyone, and Hunter made tea and toast for the family and did a final check of the room to see that everything had been gathered. Just before six, the Kerr family picked up their cases and took the back stairs down to the underground car park where two dark blue SUVs were waiting. Each of the vehicles had two plain clothes officers up front. As Hunter shook hands with the driver of his vehicle, his coat flapped loose and he caught a glimpse of a shoulder holster. He guessed each of their escorts were discreetly packing handguns, and that thought suddenly brought home to him how serious this situation was.

With no traffic hold-ups they got to the airport shortly after seven, where an Airport Security Officer was waiting. After a quick handover, Hunter and his family were whisked through priority booking, passport control, and security, to the VIP lounge, where tea and coffee and daily newspapers were on offer to them while they waited. The only people in the lounge were several flight crew members and two other passengers. It was Hunter's first experience inside the VIP lounge, and he was suitably impressed. Dawn Leggate had certainly pulled out all the stops for them. He would make sure he thanked her later.

Hunter stared at the flights board and saw that their plane was on time and that boarding would commence in twenty minutes. He checked his watch. *Not long now.* He had already been told that there would be no queuing for his family; at the appointed time, someone would be coming to take them straight onto the plane. He let out a long sigh of relief. For the first time in 24 hours, he could feel himself starting to unwind.

He walked across the lounge to where the free newspapers were and picked one up to take on the flight. As he took a quick look at the headlines, his mobile rang. Taking it from his pocket, he saw only a mobile number with no caller ID. Under normal circumstances he wouldn't have answered it, but he wondered if it was someone from airport security checking in with him.

"I've been doing some asking around, and they've told me you've gone to ground."

Hunter's heart lurched. Billy Wallace! He glanced over his shoulder. He could see that Beth was playing *Rock, Paper, Scissors, Shoot,* with Jonathan and Daniel, and his mum and dad were each reading one of the papers. He quickly made his way to the toilet, nipped inside and leaned back against the door to prevent anyone coming in before he said anything. Hunter could feel his heart pounding. "You're taking a big risk, Billy."

"That's where you're wrong, Mr Detective. This is another burn-phone, just in case you were monitoring my last one, and it will be gone once we've finished our conversation." Following a quick pause, he added, "So you're in hiding, then. Trembling in your boots? If you're not, you should be." He finished the sentence with a short laugh.

Hunter took a deep breath. He didn't want to let Billy think he had rattled him. "Not hiding, Billy, and certainly not scared of an old man like you. Just keeping our heads below the parapet for a while. You know, until they put you back in Barlinnie where you can rot."

Billy returned another short laugh. "Didn't you know I've no intention of going back there? Like I said during our last conversation, I've some unfinished business, and it won't be too long now before it's finished."

"No chance, Billy. You might as well give yourself up now."

"I think you underestimate me, Detective. Oh, and by the way say hello to that wife of yours — Beth, isn't it? And those two fine young men of yours. It's a good school you've chosen for them, but I know they're not there at the moment because I've checked."

"Fuck you, Billy." As soon as it came out, Hunter regretted saying it. He had lost it, and now he'd let Billy know he'd got to him. He tightened his grip on his phone as if squeezing the very life out of it.

The laugh Billy let out this time was a little longer. "Oh well, can't stand around here all morning chatting. Things to do, you know. Got some business to deal with."

"Oh yes. In your dreams."

"Not in my dreams. In your nightmares. I'm a lot closer than you think, Detective. In fact, I've just got you back on my radar."

"Fuck you, Billy, you worthless piece of shit." Hunter ended the call before Billy could respond. For a moment he stared at his phone. He was kidding, right? Course he was. How could Billy know where they were? Surely their escort would have checked they weren't being followed?

Hunter immediately rang Dawn Leggate and told her about Billy's phone call. She responded that she would make some enquiries, put a trace on the phone number Billy had used and get back to him.

Making his way to the sink, Hunter set down his mobile and stared into the mirror. He didn't look good at all — the blue of his eyes looked washed out and a sweaty sheen masked his face. Taking a deep breath, he held it for several seconds and let it out slowly. The Gordian knot that had formed in his stomach a minute ago had now loosened. He ran the cold tap, scooped up a handful of water and splashed his face. He did it again, rubbing his cheeks. After drying himself with a paper towel, he straightened up to his full height, swelled his chest and took another look in the mirror. Although he didn't feel it inside, outwardly, the colour had returned to his face, making him look more like himself. Pocketing his phone, he returned to the lounge.

Ten minutes later, two members of Airport Security arrived. One of them took Hunter to one side while the other instructed his family to gather their things together as they were about to be taken to the Boarding Gate. The man taking Hunter to one side was a supervisor. In a low voice he let him know that he had not long spoken with his Detective Superintendent, and that he had just checked passport control, and the day's passenger list, and no one of the name of Billy Wallace had either passed through or was listed on any of today's flights. He also reassured him that his name was on the 'All Ports Warning' system so that if he entered any airport within the UK, he would be instantly detained. Although the supervisor's words should have come as some comfort to Hunter, he was still tense as he left the VIP lounge to board the plane.

# CHAPTER ELEVEN

Their plane was a twin-turboprop 78-seater belonging to Guernsey's own airline. Hunter had never been on a propeller aircraft before, and as he climbed up the stairs at the rear of the small plane, he felt a knot of apprehension grip him. This tightened further when the seat he had been allocated gave him a direct view of the port propeller. He couldn't help but think how seemingly small it was given the size of the plane, and as it taxied onto the runway, he gripped the arms of his seat. As the plane lifted off and began its climb, he quickly realised he needn't have been so worried. Though the engines were noisy to begin with, as the plane evened out, and the throttle of the engines lessened, he was surprised at how smooth the flight became and loosened his grip from the armrests. Even more surprising was the length of the journey. It seemed that no sooner had they taken off than the pilot was announcing they were beginning their descent.

In a way, Hunter was glad the flight had been a short one. He had tried to relax, opening his paper with the intention of reading, but his concentration had been elsewhere, and after skimming through half a dozen pages, unable to take anything in, he had given up. As usual, Beth had sensed he was out of kilter with himself, enquiring, midway through the flight, if he was okay. Hunter had responded by squeezing her hand, giving a false smile and nodding his head. Seeing the stare she returned, he knew he hadn't convinced her, and he widened his fake smile and added the word "Honest." As she pulled back her eyes, he knew he still hadn't swayed her thoughts: Beth could read him like a book.

Returning his gaze to the window, Hunter got his first view of the smaller of the Channel Islands as they dropped though the clouds, and was trying to identify which of them was Sark, when he felt the lowering of the landing-gear jolt the plane. Ten minutes later, the plane hit the tarmac with a thud and Hunter found himself being thrown forward, along with the other passengers, as it braked harshly for a good twenty seconds before easing. Thirty seconds later, the aircraft turned sharply off the runway and Hunter caught sight of Guernsey's single-storey airport terminal.

Once off the plane, Hunter realised there was no more VIP treatment; he and his family joined the steady queue into the baggage collection area and waited for their cases. It was a good twenty minutes before he and his dad had dragged off all their cases from the belt, and, checking everyone was okay with their bags, Hunter led the way to the Arrivals Hall. Stepping through the automated doors into the bright and airy concourse, Hunter was faced by only a small gathering of people, and he let his eyes roam quickly among them — he had been told that a detective from the Guernsey Force would be waiting for them — and it didn't take him long to spot their bodyguard: the thickset man in a light grey suit and open-necked white shirt was holding up a piece of A4 paper with Hunter's name upon it.

Signalling him with a wave, Hunter stepped forward, pulling behind him the family's biggest case.

The forty-something man, with light brown, thinning hair and a decent tan, introduced himself as, "DC John Batiste."

Hunter shook his hand.

"I'm here to take you all to your ferry," he said softly and turned for the exit.

Their transport was a black seven-seater Mercedes. Detective Batiste helped load their luggage, ensured Jonathan and Daniel were strapped in tightly, started the engine and checked everyone was good to go before pulling away from the car park. Hunter sat up front and saw that the Detective was heading for the capital, St. Peter Port. It was a slow journey, the main roads winding and narrow and heavily congested. The officer told him that the speed limit on the island was limited to 35 mph, and it was strictly enforced. Hunter wasn't surprised in the least to learn this, given how constricted the roads were.

As the Detective drove, Hunter questioned him about police resources on the island and the nature of his job. From the conversation, he grasped that crime on the island was relatively low, with criminal damage and assault being the most common. It didn't sound too exciting in comparison with his own job, though he didn't say that. What Hunter did gather from their chat was that Detective Batiste had only been given the briefest of details about their plight; the only thing he had been told was that they were being moved because of threats to their life from an escaped convict. Hunter knew from experience that the full facts would be on a need-to-know basis, and this detective wasn't in the know, so when Hunter didn't offer up any additional information the detective quizzed no further.

As they talked, Hunter was keeping an eye on the surroundings, and he found himself captivated by the sheer quaintness of the island; it reminded him a little of Cornwall without the countryside. He especially couldn't help noticing how one location melded into the next; there seemed to be no separation between towns or villages, just an endless ribbon of whitewashed cottages and houses, and so when he saw the sign that told them they were entering St. Peter Port, it took him completely by surprise. He checked his watch: it had taken them a little over 10 minutes — it was the quickest airport transfer he had ever experienced.

Still in nose-to-tail traffic, they descended a steep hill that skirted the Capital's town centre, signposting them to the harbour. As they slowed for the junction at the bottom of the hill, the road opened out to give them a spectacular view towards the sea, the water shimmering under strong sunlight. Before them were several marinas, their moorings clogged with all manner of yachts and boats, many of them expensive-looking. The harbour was far bigger than Hunter expected. It stretched, both left and right, as far as he could see, and directly in front was a huge car park with surrounding grey walls, and a walkway and road that led to refurbished warehouses and a restaurant. To his right, at the far end of the harbour, his eyes fell upon what appeared to be a large fortress.

As if reading Hunter's thoughts, John Batiste announced, "That's Castle Cornet." He slowed the vehicle, signalling left and pulling into the nearest harbour road. "Beautiful, isn't it? Hundreds of years ago it guarded this port, but these days it houses museums and our theatre. In the summer we have quite a few concerts there. If you get chance, it's worth visiting." He drove to a hatched area designated for taxis and coaches and stopped. "Right, this is where I leave you." Pointing out through the windscreen to a metal gantry, below which was berthed a large blue and white boat, he continued, "That's your ferry." Glancing at his watch, he added, "It leaves in ten minutes. Just take your bags down to the boat; they'll load them on for you and take them off when you reach Sark. The crossing takes about fifty minutes. Once I see you on, I'm going to radio-in, and by the time you get there the island

Constable will be waiting for you. He'll take you to where you're staying."

Hunter cracked open his door, but before getting out he reached over and shook the detective's hand. "Thank you so much for looking after us."

"My pleasure. And good luck to you. You should be able to relax now." Batiste opened the driver's door. "You'll love Sark," he said, climbing out. "In fact, I guarantee you'll fall in love with the place. Everyone does."

# CHAPTER TWELVE

Hunter made sure their luggage was loaded before getting on the passenger ferry, and then made his way through the cabin seating area to the back of the boat, where he joined his parents. Beth and the boys had already secured a seat and were kneeling up on them, looking out across the harbour.

Hunter took note of the half a dozen people who had joined them outside, and then gazing back through the doorway into the seating area, he cast his eye upon the passengers who had taken up their seats. From a quick headcount, he registered about thirty people on board. Many of them looked like tourists — their outer clothing of fleeces or waterproof jackets, backpacks and cameras gave them away. Half a dozen or so, who were dressed more casually, carried handfuls of laden grocery bags, and Hunter guessed these were the island's locals who had made the journey to stock up for a week or so. He noticed that those locals were targeting the passengers with more direct looks and casting smiles. Hunter had already read that many of the islanders on Sark held three or more jobs, mostly tourist related, and he guessed that those targeted smiles were planned with a view to attracting their custom once they were on the island. One lady, who looked to be in her early sixties, with short, rather stylish white hair, aimed a smile in his direction. The smile appeared genuine, and Hunter rebuked himself for his cynicism. He returned the gesture and then took a seat beside Beth and the boys.

The water in the harbour sparkled, and the sky was full of fluffy white clouds, a splash of cerulean dotted here and there where there were gaps. Though a gentle breeze came off the sea, brushing Hunter's face, it was surprisingly warm, especially given it was the beginning of autumn. Suddenly, he felt content. The stress of the last few days had already lifted, and he switched his thoughts to the next couple of weeks. He couldn't wait to see the cottage Beth's parents had chosen for them and to explore the island. He only wished he had brought along his easel and paints.

Beth slipped her mobile out from her bag, announcing she was going to phone her parents to tell them what time the ferry was getting in.

Her voice brought back his attention. Hunter laid a hand on her wrist. "Can you just hold off until I speak with the cop who's meeting us and check what's happening?" He saw by the look on her face she was disappointed. "It'll only be a couple more hours, and then you'll have as much time with them as you want."

Tight-lipped, Beth gave him a curt nod and with a sigh returned her phone to her bag. Wrapping an arm around her, he gave her a reassuring hug.

From the back deck of the passenger ferry, Hunter watched Guernsey getting ever more distant. The lighthouse at the end of the harbour by Castle Cornet was soon just a speck of white, and he dropped his eyes upon the water, which although a beautiful ultramarine, was surprisingly choppy. That thought brought his gaze back to Beth beside him, and for the next few minutes he found himself watching her as much as the sea; she suffered from travel sickness, and boats were her worst nightmare. Every time he looked her way, she wore a weak smile, but he knew from her pallor that she wasn't enjoying this journey one bit.

Hunter had his arms across the shoulders of the boys, who were gazing out to sea. They had already spotted Sark poking above the horizon and were chattering excitedly. They suddenly gave a cry, and Hunter swung his gaze from Beth out into the Channel, where Jonathan and Daniel were pointing. Behind him passengers were making excited calls, and when his eyes landed on darkened shapes leaping out of the water, he realised why: a pod of five dolphins were springing above the waves, almost in unison, disappearing for a second and then re-appearing. Everyone's eyes were glued seaward, even Beth's, and the showmanship of the dolphins was spectacular. The acrobatic display lasted a good ten minutes until they steered away and disappeared beneath the swell. It was only when Hunter glanced right that he realised why — the rocky granite cliff face of Sark was coming into view, and its height took him by surprise. He had to crane his neck skywards to get a glimpse of the top.

The ferry throttled down, reducing its speed to a chug, and began edging in towards Maseline Harbour. The tiny harbour was nestled against the rock-face, its walls forming a right angle, the longest jetty pointing, finger-like, out to sea. In the shadow of the ominous cliffs, the water took on a shade of dark green-blue and was a lot calmer. The berthing of the ferry was relatively smooth, its gentle clunk against the harbour wall hardly felt. Within minutes, the crew had secured the mooring and began helping people off.

Hunter noticed that one of the first people off was the elderly lady he'd exchanged a smile with. He watched her switching shopping bags between hands, getting her balance before she set off. He noted how sprightly she was for her age, and he watched her skip up the steps onto the jetty and then slip into a tunnel that was cut into the rock. Its entranceway was painted white and had a sign above it, which read 'Welcome to Sark.' Everyone was following her, and he realised it was the only way out of the harbour.

Hunter waited for the crowd to thin, and then he climbed off and helped out his mum, and then Beth and both lads. His dad came out last, not requiring help. A member of the ferry crew hauled out their cases, and once they were all assembled and had gathered up their things, he traipsed after the rest of the passengers into the tunnel. Coming out of the other side, the sunlight momentarily blinded him. As the flashes behind his eyes cleared, Hunter saw that they were at the bottom of a winding track that rose steeply between a valley of trees and rocks. A signpost next to a wall read 'To the Village'. To his left, parked up, were a couple of tractors, towing open carriages with seating. One of them was already full of passengers, and people were making their way to the next one. Knowing there were no cars on the island, Hunter gathered that this was the public transport. Waiting at the end of the carriages was a squat man with a shock of iron grey hair and the facial complexion of someone who regularly worked outdoors. He was wearing a black T-shirt with a logo on the chest, cargo shorts and walking boots. He stepped towards Hunter, holding out his hand.

"DS Kerr?" he enquired.

Hunter broke into a smile. "Do I stand out that much?"

The man returned his own smile. "No, you don't actually. I was told to expect a detective with his family, and you're the only family group who's got off the ferry."

Pointing a finger at his clothing, Hunter said, "You certainly do a good job blending in with the locals. I'm guessing you're the island cop, come to meet us?"

The man, who looked to be in his fifties, gave a hearty laugh. "These are my normal clothes. I only put on my uniform when its necessary to show a presence." He stabbed a finger at the logo on his chest. "My day-job is running an adventure company on the island — corporate events, kayaking and the like. My role as the island Constable is additional."

"Certainly discreet, anyway."

He gave another burst of laughter. "I'll tell you now, there's no discreet here. There's roughly six-hundred people living on this island, and they all know each other's business." Leaning in, lowering his voice, he added, "I've already mentioned your coming. It was easier to do that than to try and be discreet and failing. I used to work in the UK, so they think you're an old colleague. Don't be surprised when they start quizzing you, but as far as they're concerned you and your family are here on holiday. Okay?"

Hunter nodded.

"By the way, I'm Paul Burgess, but everyone here calls me Budgie."

"Hunter."

Returning to talking on a low note, the Constable said, "I've been sent an email with the briefest of details about why you're here, but it is the briefest of details, so unless you want to fill me in later, I won't be asking questions. I've also been emailed a picture of this Billy Wallace character I should be looking out for. I will be showing it to a few people here who I can trust. We have a great 'ears and eyes' set-up on this island. Nothing gets past no one, as you'll no doubt find out. Any strangers normally stick out like sore thumbs." Taking a deep breath, he continued, "I say normally, because starting this weekend, and for the next ten days, it's our Festival of Light, and the island will be snided with folk, so I'm going to have to be really on my toes. But don't worry, we also have a couple of dozen Specials on the island, so I'll be briefing them and showing them the picture of Billy. You won't need to worry."

"Festival of Light?"

Budgie nodded. "It's a bit like Shetland's Up Helly Aa. There's always been a small fire festival here, going back decades, but in the last five years it's got bigger and bigger and more popular. We now get people from all over the world coming here for it. A lot of them come because we're now officially a dark skies island, and so they come to view the stars, but it's mainly about the Pagan celebration of autumn to winter, which starts with the walk of fire from the village up to Sark Henge, that's our mini Stonehenge, and finishes with a huge bonfire up on the clifftop of Hogsback. All very commercial, but it's a great experience. You and your family will love it." He paused, adding, "People will start arriving this Saturday. All the accommodation will be full. You're very lucky to get the cottage you're staying at." He looked to Beth. "It's only because your dad was able to pull some strings."

"You know him, then?" asked Beth.

"We've got to know your mum and dad very well, in the short time they've been on the island. Your dad's now our leading fire-officer for his sins." Pausing, Budgie added, "If we find out someone's got a particular skill, we abuse them." He gave another short laugh. "We might even call on you, Beth. Your dad's already told us you're a nurse. I'll introduce you to the island doctor if you want?"

Beth smiled. "No thank you. I'm here for a break."

"Only kidding. Anyway, do you want to jump on board? You could walk up to the village, but you'll find this is the easy way. It's quite a steep hill, and you've got a fair bit of luggage."

# CHAPTER THIRTEEN

The pair of tractors and their laden carriages trundled up the uneven, potholed Harbour Hill, coming to a stop by a pair of white-washed stone buildings. Between them was a courtyard containing benches. A sign on one of the end walls pointed out that it was the Bel Air Inn.

Here the tractors came to a halt and everyone started to disembark.

Budgie helped Fiona off, and ducking his head toward the buildings said, "That's our main pub on the island. Most of the tourists end up here before they catch the last ferry back to Guernsey. This is where I find that I sometimes have my work cut out, especially in summer." He dragged off one of the cases. "We have another pub, The Mermaid, which the locals mainly use. That's up in the village. If you're up for it, we can have a beer once you're settled in."

Hunter nodded but didn't reply. He wasn't sure about anything yet, and although it sounded a good offer, he didn't want to commit himself until they were in their cottage and had liaised with Beth's parents; he knew how desperate his wife was to meet up with them.

Budgie added, "I'm afraid you'll find our nightlife a bit dull. The pubs are the best venue once it drops dark."

"I'll let you know," Hunter replied.

Budgie took Fiona's case and began walking. There was still a gentle rise before they reached the top of the hill. "Your cottage is only a couple of hundred yards from here," he said.

Hunter and his family set off after him. After a few yards, as the road levelled, Hunter spotted some horses and carriages, with a cluster of tourists gathered around them.

"That's our other public transport here, but it tends to get used exclusively by visitors for sightseeing. Most of the islanders use a push-bike to get around."

Passing the group, they came to a crossroads. In front of them was a coffee and giftshop, and leading away was a line of single-storey white buildings in a tree-lined avenue.

Budgie paused momentarily until they caught up. "This is the village," he said, dipping his head. "There's a food store halfway along, and at the end is the Post Office and the Tourist Information Centre. Only half a dozen shops, but they'll cater for all your needs." He set off again, taking a left turn. "You're just down here."

The road they travelled dipped downhill and was little more than dry clay embedded with granite rock. Hunter noticed a signpost pointing them towards Little Sark, and having googled the island, he had already identified it as a place to visit. Within a hundred yards, Hunter became aware of how quiet the place was. Except for the distant clop of horse's hooves chipping the road, there was nothing.

After a hundred yards, a large white building appeared.

Leading the way, Budgie called behind him, "This is the farm your cottage belongs to. See, I told you it wasn't far."

Passing a large row of hedges, the road took a sharp left downhill, and to the right a gateway appeared, a huge hydrangea bush partly hiding a low wooden gate.

"Well, this is you," announced Budgie, deviating onto the grass path up to the gate. "I'm going to leave you here. The cottage should be all ready for you. The farm we've just passed is owned by Mr and Mrs Mauger. The family have owned this place for generations. If you need anything, just ask them. And as you can see, you're in a pretty private location." He pointed up ahead, to where a narrow footpath disappeared into trees. "That track takes you Dixcart Bay, and the road to the left takes you to Derrible Bay and Sark Henge. I'm sure you'll be exploring them over the next day or so. This place is pretty well set back, so you shouldn't see anyone or have any visitors." He handed the case back to Fiona. "Dixcart Bay is worth visiting. It has a nice beach and it's easier to get down to than Derrible. The walk there is a good twenty minutes through woodland, but it's mostly downhill. Before you get to the bay, there's a track that takes you up onto the headland. If you take that, there's a couple of hotels where you can get really nice food."

Hunter looked to Beth. "That sounds perfect."

"If you do see anyone around here, it will more than likely be a walker going to Sark Henge. There might be a few passing with the festival being on, but you'll not see them unless you're by the gate, or on the road yourselves." Shaking Hunter's hand, he added, "You've got my mobile number. I'll give you a ring tomorrow and check you've settled in, and if, in the meantime, you need me before then, you know where I am."

Hunter thanked him and watched him march away in the direction of the village. Then, picking up his case, he opened the small wooden gate into the garden. The cottage was bathed in sunlight and looked exactly like a cottage should — charming. It was made of local grey and pink granite, with a low-slung slate roof, in which were set three rooflight windows. To the right was an outbuilding, and on a flagstone area in front of that sat a large wooden table and six chairs. Hunter could already see himself sitting here this evening with

Beth, sharing a bottle of wine. As he ran his eyes over the setting, one word sprang to mind: idyllic.

The front door wasn't locked, and Hunter walked into an oak-beamed kitchen and dining area. There was a pine table with six chairs and a wooden dresser against one wall. At the far end of the dining area, a pair of doors led into a large conservatory. In it Hunter could see two small sofas and a low, round table. He walked into the middle of the kitchen, set down his case and let out a contented sigh. This place was even better than he'd expected.

"I'll stick the kettle on," piped up Jock, brushing past him. "I can see me making myself at home very quickly here."

Inside his head, Hunter echoed his dad's words. He looked around to see where Beth was; she was just disappearing through a doorway that he saw led to a stairway. He could hear the sound of Jonathan and Daniel bounding up ahead of her, shouting excitedly, seeking out where they were going to sleep.

Hunter's eyes settled on Fiona. A concerned look was etched across her face. "Are you okay?" he mouthed.

She nodded slowly. "I am now. I just hope they can catch Billy Wallace, so we can put this nasty business behind us once and for all and get our lives back again." Her soft Scottish voice sounded choked.

"They will do," returned his dad, searching the wall cupboards for cups. "Let's try and make the most of this, Fiona."

Hunter was about to reassure his mum when his dad suddenly called, "Hey, look what we've been left."

Hunter and Fiona turned to look at Jock. He was holding aloft a wicker basket. He pulled out of it a bottle of white wine.

Hunter could make out bread and biscuits poking out from the top of the basket and what looked like a large bag of crisps.

"Isn't that a lovely gesture?"

Hunter immediately agreed. This enforced break was getting better by the minute.

# CHAPTER FOURTEEN

In her new office, Detective Superintendent Dawn Leggate set down her bag on her desk, slipped off her jacket and flopped into her chair. Booting up the computer, she picked up the phone, and from memory, dialled the number of a former colleague, Detective Sergeant John Reed. As it started to ring, she spotted a note in her top tray. Recognising Grace's handwriting, Dawn picked it up, trapped the phone between her ear and shoulder and speed-read the message. Grace's memo told her that they had a forensic hit from the print lifted from the petrol container found at the rear of Jock Kerr's house — it was a match to Billy Wallace. The news immediately lifted Dawn's spirits and in a jubilant mood, while listening to the phone's ringtone, she slipped the note into her journal. She was just composing her thoughts, preparing to leave John a voicemail, when he answered.

"DS Reed."

Hearing his deep Scottish voice again instantly conjured up an image of him. Dawn wondered if John's dark collar-length hair was still as unruly and if he'd bothered to shave today. She recalled how she used to rib him about his appearance. He told her it was his designer look, and she'd tell him he just looked scruffy. It was their standing joke. She had a true fondness for John: he had been her Detective Sergeant when she had joined Stirling CID, and he'd taught her everything about detective work. That had been 14 years ago. Since then, she had risen through the ranks, and although she had been promoted to other stations within the Force area, she had returned twice to Stirling CID — once as his DI and a few years ago as his DCI

— before making the heart-wrenching decision to move to her current post, after splitting from her husband, Jack. That had been twelve months ago, and since then they had hardly been out of contact; John provided her with a much-needed fix to prevent her being homesick. Though that wasn't the reason she was ringing him now. There were more pressing things on her mind, and John was her point of liaison.

"Hello, John."

"Oh, hi Dawn. I was just thinking about you."

"Nothing bad, I hope?"

He let out a short laugh. "Would I ever think anything bad about my favourite Detective Superintendent?"

"You're such a smoothie, John Reed."

He gave out another short burst of laughter. "How's it going down there?"

"I was about to ask you that, but I've just picked out a note from my tray, and we appear to have a breakthrough."

"That's great."

"I didn't mention it to you yesterday when I rang, but a petrol container used in the attack on the PC was left behind, and SOCO lifted a couple of prints from it. I've just been told they've been identified as Billy's."

"Well, that's half the battle, Dawn, but do you have a firm identification that it's Billy, then? How's that PC of yours? Has he been able to confirm it's him?"

"He's still in intensive care. He's got twenty percent burns to his upper body. They're keeping him sedated, and then they're going to transfer him to a burns unit. It's going to be a few days, if not longer, before we can get anything from him."

"What about the neighbours who reported the prowler? Didn't you say that all that they were able to give you was the description of someone tall, wearing a dark hoodie?"

"We've got two descriptions. One from Jock's neighbours, and one from a couple walking their dog, who saw a man of a similar description sitting in a silver car about a hundred yards from Jock's house."

"So, no one has given you a good enough description that you can say it's definitely Billy? I don't want to dampen your spirits, Dawn, but you know what Billy Wallace is like. A clever lawyer would say prints on a petrol container only show he's handled it. It doesn't exactly put him at the scene."

John's comments momentarily floored her. She suddenly realised that in her excitement to put this firmly and squarely at the door of Billy Wallace, she wasn't thinking rationally. She said, "You don't want to come down here and work for me, do you?"

"What, and miss this fine Scottish weather? Nae chance. Besides, I'd miss my square sausage in the morning."

It was Dawn's turn to release a laugh. Then, on a serious note she said, "Do you know, John, you caught me not thinking straight there. I think it's because this is so personal."

There was a moment's silence, then John answered, "It's not always easy handling a case when it's one of your own. When it's a stranger, you can at least separate it from your thoughts, no matter how tragic the circumstances. When it's a cop, even though you don't necessarily know them personally, or their family, you feel like a victim. I was in that same position eighteen months ago when Billy murdered those three retired detectives up here. All I wanted was his guts."

Dawn took a deep breath and released it slowly. "Before the pair of us get all maudlin, have you managed to find out anything for me up there?"

"Nothing concrete, I'm afraid. We believe we've found the Range Rover that was used in the escape. It's been fired. We found it burned out on an industrial estate ten minutes' drive from the city centre. The Fire Brigade brought it to our attention. The number plates had been removed, and from the chassis number we've discovered it was stolen three days ago in a burglary. A couple of the premises on the estate have CCTV, but only for protection purposes, so they don't look out over the area where the Range Rover was dumped. And there's none at the entrance to the site, so we're not holding out much hope of getting anything which might identify who dumped it. A couple of my team are out at the moment, canvassing the site for witnesses, and I've made a request for footage from ANPR cameras on all roads to and from the site, but its early days yet. I've also put in a couple of calls to my contacts, but not got anything positive back yet. The moment I get anything back as to who sprung Billy, I'll let you know."

"Thank you, John."

"Nae problem. Sorry I couldn't give you some good news."

Dawn ended the call with a heavy sigh. She had hoped for an early arrest so that Hunter and family could get their life back, but it looked as though it wouldn't be any time soon. She again looked at Grace's note lying in the folds of her journal. *At least this was a start.* She pushed herself up. She had a briefing to conduct.

# CHAPTER FIFTEEN

After ringing her parents to tell them they had arrived, Beth unpacked their things while Hunter went on a tour of the cottage. Downstairs he found a utility room with a second shower and toilet, which would be handy given their number. In the comfortably furnished lounge, with its whitewashed plaster walls and beamed ceiling, he found that a built-in cupboard next to the stone fire surround, housing a log burner, was stocked with games, puzzles, and DVDs, and next to the smaller of two leather sofas was a cupboard crammed with all manner of books. It certainly catered for their needs, he thought, as his eyes roamed around the room.

Entering the conservatory, bathed in warm light, Hunter found another bookcase, and on top of that a 50s Crosley record player with a couple of dozen albums stacked beside it. He hadn't played vinyl since he'd left his parents' house, and he picked up half a dozen of the records. The first two were easy listening albums, but the third one sparked an instant vision from his teenage years: *Human League, Dare*. He read out the title inside his head. *Now that brings back memories.* The fourth ignited an even bigger spark and also brought about a huge tug on his heartstrings — *Thompson Twins, Into the Gap*. This had been Polly's — his first love's — favourite band. They had played this album relentlessly up in her room. He could see himself with her, lying side by side, talking about school stuff and what they were going to do with their futures. And then hers had ended when she was sixteen, and his had changed dramatically.

He quickly shook the sad thought from his head and placed the records back on top of the pile. He'd go through them in a couple of days' time, and maybe play a few for old times' sake, he told himself, turning his eyes to the garden. It had the picture-postcard cottage look with borders full of blooms and a good size lawn that had been recently cut. A chest-high hedge surrounded it, and beyond that was a thick bank of trees, which he guessed was the beginning of the woods leading to the bay Budgie had mentioned. Surprisingly, in spite of the trees, the garden was blanketed in bright sunlight and he unlocked the conservatory doors and stepped out. The first thing that struck him again was the quietness. All he could hear was birdsong. He took in a deep breath, as if sampling air for the first time, and held it for a few seconds before releasing it slowly. It was just as Detective John Batiste had said — Hunter was already falling in love with the place. He couldn't wait to explore.

Back in the house, he suddenly caught the sound of laughter and yells from Jonathan and Daniel coming from upstairs. It sounded as if Jock was play-fighting with them. He could hear Fiona telling him not to be so rough, and for a split-second Hunter's thoughts were transported back to his childhood: a time of happiness, security and love. His dad had played with him similarly so many times. He was still finding it difficult relating that version of Jock to what he now knew about him. In a way, it felt like Jock had betrayed him for years, even though he now knew the reason why he had never been told.

Suddenly, Hunter's mobile rang, making him jump. Pulling it from his jeans pocket, he saw it was Dawn Leggate. He answered, "Afternoon, boss."

"Afternoon, Hunter, I'm just checking in with you. I'm presuming you're in your cottage on Sark."

"Got here about an hour ago. It's gorgeous and the weather's beautiful."

"Don't rub it in; its throwing it down here."

Hunter thought her voice didn't have the normal upbeat sound to it. He said, "You sound tired, boss."

"Tired is an understatement. I'm knackered. I seem to be going from one crisis to another. I've got my trusted colleagues up in Scotland doing their best to track down an ugly-looking twat who gets his kicks from killing people, I'm overseeing the move to our new HQ, and I'm trying to look after one of my favourite detectives and his family several hundred miles away. Being a detective superintendent is not as nice a job as you think it is. Remember that when you go for promotion."

"I think I might just give promotion a miss, then."

Letting out a short laugh, she said, "Don't let me put you off. I'm just feeling sorry for myself. I was on call last night, just for my sins, and I had to turn out to a domestic murder in Rotherham. It was four o'clock this morning before I got back to bed."

"Well, I'll just get on with my nice holiday with my family on this beautiful island and wait for your call to tell me you've caught that ugly-looking twat, Billy Wallace."

"Very funny, Hunter, very funny. Well, you know where I am if you need me. Speak soon." With that, she hung up.

For a few seconds Hunter stared at the screen of his mobile, a smile across his face. Then, slipping it back into his pocket, he took another look out over the garden before returning inside.

Given that they hadn't enough time to shop, and the items in the basket of goodies left for them were snacks, the Kerrs decided to try out one of the hotels that Budgie had mentioned. On the top of a coffee table in the conservatory, Hunter found a well-used tourist information map of the island, and finding and tracing the hotel's location, he checked that everyone was up for tackling the walk. Everyone was, and after a quick wash and change of clothing, putting on their stoutest, most comfortable shoes, they set off along the track outside the cottage gate. It was extremely narrow with overgrown hedgerows, and they had to travel single file.

A hundred yards along, as they rounded a bend, they saw a sign for Dixcart Bay pointing them into dense woodland. Within thirty metres of entering the wood, they found that the light had diminished, and the gradient of the track changed to one that was downhill, and although not too dramatic a drop, the going became precarious, not only because of the lack of daylight, but also because of the vast number of tree roots that criss-crossed the path. In parts it was also covered in wet leaves, and Hunter kept looking around to check how Fiona and Beth were handling the conditions.

Just over ten minutes in, Hunter noted dappled light dancing before them, and then the blue of the sky appeared as the woodland thinned out and a row of granite cottages came into view. Like the one they were renting, these had the same picturesque look with well-tended lawns, and Hunter paused for a minute to admire them and to let everyone catch up.

The track briefly skirted around the cottages' front gardens before leading them back into woodland, where they came across a bridge of wooden sleepers spanning a narrow stream. Daniel and Jonathan skipped across easily, but Fiona and Beth needed a helping hand. After another few hundred metres, the path exited the woods, giving them their first sight of the sea. The view was spectacular, though they couldn't see the bay; the track dropped away beyond their line of sight.

Hunter stopped and checked his bearings against the map. Just off to the right, another narrow path ran up the side of the hill, disappearing into a line of trees. "According to the map, that path takes us up onto the headland, and the hotel we want is a few hundred yards beyond."

The steepness of the path made the going slow, and by the time Hunter had reached the top even he was blowing heavily. He turned around to the stragglers. "I think we've certainly earned ourselves a drink," he said, as the track evened out. At the top, the view was even more breath-taking. Huge rocky masses with coves and inlets stretched for miles, and the sea was so calm. There were barely any waves. "That's Little Sark," Hunter announced, pointing to the farthest headland. "We'll go there tomorrow."

At the top of the rise, the track widened into a substantial footpath, taking them through a gate, where, after another fifty metres, they came to the Dixcart Bay Hotel, which was a long stone building with a cobbled courtyard, on which was set half a dozen tables all laid with blue-and-white checked tablecloths. They entered a building that was charming and elegant, with high wood-beamed ceilings, and although the setting was old-worldly, its furnishings had been brought up to date.

The menu was à la carte with a special 'dish of the day'; Hunter saw that this was freshly caught turbot, which he hadn't tried before and so looked no further.

Service was swift. Inside half an hour, their food arrived piping-hot. Hunter's choice came with Jersey potatoes and a range of vegetables, and he attacked it with gusto, savouring each mouthful, swilling it down with another pint of the locally brewed beer. It was one of the best pieces of fish he had tasted in a long while, and Beth and his parents, who had all chosen sirloin steak, commented similarly on their meals.

By the time they left the hotel, the day was giving way to dusk, and walking back through the woods in the low light was not only precarious but also spooky. Hunter reminded himself to bring a torch next time they ventured out this late in the day.

Once back in the cottage, the boys immediately made for the TV and began flicking through the channels. Jock asked if they all wanted coffee, but Hunter took one look at Beth and asked if she would prefer the wine they had been left. Her face lit up.

Hunter started searching the cupboards for glasses. Over his shoulder he said, "Fancy going into the garden with it? It's still warm outside."

Before Beth had time to answer, Fiona said, "You two go out and relax. I bet it's a long time since you have done. Me and your da will sort the boys."

Hunter checked Beth's expression to see if she was okay with that, and seeing her nod, he grabbed the bottle of wine and followed her out into the front garden to where the table and chairs were. It was the perfect end to their hectic day.

# CHAPTER SIXTEEN

Hunter woke in the middle of the night drenched in sweat; he had come out of a nightmare where dark shadows and phantoms from previous cases had attacked his sleep. Among them Barry had suddenly appeared, and it had been his ghost that had jolted him awake. For a moment, as his eyes registered only darkness, fear gripped him, and then the sound of Beth softly snoozing anchored his reasoning, reassuring him that it was all a dream.

His head remained stationary on the pillow, his eyes staring upwards. It was far darker than their bedroom back home, and he could just make out the beams in the ceiling. He lay there, slowing his breathing, reflecting on the people he had seen in his sleep. At that moment, Billy Wallace broke into his thoughts, reminding him just what he was capable of. Hunter tried to shake the image out of his head, but it refused to go away, and after a few minutes he realised that there was no way he was going to get back to sleep anytime soon, and so decided to get up and make himself a cup of tea.

He rolled over gently so as to not disturb Beth, and slipped out from the duvet. In semidarkness he found his shorts and quietly made his way down the stairs. Opening the door into the lounge, he stopped in his tracks. A dim light was coming from the kitchen. He was the last one to retire and he thought he had turned off all the lights. A sudden noise from that direction made him jump, and his heartrate picked up. He clenched his hands into tight fists and caught his breath. Another sound came. He recognised this one — the chink of bottle against bottle told him it was the sound of the fridge door opening. *Burglars don't root around in fridges*, he told himself, and, releasing his fists, made his way into the kitchen.

Entering, Hunter saw his father pouring milk into a cup.

Jock stopped and looked his way. "Couldn't sleep as well, son?" he said. "I've just boiled the kettle. Want one?"

Hunter nodded, rubbing a hand through his tousled hair. Watching Jock put aside the bottle of milk and line up another cup, he couldn't help but think how drained and washed-out his father looked. For the first time, he saw him as an old man. Jock's muscular, sinewy frame, sculptured by years of boxing and training, suddenly appeared withered and bowed. There was a moment's silence between them.

Jock spoke first. "I never wanted this, Hunter. For you or your ma."

"We've had this conversation before, Dad," Hunter returned, squashing the tea bag with a spoon. He watched the hot water slowly turning golden brown.

"I know, but I feel so guilty about all of this. If I'd have thought all those years ago that driving two dodgy guys around was going to cause me all this grief — not just me, but my family as well — I can assure you I'd have walked away."

Adding milk to his tea, Hunter gave it another stir and brought the cup up to his chest, clasping it with both hands. Meeting Jock's eyes, he said, "You've told me the story of how you came to be driving Billy and Rab around that night they shot that woman and her daughter, but what's always puzzled me is how you got mixed up with them in the first place. It wasn't as if you didn't know that Billy was a dodgy guy."

Hunter's dad returned a down-at-heels look. "Yes, you're right. I did know Billy was dodgy, and to be honest, son, I also knew his dad was a wrong 'un. Everyone knew they were into dodgy stuff, and yes, there were also rumours about some of the things they had done, beatings and the like, but because I lived on the same street and had known the Wallaces all my life, I just saw them as a family who were always having run-ins with the law.

"Billy was younger than me, and I didn't mix with him, so I didn't know him well. Billy's old man, Gordon, was someone who had a bit of a reputation for being a hard-man, but he always seemed to look after his neighbours, and I knew him from boxing. It was Gordon who provided the venues for my fights and brought in the crowds. When I got that nasty cut above my eye, and was told by the surgeon that I couldn't fight anymore, it was Gordon who said he could put some business my way as a doorman. I was twenty-two, without a job, no skills apart from boxing, and with a flat to pay for and your ma to look after. It was an offer I couldn't refuse. And the pay was good. I ran the doors on a number of his clubs and did a good job.

"Then, one night, Gordon came to me and told me that his son Billy was having trouble with one of the rival gangs, and he wanted me to look after him, driving him around and acting as backup muscle. I genuinely didn't know what exactly Billy was involved in until that night. When I realised I was running him around to collect his drug money, I'd already decided that at the end of that night I was going to tell Gordon that I was having nothing more to do with him.

"Then, as you know, there were the shootings. We'd gone to these tenements, where Billy said this guy owed him a couple of hundred quid. He and Rab went to find him, and they'd been gone about twenty minutes when I heard the gunshots. Billy came running back to the car covered in blood, with this really nasty cut to his face. He told me that he'd been attacked with a knife and that he'd shot them in self-defence. I didn't know it was a woman and her bairn he'd shot, I swear. I thought it was the guy they'd gone for. He told me that he had to get rid of the gun, so I drove them to the Clyde and Billy threw it in. Then I drove them home."

"So, how did you caught by the police?"

Jock shrugged his shoulders. "A few days later, three of those detectives that Billy murdered eighteen months ago turned up at the gym where I was training, and said they'd been given my name for the shooting and they arrested me. I was absolutely terrified at what was going to happen to me. They just kept telling me I was going down for life, and so I told them the truth and took them to where Billy had dumped the gun. Then they told me if I made a statement, and was prepared to give evidence, they would make sure your ma and I got police protection, and we'd be looked after, otherwise they'd make sure I went down as well, as an accessory. My solicitor advised me the deal was the best I could hope for under the circumstances, and so I helped them. In return, they helped me with the house in Barnwell and the paperwork to change my name. As time went on, I thought it was all behind me — that was until eighteen months ago when Billy and Rab got out from prison, and you know what happened then." Jock sipped his tea, and swallowing hard continued, "I thought when he got caught again, and got convicted for all those murders, that would finally be the end of things. How wrong I was."

Watching his father's crestfallen face, Hunter felt a sudden sense of powerlessness and sorrow for him. "I'm sure Billy will be caught again soon, Dad, and then we can all relax again and get on with our lives."

"Well, I hope it's sometime soon," Jock responded, shaking his head. Hunter's thoughts echoed his dad's words.

# CHAPTER SEVENTEEN

Hunter awoke with an arm across Beth. He had finally dropped off after returning to bed just after 3 a.m. Now, sunlight was streaming in, and he remembered he had opened the curtains before slipping back into bed because of the privacy of the garden the window overlooked. He felt surprisingly refreshed given his disturbed sleep. Draping a leg over Beth's thigh, he pulled her closer, feeling the warmth of her body. He moved her hair to one side and kissed her neck.

Beth returned a moan that registered tiredness as well as pleasure.

"I'll make us a cuppa," he whispered, pulling back his leg and slipping out of bed.

After taking Beth a cup of tea, checking the boys were still asleep, he returned back downstairs and drank his tea in the conservatory, looking out across the rear garden. Dew covering the grass glistened, and above the trees, the sky was beginning to show bright patches of blue. For a moment, snippets of last night's conversation with his dad entered his head. If this was how they were going to spend their time in hiding, he thought, it might not be so bad after all.

Showering and dressing, Hunter and Beth came downstairs to a laid-out kitchen table. Hunter's mum had made a pan of porridge and a pile of bacon sandwiches for breakfast, and Jonathan and Daniel had already pulled up chairs and were tucking in. It instantly brought back a memory for Hunter of Sunday mornings at home, eating breakfast with *The Archers* on the radio. He fondly ruffled his hands in both his sons' hair as he took a seat. He went straight for the sandwiches, lavishing brown sauce between the slices of bread. As he took a bite, he was reminded of being a teenager again. As he chewed, he mumbled, "I think I've just died and gone to heaven." Everyone looked at him and chuckled. Afterwards, he and his Dad washed and dried the pots, and then they all got ready to go and meet Beth's parents: Beth had phoned them earlier and arranged to meet near the Information Centre in the village.

By the time they set off, the weave of clouds they had woken up to had broken up, and although it was the first week of October the sun was throwing out enough heat for them to not need coats. They took the route they had used the previous day and within five minutes were entering the village. Hunter had expected the place to be small, but it was a lot smaller than he had envisioned. Just over a dozen single-storey buildings, clustered either side of a long straight lane, made up the shopping area, a line of trees separating them. It was jostling with tourists, and they meandered along, stopping every few yards for a quick window-shop as they made their way to the end, where they came to the Information Centre. Beth's parents were sitting on a bench by the door, and Jonathan and Daniel yelled excitedly upon spotting them, bolting and quickly embracing them.

Beth's parents were younger than Hunter's — they were both in their mid-fifties. Ray had been a firefighter, retiring two years ago. Sandra had been a primary school teacher, who had taken early retirement within two months of her husband leaving, and the pair had quickly settled into their new lifestyle. It had been so convenient having them around, especially with Hunter's unsettled work pattern and Beth working three days a week. Then, six months ago, things had taken a dramatic shift. Ray and Sandra had turned up one Friday evening with the news that they had taken a year's lease out on a cottage here on Sark and were renting out their own home to subsidise their move. Hunter knew from many chats with them over the years, even before he and Beth had married, that this was their favourite holiday destination, and they had constantly talked about one day getting a place here, but neither he nor Beth saw the announcement coming. It had been a shock at first, especially for Beth, but he knew from the many phone calls since that she was happy for them. And he knew it was a decision Ray and Sandra were so glad they had made. They were already negotiating to stay on for a second year. Hunter also knew from their calls and texts that they had ingratiated themselves with the people here — Ray had become the leading firefighter among the volunteers and Sandra was a volunteer at the school.

Beth hugged them both. As she pulled away, Hunter caught the beaming smile on her face. It was good to see her happy again.

Hunter shook hands with Ray and cheek-kissed Sandra, and as he looked them up and down he couldn't help but think how healthy they both looked. Ray was a broad-shouldered man who had looked after himself. His short hair, the colour of brushed steel, and tanned complexion gave him a distinguished look. He was wearing a blue Ralph Lauren polo with cargo shorts and walking boots. Sandra, wearing a white sleeveless top and light blue shorts, also had a glowing tan. She looked younger than her age; except for a few laughter lines around her blue eyes, her skin was flawless. Beth had inherited both her mum's attractive features and her slim, leggy build.

"How's the cottage?" Ray asked.

"Perfect, Dad," Beth answered.

"What's made you decide to do this?"

"We all had some time we could take and just made the decision to go for it," interjected Hunter. The last thing he wanted was for Beth's parents to worry unnecessarily about their predicament.

"Well, its lovely to see you all. Why don't we all have a coffee and then take a stroll? Have you been down to Dixcart Bay yet?"

"Not yet. We haven't had time. We went past it when we went to the hotel last night for some food," Beth replied.

"Well, why don't you show us around the cottage? We've only seen it online. Then we'll go down to the bay. It's the best one on the island."

They grabbed a coffee next to the Information Centre, where a resident had opened up their large garden to serve drinks and sandwiches, and then, on the way back to the cottage, called in at the only supermarket, where they picked up enough provisions to last them a couple of days. Back in the cottage, Fiona made them all a hot drink, while Beth and the boys showed Ray and Sandra around the house and garden. Beth's parents both commented on the seclusion and quaintness of the place, telling them that one of ladies at the Visitor Centre had recommended it.

"Perfect choice," said Beth and asked them to pass on her thanks to the woman.

"Right, shall we go down to the bay, then?" said Ray, putting his empty cup in the sink and wringing his hands excitedly. "You'll love the place. To be honest, I haven't found a bad bay on this island. Just you wait till we show you around Little Sark and the view across to Brecqhou, where the Barclay Brothers live. And I guarantee you'll love the stacks at Port du Moulin. They'd make a great painting."

Packing spare T-shirts, jeans and trainers for Jonathan and Daniel, Beth handed Hunter the knapsack and they all set off for Dixcart Bay. The first part of the troupe's journey was along the path Hunter and his family had taken the previous night, but once out of the woods, instead of taking the hill climb they took the steady sloping path direct to the bay. As they got to the end of the straight, Hunter saw it was exactly how he'd thought yesterday — the path branched off downhill, where there was a concrete stairway to the beach. At the top of the steps, Hunter stopped and looked across the bay. It was horseshoe-shaped with a sand and stone beach encased by steep cliffs. The cliff-face to the right had a natural arch, and Hunter could just see that there was another bay through the gap. Except for themselves, the place was deserted.

Jonathan and Daniel pushing past him brought back Hunter's attention. He watched his sons skip down the narrow steps, holding onto the metal handrail so they didn't fall. They had reached the sloping beach before any of the adults took a step down. By the time Hunter made it to the bottom, holding Beth's hand tightly, Jonathan and Daniel were by the shoreline, skimming stones into the gently lapping waves.

Putting an arm around Beth, pulling her close enough to get a delicate whiff of her perfume, Hunter felt the best he had been in a long while. For once his head was not full of work, and although Billy Wallace was floating in and out of his thoughts, he wasn't troubled. Out of the corner of his eye he saw his mum and dad drift away with Beth's parents, chatting and strolling steadily, and he gave Beth a squeeze and set off after them. "Feeling better?"

Beth dragged her eyes away from the boys and met his gaze. She leaned her head in closer, brushing his neck and shoulder. "I am now."

"I got up in the middle of the night. I couldn't sleep. I went downstairs to get a drink and Dad was there. We had a chat. He's genuinely sorry about all this, you know."

"I know he is. I shouldn't be blaming him. I was just pretty pissed off with being uprooted like we were. Coming here has more than made up for it. The boys are pretty happy, and it's great to see Mum and Dad again."

"They seem happy."

"They are. This was always one of their favourite holiday places. You know how long they've talked about living here when they retired."

"And the good thing is they're still young and fit enough to enjoy it."

"I'm hoping it's the same for us when it's our time."

"Stop wishing our lives away, Beth Kerr." Hunter gave her a squeeze and she giggled. As she stopped, Hunter suddenly became aware of the lack of noise. Specifically, the lack of shouting from Jonathan and Daniel, and he turned his head towards where he had last seen them, but found himself staring at the open sea. He whipped his head in all directions. All he saw were their parents strolling in front of them. Jonathan and Daniel were not with them and nowhere to be seen. He felt his heartrate increase. "Where are Jonathan and Daniel?" He tried to prevent the note of concern from creeping into his voice, but failed.

Beth was following his gaze around the bay, and Hunter could see the frantic look on her face. "Where are they?" she said.

Hunter returned his look to the sea, just in case they had gone into the water, but the only activity he could see was the gentle roll of a small wave. Without warning, their faces flashed inside his head and a darkness he had never experienced before suddenly shadowed him, making him feel sick. *Jonathan, Daniel, where are you?* Hunter was about to bomb back up the stairway, retracing his steps, to see if they had made their way back up the cliff, when he thought he caught the sound of Daniel's voice somewhere to his right. He quickly looked at Beth. He could tell from her expression that she had also heard their son's voice.

Hunter shot a look in the direction the noise had come from. There it was again. This time, it was followed by a whoop of delight. He couldn't see Daniel, yet it seemed to be coming from the rocks, and then he remembered the natural arch he had seen when he'd first stepped onto the beach. He set off at a sprint, with Beth following. The sand made it hard going, and within seconds he was clawing for air. Taking a deep breath, he took the edge off his pace as the rock face opened up, giving him a view of the arch. Now he could hear Daniel's cries a lot more clearly. He jogged through the gap and found himself in another horseshoe-shaped bay, this one slightly smaller and filled with rocks and boulders, where he saw both Jonathan and Daniel, their backs to him, bending down, scooping something out of the sand.

Daniel was nearest, calling excitedly, "Got one."

Hunter's heart instantly lifted, but at the same time he became overwhelmed by irritation and frustration, and he dashed towards them, yelling, "What the hell do you think the pair of you are doing?"

Both boys turned sharply and looked up.

Hunter grabbed Daniel by his arm, giving him a shake. "What on earth do you think you are doing, coming through here without telling us?"

Daniel shrank away, his face taking on a frightened look, eyes starting to water.

Beth took a hold of his wrist, and Hunter relaxed his grip and stopped shaking Daniel.

Glancing quickly at Beth, he returned his focus to Daniel, softening his voice. "You scared the life out us. We didn't know where you'd gone."

"I'm sorry; that was my fault."

The female voice took Hunter completely by surprise. He spun sideways, setting his eyes upon a slim, sixty-something, white-haired lady, wearing a light grey fleece and jeans, appearing from behind one of the boulders. He immediately recognised her from the ferry crossing.

She came towards them. "I spotted your boys playing through the arch, and they saw me. They asked me what I was doing, and I told them I was collecting shells and they asked me if they could help. I saw you strolling on the beach and didn't think you would mind. I'm so sorry. I didn't mean to cause you concern."

Hunter noted that the lady's soft, throaty voice had a slight North-East accent. Not quite Geordie.

Beth squeezed Hunter's wrist. "You need to apologise. You scared them," she said softly.

Beth's comment hurt him. It felt like a rebuke. His heart had still not slowed — it was beating ten-to-the-dozen. He swallowed hard, wrapped his arm around Daniel and met the woman's eyes. "I'm sorry, but I thought something had happened to them. One minute they were playing on the beach, and the next they were gone. I didn't see them disappear."

"That's understandable," the woman replied. "I haven't got any children myself, but I've taught enough in my time to know the concerns of parents. I should have shouted and let you know they were with me, but they just came through and we started looking for shells together."

"You're a teacher?" asked Beth.

"Used to be. Been retired almost ten years."

"You're not local, though?" said Hunter.

She shook her head. "Oh no."

"I didn't think so. I noticed your accent. North East?"

"Very perceptive. Bulmer. Little village on the east coast. Not far from Holy Island. You might have heard of it."

Both Hunter and Beth and shook their heads.

"I don't live there now. I moved when I got my last teaching job."

"You're here on holiday? Or do you live here?" asked Beth.

"No. I'm here for the Festival. It's always been on my bucket list. I've got a friend coming to join me for it. I've rented a cottage back there in the woods."

Hunter nodded, recalling the cottages they had passed to get to the bay.

The lady said, "Are you on holiday?"

"I've come to see my parents," Beth replied. "They're staying here on the island."

Hunter admired how quickly Beth had responded without needing to lie.

"They are lucky. It's a beautiful island. Where else can you find somewhere like this in this day and age?"

Hunter and Beth nodded.

"So, are you here for the festival as well?"

Beth replied, "Yes, we can't wait. It sounds wonderful."

"It is. Or so I've been told. For now, I'm just exploring the island. I thought I'd got the bay to myself until I heard your charming boys here."

Hunter caught the twinkle in her vivid blue-grey eyes and suddenly felt guilty. "I bet you think I'm a right father, going off like that."

She laughed. "Not at all. When you've dealt with as many parents as I have, I can understand your concerns. It should be me apologising." She paused and added, "I'm Hazel, by the way."

"Hunter."

"Beth."

"Well, I'm very pleased to meet you both, and now I've collected enough shells, I'll leave you in peace." She held up a carrier bag that was a quarter full, turned and began walking away. After a few yards, she called back over her shoulder, "I'm sure we'll be seeing one another again."

Hunter watched her climb the steps and then turned to face Beth. "I didn't mean to react like that."

Beth shook her head and with a straight face said, "That lady'll be reporting you to Social Services." A couple of seconds later, her face broke into a grin. "I know you didn't. I panicked as well there for a moment. I hope for all our sakes they catch this Billy Wallace guy soon, and then we can all relax again. My nerves can't take any more of this."

# CHAPTER EIGHTEEN

Hunter awoke from yet another nightmare. In this one, Jonathan and Daniel had been abducted by Billy Wallace. He was lathered in sweat and the duvet was damp around him, making him shiver. The room was in darkness, and he rolled over and tapped his phone on the bedside table. The screen lit up, informing him it was 03.41. *Stupid o'clock again*. Letting out a frustrated sigh, he slipped out of bed and made his way to the bathroom. Washing his face, he knew he wouldn't be getting back to sleep anytime soon, so he decided to go downstairs, make a drink of warm milk and scour the bookshelves for something to occupy his mind.

He had always suffered an irregular sleep pattern; usually it was aspects of the job that kept him tossing and turning. Now, though, it was something far more serious that was troubling his thoughts. The recent encounters were playing out like a horror movie inside his head. Reading had always been a way he had been able to spark his imagination away from the day's disturbance, tiring his brain and taking him to a point of sleep, and he was hoping the same would happen tonight.

Tiptoeing downstairs, avoiding the second from bottom step which creaked, Hunter sauntered into the kitchen, where he poured milk into a mug and put it in the microwave. Setting the timer, he made his way to the lounge, switched on the light and began searching the bookcase in the alcove next to the fireplace. There was a wide variety of books — crime and thrillers, romance, and historical fiction, as well as a couple of celebrity biographies. He spotted a Peter Robinson title he'd not read before and he picked it out. Robinson was one of his favourite authors, and it especially helped that he was familiar with many of the Yorkshire settings. He tucked the book under his arm, collected his hot milk from the microwave and went to sit in the conservatory. The light from the lounge strayed far enough inside to allow him to read, and he set down his steaming mug on the tiled floor, stretched out on the sofa, and opened the book.

Hunter read for just over an hour, after which he could feel his eyes beginning to droop; as ever, reading had been his saviour. Walking back into the lounge, he switched off the light and stayed there for a moment, looking into the conservatory. Initially, all he saw was a wall of blackness, but as his vision adjusted he caught sight of the sky. The stars were so bright. They looked like sparkling jewels against black velvet. Hunter stepped inside the conservatory for a better view, and for a few minutes he stood rooted to the spot, entertaining himself with the majestic spectacle of the heavens. He had seen it mentioned in one of the information leaflets that Sark was one of the world's first Dark Skies Islands, and here he was experiencing it.

He had just dropped his gaze to the tree line at the bottom of the garden and was about to turn away when he thought he caught a movement. He flinched, and the hairs on the back of his neck bristled. Intensifying his focus on where he thought he had seen something, he held his breath. Within a few seconds, he caught the movement again. It was fleeting, and although he couldn't make out any shape he saw that there was definitely something shuffling among the trees. Someone was watching him. He slowly let out the breath he was holding, remaining motionless. He stayed like that for the best part of a couple of minutes, scouring the mass of trees, but nothing further happened — whoever, or whatever, was there had gone.

In that moment, for some reason an image of the Gruffalo, a story Hunter had read many times to his sons in the past, appeared in his mind's eye, and he chuckled to himself. Now he knew his imagination was running riot. After all, the island must be full of wildlife. It could have quite easily have been a fox. Despite telling himself *You're losing the plot*, he remained rooted to the spot for a few more minutes, staring out over the garden. Seeing nothing further, he cursed himself for allowing his mind to stray and made his way back upstairs.

# CHAPTER NINETEEN

When Hunter got up the next morning, he found his mum and dad having breakfast in the conservatory. He made a pot of tea, took a cup up to Beth, who was still half-asleep, and then returned downstairs. Jock had stepped out of the conservatory and was in the garden, and Hunter joined him. There was a noticeable chill this morning, and Hunter hugged his mug close to his chest, warming himself. He stood next to his dad in silence, looking out over the garden. Suddenly, a black cat appeared from the treeline and stopped and stared at them for several seconds, before sloping back into the woods. Hunter let out a short laugh, followed by the words, "Bloody cat."

"Why do you say that?" his dad returned, looking sideways at him.

"I got up in the middle of the night again, couldn't sleep, made myself a drink and read a bit. I was just standing here before going back to bed and thought I'd seen something moving in the trees, and you can guess what I was thinking."

"Billy Wallace," Jock answered on a low note, glancing over his shoulder to where Fiona was.

"Exactly, and all along it was a bloody cat."

They both let out a short laugh.

Jock placed a hand on Hunter's shoulder and on a low note said, "Hopefully your lot will catch him soon, and then we can all get back to normal." Giving him a quick squeeze, Jock finished the last of his tea and returned to the conservatory.

Hunter stayed, scoping the trees to see if the cat would make an appearance again.

Following breakfast, they all slipped on jackets, locked up the cottage, and made their way to The Avenue, where they had arranged to meet up with Beth's parents. When they got there, Ray and Sandra were standing beside a horse-drawn carriage and its driver. They were introduced to Phil and his horse Paddy and told they were going on a tour of the island. Jonathan and Daniel gave a whoop of delight and jumped up onto the back, while the driver helped everyone else to board.

Checking everyone was comfortable, Phil clicked his tongue and the horse set off at a gentle clop along the village avenue until they reached the Post Office, where the driver steered right, telling them that they were heading up to the far north of the island first, before doubling back towards Little Sark.

The sun made an appearance, but it was behind a haze of wispy grey cloud, providing a milky light that once again reminded Hunter of Cornwall, and although not as warm as the last couple of days, the temperature was pleasant. As they ambled along, Phil began to tell them a little of the island, pointing out things relevant to his well-versed tour as they went. It took them half an hour to reach a place Phil announced as 'Les Fontaines', where the uneven road came to an abrupt end at a gated entrance and a dirt track began the other side.

"You can get off here if you want and check out the view, but it's a fair distance to the end of the headland. It'll probably take you a good quarter of an hour to walk it, and I'm afraid I don't have time to hang around. I can tell you that it's worth coming back here and visiting the carved Buddha stone at the end."

"That sounds interesting, what's that?" asked Fiona.

"A Tibetan Buddhist monk and his friend came here in nineteen-ninety-nine and carved a large rock with Buddhist blessings to mark the millennium. They started off using a hammer and chisel, but hadn't counted on the granite being so tough, and they ended up using a small pneumatic drill," Phil laughed.

The group decided not to get off, agreeing among themselves to return tomorrow on a walk, and Phil clicked his tongue again and the horse jolted forward and began retracing its journey.

On this part of the journey, they caught up with three other horse-driven carriages that were full of tourists, and they also passed a number of individuals and groups. Hunter was surprised at the numbers strolling around, especially given how small and remote the island was.

"Is it always like this?" Hunter asked Phil.

"During the day it is. Most of the tourists catch the four o'clock ferry back, so we get the island to ourselves in the evening. Come the end of this month, we'll get very few visitors until next spring, so we have to make the most of it when we can to make our living. In the winter months, we do bits of garden tidying and road repairing and the like." Following a short pause, Phil continued with his tourist preamble, pointing out a track that took them to a place called Les Autelets and Port du Moulin. "That is also a great area to walk. Some great rock structures if you're into photography. And you get a really good view of Brecqhou from there."

Phil's comments about the places reminded Hunter of his father-in-law's mention of The Stacks being a good subject to paint, and he quickly determined that he would try and get a good photo of it.

Traveling slowly along the backbone of the island, Phil pointed out a chapel and an old mill, giving them a potted history of the structures, and then a quarter of an hour later they came across the view Hunter had been waiting for. He had seen it a few times already, but only in photographs — the La Coupée — the narrow stretch of road that travelled across the isthmus, connecting Sark to Little Sark. Hunter saw that the road ahead initially dropped down at quite a steep angle before reaching the gentle sweep of track, and was just wondering how the horse was going to negotiate it with the weight of the carriage, when Phil pulled hard on the reins and slowed to a stop.

"I can't take you any further," he said. "I'll pull in here and you can get off and have a stroll across. Shall we say ten minutes? Then we'll make our way back." He helped them all off, pointing to the far end of the La Coupée, where he told them there was a natural viewing point that gave them a great outlook to both parts of the island.

Jonathan and Daniel went off ahead at a trot, while the adults made their way steadily down the incline. Remembering yesterday's saga, Hunter kept his sons firmly in his sight the entire time until joining them at the beginning of the single-track concrete strip. Here they all took a few steps onto the causeway and stopped to admire the view. It was breath-taking. Either side the sea rolled and swelled, gradually disappearing into the warm haze of the sky. The road was narrower than Hunter had thought, and down to his left there was an almost 150-foot sheer drop, which he found uncomfortable viewing. The other side of the track, the hillside sloped away less sharply to a long sweeping bay of dark sand. He could just make out a series of steps and a footpath meandering down the gradient. What he also noticed was the wind. It had been hardly noticeable until now, but here they were obviously exposed. Hunter could imagine that if the wind picked up, this would make for a very unpleasant crossing.

They found the viewing point on the opposite side, and it certainly gave Hunter a great outlook. In the distance, breaking through the haze, he could make out an island, and guessed it was Brecqhou. Hunter took a photograph with his phone camera, but he could see the shot didn't do justice to what was before him.

Returning to the horse and carriage, they climbed aboard and began the journey back to where they had started out two hours earlier. Five minutes in, Hunter felt his phone vibrate. He fished it out of his pocket and saw that he had a text. It was from Budgie: *Can you meet me in the Bel Air pub at 2?*

He showed it to Beth, whispering, "I wonder if he's got some news? Is it okay if I go and meet him?"

She nodded. "You'd better. We'll go back to the cottage, and I'll get us all some lunch. I'll stay with the boys, and I'm guessing mum and dad will want to hang around. I might suggest we all go back to the beach for the afternoon."

Shortly after lunch, Hunter went off to meet Budgie at the Bel Air Inn. Budgie was already waiting for him, seated at a table in the courtyard. Hunter asked him what he wanted to drink before stepping into the bar. There were only three people seated at it, and a dark-haired woman in her late thirties was behind it, singing along to an eighties song playing from the music system. Hunter knew the song — 'Hold Me Now' by the Thompson Twins, and he remembered the album he'd been re-introduced to back at the cottage. *What a coincidence.* He hadn't heard this song in a long time, and he joined in with the words inside his head. He and Polly used to sing along at the top of their voices to this one in her bedroom, causing her parents to shout up, telling them to turn the music down.

For a couple of seconds, a flashback hurtled into Hunter's thoughts, but just as quickly it was broken when the landlady stopped singing and asked him what he wanted. Hunter spotted good old Yorkshire 'Black Sheep' on draught, ordered a pint and a Coke and then returned outside. Only two other tables were occupied, both by couples, and Hunter gave them the once-over before joining the Constable, who was again wearing cargo shorts, T-shirt and walking boots. *He'd make a great undercover cop*, thought Hunter, sitting down and handing over his Coke.

"Suspicious?" asked Budgie, flicking his eyes to the two couples at the tables, a wide grin across his face.

Hunter returned the smile. "The job never leaves you."

"I'd already checked them out myself. You've got me looking at everyone with suspicion since you arrived."

"One thing I've learned over the years is that you can never be too careful."

"I guess not. Thankfully, I don't have the same problems as you. Except for the odd drunken idiot or two in the summer to deal with, my work on the island is a lot more sedate."

"And on that note," said Hunter, taking the head off his beer, "I got your text. Have you got something?"

"No, but I just wanted to give you an update. I've put the word out, and I've shown Billy's picture to a few people and no one remotely fitting his description has been seen. If he uses any of the facilities here, or does any shopping, I'll know. I've also spoken with the fishermen; they know these waters and bays like no one else, and if they see anything unusual they'll let me know. No one can be a stranger here for long. People are already talking about you lot." Budgie gave a half-laugh. "If he turns up, I'll be the first to know. Trust me."

Hunter took a longer drink of his beer. Then, exchanging looks with the Constable, he said, "I hope this doesn't come across in the wrong manner, but Billy Wallace is a real nasty character. He'll kill you as soon as look at you. He's killed half a dozen people to my knowledge, and I've just been told he's attacked another cop back home — poured petrol over him and set fire to him. If he turns up, it's going to need more than a couple of you to take care of him."

Budgie's mouth set tight. "And no offence taken. I do understand where you're coming from. If he does turn up here, I'll put in an immediate call to Guernsey and a team will be scrambled straight away."

"How long will it take for them to get here?"

"Roughly forty minutes. They'll come on the Leopardess. It's the main patrol boat used by police and customs. Faster than the ferry."

Hunter took a deep breath. "Forty minutes is an awful long time."

Budgie locked eyes with him. "Look, I know this might seem a backwater to you, but there are almost two dozen Specials on this island, plus we have ten Reserve Firefighters. These are all resources I can call upon, and while they are all not as highly trained as the cops are back in the UK, these guys all work on the land and are quite tough so-an-sos when riled. Believe me, I've seen some of these guys scrap and I'm glad they're on my side. Billy will have his work cut out if he shows his ugly mug round here." Budgie drained his glass. "Just relax and enjoy your time here. Now, drink up and let me buy you another beer."

# CHAPTER TWENTY

Billy Wallace heard the ringtone of his new phone and dug into his jacket to pull it out. Before answering, he glanced at the screen. No name was displayed, but he recognised the number and answered, pressing it close to his ear.

"He's here," the voice said excitedly.

Billy smiled, and he took a step sideways out from the queue he'd been standing in and found a space against a wall in the fast food restaurant. "Jock?" he answered mutedly, checking around him to see if anyone's eyes were on him.

"Yes, and that family of his. Looks like the entire lot of them. There's another couple that's joined them, man and woman in their fifties. They look pretty close to the lot of them, especially with that detective's wife, so I'm guessing they're her parents."

"Staying together?"

"Don't know. I haven't found where they're staying yet. I didn't want to make myself conspicuous, especially with that detective. It shouldn't be too difficult to find out, though. There aren't too many places they can be. I'm going to hang around in the village and wait for them to show their faces, then I'll try and follow."

"Okay. Sounds like a plan."

"You joining me soon?"

"Yeah, should be just a couple of days. I think I've found someone who can bring me across on a boat. Just got a few things to sort out."

"Okay, don't be too long."

"Don't worry, I won't." Billy ended the call without saying cheerio, looking at the screen for a few seconds before pocketing the mobile. His smile became menacing. *No one messes with Billy Wallace.* He had been planning this ever since the guilty verdict. All he had thought about for the last eighteen months, while banged up, was how he was going to make Jock suffer. He cast his gaze around the restaurant again, looking for anyone whose look lingered longer than normal. Happy with what he saw, he re-joined the queue. Suddenly, he was famished.

# CHAPTER TWENTY-ONE

"Morning, Dawn, where are you? I've just tried your office."

It was DS John Reed. Dawn answered her mobile while looking in the hall mirror, checking her face and hair. She pulled at the collar of her white blouse, re-arranging the neckline. "I'm just on my way in."

"Having a lie-in? That would never be allowed on my watch."

"You cheeky devil, John Reed. I was on call last night and didn't get into bed until

three this morning."

"Well, you wanted the promotion. Don't gripe with the responsibilities it brings."

"I wasn't griping. I was just telling you… Argh!" Dawn let off an exasperated cry. "Anyway, what do you want? What's so urgent it can't wait until I get into the office?"

"We think we've found him!"

"Billy Wallace?"

"Yes, we think he's holed up in a flat in Motherwell."

"How did you find this out?"

"A snout of mine overheard a conversation in a pub a couple of nights ago. I'm just following things up — doing a few checks. I'm told the flat is owned by an ex-squaddie, who's now on civvy street, doing security work. Apparently, he's been flashing loads of cash around and telling people he 'got it doing a job that's in all the papers.' I've been given a name, but there's nothing on him on our system. But I've also been told the guy did a couple of tours in Afghanistan, so I've put in a request to army records. I'm waiting for them to come back to me. I've got a couple of my team going over to the flats this morning to make some discreet enquiries and see if I can get confirmation. Even better, try and get a sighting of Billy. If I get anything, I'll come back to you. Could be later today. You're going to be in the office, aren't you?"

"Do I detect sarcasm there, John Reed?"

A burst of laughter came down the phone. "I'll get back to you later, Dawn, one way or the other."

"Thanks, I'd appreciate that." Ending the call, Dawn returned her mobile to her bag, picked up her car keys from the hall table, checked her hair again in the mirror, shouted 'cheerio' to her partner Michael, and let herself out.

# CHAPTER TWENTY-TWO

In the Operations Room at Glasgow Central Police Station, there was a piquant atmosphere. Chief Inspector Ian Hamilton was acting as Gold Commander, directing the operation to capture Billy Wallace, and was currently viewing body-camera live-feed on the large screen monitor at the front of the Ops Room; the heavily armed contingent had just sneaked out of the back of the white van they had been transported in and were approaching the flat where Billy had been tracked to. Behind Ian, looking over his shoulder, was DS John Reed, keeping up with the jerking images as the team dashed through the foyer entrance and made for the stairwell.

The raid party were kitted out with Kevlar vests and MP5s, with tasers and Pava spray for backup, because this was a no-chances takedown; guns had been pointed at prison staff to assist Billy's escape, and it was more than likely that the guys in the flat with Billy still had their weapons. On the landing of the second floor the footfall suddenly came to a halt, and the screen became filled with the top section of a green door, number 24, coming into focus. For a brief moment, there was a jigging around as the officer wearing the body-camera stepped back to allow the cop with the big red key to move forward. The shout of 'Armed Police' went up, and then the steel enforcer bashed open the wooden door after two solid thrusts.

Suddenly, everything became a blur. Brief glimpses of a staircase, part of a hallway, and figures in black fatigues flitted in and out of frame as they burst into the flat. To an onlooker it might have been seen as chaotic, but John Reed knew this was a carefully orchestrated assault to capture an escaped psychopath. After several calls of 'Clear', which John knew was the signal that rooms had been visually swept, and their intended target wasn't present, there came another cry that they hadn't anticipated. "We have bodies!"

Ian Hamilton quickly looked over his shoulder, met John's eyes and returned to the screen. The officer wearing the camera was now mounting the flat's staircase at a fast pace. As he reached the upstairs landing, he came to a stop. A man's body came into focus. He was half-slumped, with his legs spread awkwardly across the floor and his back pressed against the wall. His dark-haired head hung down, chin resting on his upper chest. There was a long stream of blood staining his white T-shirt and running onto his upper arm. As the camera settled on his face, John could see it wasn't Billy. He could also see the neatly punched dark hole amid the dried blood-splatter, just below the right eye, that told him he had been shot.

The camera jerked again as the officer stepped over the prostrate body, moved across the landing and entered a bedroom that had the light on. Within a few seconds, the officer became stationary once more, and images of a man and a woman slumped on a bed came into view. The man's head was flat against the pillow, a pool of blood haloed around it. His eyes were shut and his mouth open. He was bare-chested, a duvet covering him from the waist down. Again, it wasn't Billy. Next to him lay a dark-haired woman, who looked to be in her late twenties. Her head rested to the side, below the pillow. She was wearing a white cotton sleep-shirt. Where her head lay against the bottom sheet there was a splodge of dried blood. Both had been shot in the head.

"Any sign of our target?" Ian Hamilton asked over the airwaves.

"Target not here," came the response. It was the female Sergeant leading the raid.

Chief Inspector Ian Hamilton looked back over his shoulder. "Well, that's not gone accordingly to plan, has it?" Sighing, he added, "You'd better get over there, John. Looks like you've got a crime scene to take charge of."

After checking that there were a couple of forensic suits in the boot of the CID car, DS John Reed tore over to the bloodbath in Motherwell. He arrived at a scene where the approach was already organised; blue and white tape had been strung across the road, and officers in high-vis were deflecting unwanted attention.

As he parked the car, John saw the press were already there in numbers, including a film crew, and he was mightily glad the security had been put in place to prevent them tramping around. Being as furtive as possible, keeping himself tucked behind the rear of the CID car, he climbed into his forensic all-in-one, keeping his eyes on the gaggle of journalists chatting among themselves. The last thing he wanted to do was draw attention to himself and get caught in their swarm, especially knowing the story so far. It was certainly going to make the leading news by lunchtime. The Prison Service was in for a bashing, there would be criticism of government cuts, and his Force would be under pressure to capture Billy Wallace — and soon.

John knew this was a high-stakes investigation — his career could elevate or fall depending on the outcome — and the last thing he wanted was to be pressurised into making a comment that he might regret later. Pulling up his hood and keeping his head down, he quickly made a beeline for the outer cordon. Edging quickly around the group, he avoided their questions, flashed his ID to the two officers guarding the sterile area and made his way to the block of flats. DC Craig McDonald, one of his team he had assigned to the raid, was standing by the entrance. He was also in a forensic suit, its hood up, but mask dangling below his chin.

John greeted him with a nod. "Well, this is something I hadn't planned for, Craig. Can you fill me in?"

"As you know, Serge, we have three bodies, all shot in the head. The flat is registered to an Alec Jefferies and his partner Mary Brown. We haven't confirmed it, but we believe they're the ones in bed. We don't know who the dead guy on the landing is, but we're guessing he was probably the other person involved in Billy's escape."

"And no sign of Billy?"

The DC shook his head. "The team have done a full sweep of the place. No sign of him. We're just starting house-to-house."

"And forensics?"

"Team on their way. So is the pathologist."

"Good. What's it look like to you? Do you think they've been dead long?"

"I wouldn't have thought too long. Although the blood is dry, there's no smell to suggest they've been like that for more than a day or two."

"And the weapon?"

"We've found a gun under the bed, where the couple are, but we don't think it's the gun that killed them. It was between the bed and bedside cabinet. Its position would suggest it was just in reach if you needed it. It's my guess that it was there for protection, but the guy never had time to get to it. Looks as though they were popped while they were both asleep."

John lifted up his mask. "Okay, Craig, let's take a look-see."

111

At eight-fifteen that morning, Billy Wallace was awakened by his phone alarm. He lurched upright, nervously taking in his surroundings. It was the first time in days he had managed to sleep. It had been a deep sleep, and that was why, for a brief moment, he fell into a state of panic. He'd let his guard down.

He reached beneath the pillow in search of his gun. It was still there, and the panic subsided. Wrapping his fingers around the butt, he slid it out. "PSS silent pistol." He was mouthing the words of Alec, who had shown him the two guns he and Frankie had used to spring him. "Used by Russian Special Forces. Smuggled them out of Afghan on my last tour," Alec had added.

In the gloomy surroundings of his hotel room, Billy locked eyes on the handgun that felt comfortable in his hand, a smile breaking across his face. *Loose ends tidied up*, he thought to himself. And now there was just one more score to settle.

# CHAPTER TWENTY-THREE

"He's slipped the net, I'm afraid, Dawn," said John Reed, over the phone.

Dawn Leggate was at her desk, resting on one elbow, with the phone clamped to her ear. Her former Detective Sergeant had already told her about the three new victims and described the crime scene. She sucked in a deep breath. "And there I was hoping you were going to bring me some good news, John," she interjected as she detected a break in his speech.

"So was I, believe me."

"And you believe Billy's responsible?"

There was an elongated pause before John replied. "Given what my snout told me, and given Billy's previous, this has his trademark all over it. Forensics have recovered loads of dabs and DNA, but we won't know anything for the best part of a week. My team are still going over the place and doing house-to-house. We have a sighting from one of the residents in the flats, who says he bumped into a guy hurrying down the stairs shortly after midnight, two days ago. The resident was just coming back from the pub. The description he gives certainly fits Billy. Even down to the scar across his face. And that fits roughly with the timing of the murders."

"And you've no idea where he is?"

"Sorry, Dawn. The last sighting was two days ago. We're checking around the site to see if there's any CCTV that could help. The flats themselves don't have any. But we don't think Billy left on foot. We've found documents in the flat that lead us to believe that the ex-squaddie who's down as renting the place owns a white Kia Sportage, but we've not found any car keys, and there's no sign of it anywhere on the complex, so we believe Billy has taken it. We've put out a request for sightings, so if he's driving it still, it'll ping up on ANPR. That's our best hope at the moment."

"What's the reg number?"

John gave her the details and added, "I believe, in the sequence of things, that he popped these three before he made his way down to you and did the cop."

"Anything else?"

"The District Commander up here is going to do a press appeal this afternoon, saying we want to trace Billy in relation to the killings, and we'll be showing a recent photo of him, so I'm giving you the head's up now, so that you can have something in place if there are any sightings down your way."

"Is it likely to go out on the main news?"

"It's a pretty quiet day news-wise, so I think it will get an airing. There's certainly enough interest up here."

"Okay, I'll make sure I text Hunter and make him aware. His parents and Beth must be at their wits' end with all this, so if I let him know, he might be able to do something to stop them seeing the news and prevent them from worrying more than they have to."

"Right, I'll leave it with you, Dawn. If I get anything pressing in the meantime, I'll give you a call."

Hunter locked up the cottage, slipped the key into his jeans and zipped up his fleece — he had noticed a distinct drop in temperature this morning, and he and Beth were off to the north of the island for a walk around the headland, where he guessed it would be a few degrees colder. He glanced at his watch as he followed Beth down the path to the gate. It was just after 10 a.m. — they had a whole four hours to themselves. Jonathan and Daniel had gone off with Sandra and Ray, and Fiona and Jock had gone off to visit the La Seigneurie House and gardens, and on the way back they were going to get more provisions from the Village Store. They had all arranged to meet back at the cottage at two o'clock and have a late lunch.

Hunter and Beth set off with purpose, bypassing the village, taking another road they hadn't tramped before that signposted them to the Eperquerie, the northern tip of the island. They passed mostly ploughed farmland, until they reached a point they recognised from yesterday's trip with Phil, which was where the road ended and became a dirt track. It was here the landscape changed as well; they left behind relatively well-trimmed hedgerows to be faced by shoulder-high gorse, flanking a narrow path.

A hundred yards along, the track opened up to heathland, giving them a panoramic view of headland and sea that was stunningly dramatic. Hunter dragged out the map from the cottage to gather his bearings. Darting his gaze between landscape and map, he made out the island of Brecqhou to his left, a place he had already earmarked to get a better look at, and he picked out a path with his eyes that he thought might lead them that way.

Within ten minutes of taking a left, he and Beth found themselves at a granite outcrop, and immediately realised they had found the Monk's Rock with the Buddhist blessing carved upon it. With careful steps, they took the rocky path down to it and spent a few minutes eyeing up the carving, Hunter running his hand over the smooth artistry of the work, before heading back up the path, finding an offshoot that looked as if it took them in the direction of Brecqhou. They instantly noticed that the wind had picked up here, and although it wasn't as cold as

Hunter had anticipated, it lashed at their faces, forcing them to hitch up their collars and dip their chins.

Following the track, Hunter was surprised to find it returned them to the main road, taking them away from the headland, and after consulting his map again, he discovered another route through farmland and took it. The deviation was worth it. As he rounded a bend, and looked out to sea, he was faced with the most breath-taking sight of four monumental rocky stacks towering out of the sea against an escarpment of huge dark cliffs. The granite blocks were suffering an onslaught of vicious sea-troughs and crashing waves, the thunderous sound echoing around the bay, and Hunter was mesmerised. It was the most spectacular sight he had ever encountered in a coastline, and he pulled out his mobile to photograph it. It was as Ray had said; it would make the most perfect painting, and as he snapped several shots, in his mind's eye, he could already see it on the wall of their lounge back home. He took at least twenty photographs before Beth nudged him.

"Come on, Constable, I'm ready for a drink."

Hunter turned and smiled; he knew she was referring to the artist and not his job. He put away his phone and glanced at his watch. They had been walking for over an hour and a half. Taking one last look at the scene, he pulled Beth close, kissed the side of her face and set off back in the direction they had come. "Sorry, got carried away again."

"You can treat me to a cider; that'll make up for it."

"Bel Air?" he returned.

"That sounds good to me."

The road back was well signposted. It took them past the church and into the village. Half an hour later, they were entering the courtyard of the Bel Air. The weather had improved; the clouds had shifted and the sun had broken through, and although it wasn't as warm as the previous few days, it was still comfortable enough to sit outside.

One couple, a young man and young woman, were at a table by the door, and as Hunter eyed the man drinking a beer he was already hoping they still had Black Sheep on draught. They selected a table up the steps on the terrace, out of earshot of the young couple, and after checking that Beth still wanted a cider, Hunter nipped into the pub. There were only four people in the place: two men standing at the bar, and an elderly couple seated at one of the tables near the fire. It looked as if it had just been lit; small flames were licking around a couple of logs, but very little heat was coming from it.

Hunter made his way to the bar, the barman just appearing from the back, throwing a towel over his shoulder. As the steel-grey, short-haired man in his early fifties met his look, Hunter thought he recognised him, and judging by the reaction from the barman, the feeling was mutual. Hunter quickly searched his memory banks, but before anything came to him, the man pointed a finger and said, "You're Barry Newstead's mate."

The cogs in Hunter's brain went into overdrive, and then it came to him. 1991. This man had given them some information which had helped them detect a robbery and a murder. It had been his first murder case — he had just started his CID aideship. He stared hard at the barman, trying to bring back his name; there had been so many more jobs and informants since then.

"Your name will come to me," said the man.

"Hunter. Sorry, I can't remember your name, it's such a long time ago."

"Mick, Mick Woods."

Suddenly, everything came back to Hunter. 1991. Just before Christmas. He hadn't been in the job long. He was on attachment to CID and working with Barry. A nasty armed robbery, where the owner had been shot. Three young men had been involved; they'd then driven on to a disabled man's house because they hadn't got much loot, and they'd shot him dead and robbed him. Mick had given him and Barry the names of those involved.

"How's Barry going on? It's years since I've seen him. He must have retired by now; I'm fifty-seven."

A lump emerged in Hunter's throat. He swallowed hard. "He's dead," he replied, stumbling over his words.

"Oh, I'm sorry to hear that. Nice bloke … for a cop." Mick let out a half-laugh.

The two young men standing at the bar whipped their heads sideways, just for a split-second, before returning to face the bar.

Hunter felt his face flush. Quickly changing the subject, he said, "It's a small world. How come you're here?"

"Long story short, since I finished at the pit, I've done loads of travelling. Been all over Europe, and one of my journeys was here, to the Channel Islands. I came here for a couple of days six months ago and saw this place up for lease. I've always fancied running my own pub, so I thought I'd give it a go. And I've not regretted one minute, so far. Are you here on holiday, or are you working? Are you still in CID?"

The two men were still facing the bar, but out of the corner of his eye Hunter could see the guys were earwigging the conversation. He smiled to himself. "Holiday. I'm here with the family."

"Here for the festival?"

"Should be."

"Seen much of the island?"

"Only been here a couple of days. This morning we've just been up to the north of the island and walked down to where the stacks are."

"Great views, aren't they? I've got to know the island like the back of my hand now. There are some great places to visit. Did you see the Window in the Rock while you were near the stacks? They're called 'Les Autelets', 'The Alters', by the way."

"Window in the Rock?"

"It's the other side of the headland, opposite side of the stacks. Some entrepreneur, who used to live on the island, blew a hole in the rockface as a tourist attraction so you could look through to get another view of 'The Alters'. It's a great view, but you have go careful; there's a sheer drop of a couple of hundred feet the other side of the Window. It's marked on the map next to Port du Moulins. You need to pay it a visit."

"Thanks, I will do."

"Now, what can I get you?"

Hunter saw Black Sheep was still on draught, and he ordered a pint and a local cider for Beth. After thanking Mick, he took them outside and set them down on the bench. He told Beth about his meeting.

"Gosh, that's weird. You come hundreds of miles to a small island like this and end up bumping into someone who's from your own neck of the woods. Good job you're not having an affair." She laughed.

"I never thought of that. I should have said I was. That would have set tongues wagging."

Hunter tucked into his pint. He had just taken the head off it, gazing around the courtyard, when his eyes settled upon a man with collar-length, straggly, brown, greying hair and a rough beard, who was sitting alone at one of the tables, looking in their direction. As Hunter caught his eye, the man pulled back his gaze and dropped his head, as if trying to hide the fact he had been watching. Hunter felt his heart leap and pick up several beats. He kept his eyes upon him for several seconds, watching the man take out his phone, swipe it and begin staring at the screen as if reading something, though Hunter felt the action was false.

"Something the matter?" Beth asked.

Hunter dragged back his eyes and met hers. "No, of course not," he lied. "Just thinking about the barman."

"What a coincidence, hey?" She smiled and sipped her cider.

For the next quarter of an hour, Beth talked about how much she had enjoyed their walk and time out from the boys for a change. Hunter half-listened, nodding while drinking his beer, breaking away his gaze a couple of times to catch a glimpse of the lone man. On one of those occasions, he had caught him looking their way again, but he quickly shied away, acting like a child who had been caught doing something he shouldn't, which again unnerved Hunter. He freeze-framed his thin angular face with high cheek-bones, storing it to memory.

"It's time we should be getting back." Beth's words brought back his attention. She had finished her drink and was holding up her watch, tapping its face. "We said we'd be back at two for lunch. It's almost quarter-to."

Hunter quickly nodded, glanced at his pint, and seeing that he only had the dregs left downed them in one gulp. Then, setting down his empty glass, he pushed himself up from the bench, shooting another look in the lone man's direction. His straggly-haired head was down once again; he appeared to still be looking at his phone.

Beth got up and slipped her arm through Hunter's. "I enjoyed that."

"Me too," Hunter returned, although he hadn't exactly. The stranger's shifty actions had unsettled him. As he stepped away, he so much wanted to spin around and see if the man was staring at them, but he didn't want to panic Beth, and so, taking a deep gulp of air to steady his breathing, he picked up his pace and headed back to their cottage, all the time feeling as if a stare was boring into his back.

# CHAPTER TWENTY-FOUR

Hunter and Beth returned to the cottage to find the kitchen table laid out with an array of sandwiches and nibbles, and everyone was waiting. Making their apologies, they washed their hands and joined them. Lunch was a chatty affair, with Fiona and Jock telling everyone about their visit to the Seigneurie Gardens. Hunter tried to be part of the conversation but found himself zoning out, thinking about the man with the straggly hair and beard, deciding to keep a lookout for him from now on.

After lunch, his and Beth's parents went into the conservatory and he helped Beth tidy up the table and wash the dishes. Then he went into the garden, where Jonathan and Daniel were kicking around a ball they had found in the outbuilding, and he joined in. The kick-around quickly worked him into a sweat, and it broke his thoughts away from the stranger. Twenty minutes later, Daniel had had enough and returned indoors, leaving him to pass the ball around with Jonathan. It didn't last long, and soon they came together, catching their breath. Hunter noticed that the day was ending as it started, with the sky awash with thick clumps of grey cloud. Dropping the ball and kicking it down towards the trees, Hunter leaned in to Jonathan and fussed affectionately with his hair.

Jonathan quickly drew away his head. "Dad!"

Hunter gazed downwards at his son. Jonathan was staring at where the ball had ended up, his head bent to one side. For a moment, Hunter felt put out by his son's reaction, but as he stared down it suddenly dawned on him that Jonathan had probably got to that time in his life where he didn't want his dad fussing over him anymore. *He's no longer a child.* This year, he seemed to have shot up — thin and lanky, like Hunter used to be — and his collar-length dark brown hair had thickened, reminding him of how his own once was.

Next year, Jonathan was starting comprehensive school, and unlike himself, Jonathan had no artistic talent whatsoever. Instead, he was sports-mad, especially football, and far better than Hunter had been at his age. He had already been approached by Rotherham Football Club Academy and was training with them. The downside was his lack of educational focus, and he and Beth had worried over it, especially Beth. They had no worries on that subject with Daniel. He was certainly the most studious — his head was constantly in a book, or he was writing his own adventure stories on the laptop.

"Is Granddad in trouble, Dad?" Jonathan looked up at Hunter, and for a moment father and son locked eyes.

"Why do you ask that?" Hunter responded, breaking from his thoughts.

"I heard you and Mum talking before we came here. You were telling Mum about someone escaping from prison who was after Granddad."

Hunter felt his chest tighten. Taking a quick breath, he replied, "You must have got it mixed up, Jonathan. It wasn't Granddad I was talking about, it was just about work. I was telling her about a job I'd heard about. I was talking about someone else's granddad. Nobody you know."

"Oh, okay." Jonathan pulled away his eyes and dropped silent. A few seconds later, he said, "I'm glad about that. I wouldn't like anything bad to happen to Granddad."

"Neither would I," answered Hunter. "It won't." Putting his hand on Jonathan's shoulder, he was determined to bring this line of talk to an end. "And now, young man, let's go and see what both Nannans and Granddads are up to. I think Grandad Ray and Nannan Sandra are off home soon. You and Daniel are having tea with them and staying over at their place tonight. Me and your mum are going out for a meal, and Granddad Jock and Nannan Fiona are having a night of peace and quiet."

After packing off Jonathan and Daniel for the night with Beth's parents, Hunter put in a call to the family-run, four-star Stocks Hotel, which he had seen great reviews about, and reserved a table for Beth and himself. Then he showered, had a wet-shave, and selected a white Oxford shirt, with his dark-wash Levi's and tan brogues. Taking time with her make-up, Beth piled up her hair and chose a black and white A-line dress with flat black shoes.

At just after 7 o'clock that evening, Hunter and Beth set off from the cottage, leaving Fiona and Jock watching television, sharing a bottle of wine. As he made his way down the path to the gate, Hunter's head was still swilling around thoughts of the stranger in the Bel Air and Jonathan's earlier comments, and he was hoping against hope that by the time he sat down for his meal, his head would have emptied out its problems so he could enjoy himself.

Their route was along The Avenue, through the village, and as they strolled, Beth grabbed Hunter's hand and told him how much she had enjoyed their day together, that it seemed ages since just the two of them had done something and how much she was looking forward to the meal. Hunter immediately engaged with the conversation, echoing Beth's thoughts, and by the time they stepped onto the cart-track, signposting their way to the hotel, his thoughts had drifted away from the worry that had been taxing his brain to which beer he would have before his food. That light chat was just what he needed, and as they stepped through the reception door, Hunter squeezed Beth's hand and kissed her cheek.

"What's that for?" she asked, smiling.

"For just being you."

Beth returned the squeeze of his hand. "You can be so romantic sometimes, Hunter Kerr."

"Only sometimes?"

She let go of his hand and bumped his shoulder. "You know what I mean."

They followed the passage to the Smugglers Bar, entering a soft-lit, cosy bar, furnished with tub-chairs, low-tables and a leather two-seater sofa. The room had a low ceiling, whitewashed walls and dark wooden beams. The name suited the area. There were only two customers — a man and woman, who looked to be in their mid-forties. They were seated on high chairs at the bar, chatting with a young-looking barman. They all turned as he and Beth entered, and each of them offered up a welcoming smile, and yet Hunter found himself eyeing them suspiciously. His thoughts had returned to that afternoon, and he cursed himself.

"Have you booked a table?" the barman asked, sliding towards them.

Hunter caught his Scottish accent, replied that they had, gave his surname and said, "Whereabouts in Scotland are you from?"

"Musselburgh, near Edinburgh."

"I know Edinburgh. Been there a few times."

"Oh aye?"

Hunter nodded. He was about to say his parents were from Glasgow, when he decided it wouldn't be wise. Instead, he said, "Been to the Tattoo a couple of times. What are you doing so far south?"

The barman let out a light laugh. "Finished uni in May. Doing a bit of seasonal work in-between sightseeing before I start a proper job. Going on to France after Christmas, when this place closes for winter."

"Sounds good."

"Aye, it is." Pausing, the barman continued, "Can I get you a drink?"

Hunter asked if they had any local beers, and the barman told him they had. He offered him three types, and Hunter chose the IPA and ordered a large glass of Chardonnay for Beth.

"If you'd like to take a seat, I'll bring you over your drinks and the menus."

Hunter targeted the two-seater sofa against the far corner — it looked well-used and comfortable — and made a beeline for it. Slipping off her coat, Beth settled into the sofa, setting her handbag down on the coffee table. Hunter joined her, sinking down into the cushions.

"This is lovely," Beth said, running her eyes around the room. "I'm glad we did this."

"So am I," Hunter replied, watching her glistening blue eyes scope the plush surroundings.

The approaching barman grabbed back their attention. He set down their drinks and slipped out two menus from under his arm, as well as a drinks list. "We have a set menu and also à la carte tonight. Just let me know when you're ready to order," he said, and returned back to the bar.

Hunter picked up his beer. It had the perfect head and was chilled. He took a long hit, savouring its hoppy taste. He could already feel a calm descending and decided he was going to have another before the meal. After another long swallow, he set down his glass and picked up the menus, opening them up and leaning in to Beth. He saw that she had taken a good drink of her wine.

As she set the glass down on the table, she said, "God, I needed that."

They scoured both menus. Both looked very appetising, but Hunter saw that on the à la carte selection, moules marinière was available as a starter. It was one of his favourites, and he underlined it with his finger, locking eyes with Beth. It was one of her favourites as well. Her eyes lit up and she nodded. Hunter also saw that 21-day matured sirloin steak was on the menu and instantly made up his mind as to what he was going to order. "That was easy. I've chosen," he said, handing over the menus to Beth. He picked up the wine list. "Red or white?"

"What are you having to eat?"

"The mussels and sirloin."

She gave the menus another quick look, and folding them, responded, "I'll have the same. Shall we order a red with the steak?"

"Sounds like a good plan."

They finished their drinks at the same time, and the barman returned to ask them if they wanted another and if they had selected their order. They ordered the same round of drinks and gave the barman their menu and wine selection, both stating they wanted the steak cooked medium. As he walked back to the bar, Hunter saw, over his shoulder, another couple coming into the room, and after a steady up-and-down glance, he told himself they weren't a threat and returned his attention to Beth.

Halfway through his second drink, Hunter became aware of someone standing before him and looked up. It was a young lady wearing a black knee-length dress and white apron, and he realised she was the waitress. She told them their table was ready and asked if they would like to follow her. He also noticed that there was now a dozen or so people dotted around the room. He had been so wrapped up in his conversation with Beth he hadn't spotted any of them arriving. He instantly told himself that had to be a good thing, and as he rose from the sofa he could feel his mood lifting.

The restaurant was up a flight of stairs, in a large wood-panelled room, its windows covered by heavy drapes and its furnishings Victorian — all very tasteful and keeping in with the hotel. There were fifteen tables, all laid for fine dining, and every one of them had been placed far enough apart so as not to overshadow the next diner. Five of the tables were taken, all by couples. Beth gave Hunter a quick happy look as they were shown to their table. He knew what she was thinking — this was perfect. The mussels in white wine, onion, garlic and fresh cream, served with freshly baked bread, still warm, was to die for and Hunter savoured every mouthful. As the dishes were cleared away, Hunter topped up their wine glasses and searched out Beth's eyes. He said softly, "Have I told you how gorgeous you look?"

A smile broke from her lips. "No, you haven't, and I've made such an effort tonight."

"I can tell, and I apologise. You look gorgeous."

"And you don't scrub up bad yourself."

He held up his wine as a toast, and they gently chinked glasses. "To us. And many more happy years."

The second course was just as delicious. The sirloin was served with Jersey Royal potatoes, and runner beans and baby carrots cooked al dente. Hunter commented to Beth that it was the best cooked piece of steak he had tasted.

They were too full for dessert and gave up on the coffee and mints. Hunter settled their bill, helped Beth on with her coat and they left the hotel. Outside it was a full moon, and Hunter was very thankful, because it had slipped his mind to bring a torch. Huddling in close, Beth grabbed his arm, gave it a hug, and they slowly made their way back, a silvery thread lighting their way.

Opening the cottage gate, Hunter saw the downstairs lights on and wondered if his parents were still up. "Fancy a nightcap?" he said, turning to Beth.

"I could drink another glass of wine, if your mum and dad have left any."

"What are you trying to say about my parents?"

She chuckled.

Hunter was just securing the gate when he felt and heard his mobile ring. He instantly thought of work and reached into his pocket. "Will you pour me a small whisky? I'll just get this," he said, taking out his phone while watching Beth making for the door. He checked who was ringing. It was a mobile number he didn't recognise, though he could guess who it was. He answered but didn't say anything.

After a couple of seconds of listening, Hunter picked up the noise of someone breathing and said, "Who is this?"

"Your old friend, Detective."

He instantly recognised Billy Wallace's gravelly Scottish voice. "You're no friend of mine, Billy."

There followed a long snort, and then Billy said, "I'm sending you something."

Hunter's phone pinged and he withdrew the phone from his ear and viewed the screen. There was a video waiting. He tapped the screen, saw an image of a group of people huddled together and hit play. The video was of his family walking down the passenger gantry at Guernsey, and as it ended, he felt his stomach empty and icy fingers run down his spine. Someone had watched them boarding the ferry to Sark. That could only mean one thing — Billy knew where they were. The vision of the straggly grey-haired man at the Bel Air flashed into his brain, as did the young barman he had been talking with earlier.

"Did you think you could escape from me, Detective? I told you I had some unfinished business with your da, and you should keep out of it. You've made your choice, and now all of you will suffer."

"You sick fuck," Hunter growled.

Billy let out a long laugh, and Hunter felt a chill run down his back. "When I've finished with you and your da, I'm going to rape that beautiful wifey and ma of yours up the arse."

Before Hunter could respond, the line went dead.

For a few seconds he stared at his phone, bringing his breathing and racing heartbeat back under control. The last thing he wanted to do was look agitated when he entered the house. Beth would immediately pick up on it and realise something was wrong.

A minute later, feeling he was back in control, he slipped his phone back in his pocket and took a last steadying breath as he took a step toward the door. He had just turned the handle when a scream from his mother froze him in his tracks. For a brief moment the shock stunned him, but it was only momentary. Slamming down the handle, he leapt into the house. He instantly saw Fiona, Jock and Beth all clustered around the conservatory door, peering into the garden. Fiona and Beth had their hands to their faces. Hunter bolted across the kitchen, into the lounge and into the conservatory, forcing himself among them. Following their gazes, he saw what they were all looking at. Directly outside the set of doors, stretched out on a stone flag was a dead black cat. It looked like the one he had seen that morning.

"Oh, poor thing," said Fiona. "Looks like a dog's got hold of it."

Hunter dropped to his haunches and took a lingering look at it through the double glazing. Its mouth was agape, tongue lolling out. The instant he saw the bulging eyes, he knew this cat hadn't been attacked by a dog. Bulging eyes could only mean one thing: strangulation.

Hunter lay on his back in the dark, listening to Beth's steady breathing beside him. He had tried to get to sleep but failed miserably. That video, Billy's comments, and the dead cat had tortured his thoughts from the moment he'd closed his eyes. He had not even been able to drink the whisky Beth had poured him. And now he had indigestion to add to the sickness in his stomach, and his throat was as dry as a bone. He needed a drink.

Rolling over gently, he pulled on his shorts, grabbed his T-shirt and slipped quietly out of the bedroom. Out on the landing he stood for a moment, listening. The house was quiet. He pulled on his T-shirt and tiptoed downstairs. He was in no mood to read tonight, but he hoped a cup of tea might settle him.

As Hunter stepped into the kitchen, he heard a noise. It was just a small sound of something, or someone, shuffling outside, close to the back door. He froze, balling his hands into tight fists, straining his ears. There was definitely a noise outside. He focused on the kitchen door. A sliver of moonlight poked through the gap at the bottom, creeping onto the wooden floor. Suddenly, a shadow passed across the base, temporarily cutting off the light and Hunter's heart skipped a beat. On the kitchen table he spotted an empty wine bottle, and he snatched it up and moved quickly towards the door. As he reached for the handle, he could feel his chest tighten.

In one swift motion, he turned the key and sprang open the door. All he saw was darkness. The moon had disappeared behind clouds and it took him by surprise. Then, movement at the periphery of his sight startled him, and as he spun, a whooshing noise fractured his hearing. Before instinct told him to duck, a heavy blow smashed his forehead. A sharp pain tore through his head to the back of his neck. At the same time, flashes of red and white exploded behind his eyes and he became light-headed. Then, his legs buckled beneath him. That was the last thing he remembered as blackness overcame him.

# CHAPTER TWENTY-FIVE

A jumble of noise, voices of panic, brought Hunter round, and snapping open his eyes he was confused to see his dad leaning over him. For a second, he was disoriented; he was lying on the path outside. How had he got here? Suddenly his head was hurting, and it came to him in a flash. Someone had whacked him.

"Just stay where you are. Try not to move. We've called for an ambulance and the police," said Jock.

Hunter tried to raise himself, but his sight was cartwheeling and he stopped, dropping back onto one arm. Behind him he could hear Beth's voice calling Fiona's name, and he was confused. He was the one who was hurt. Lifting his head, he turned to get a look back inside the cottage. What he saw threw his thoughts into a state of alarm. Fiona was lying on the kitchen floor in her dressing gown, one leg tucked awkwardly beneath the other. Beth was on her knees beside her, holding her head, supporting her. Fiona's complexion was extremely pale, almost alabaster. Hunter jerked up onto an elbow and his vision started to spin. He froze, and in a second, he was focused again. His mother was unconscious. He met Beth's eyes. "What's happened to Mum?"

"She collapsed after we found you."

He felt sick and his head started to pound.

"Her breathing's rapid, Hunter, but she is breathing. We've dialled 999 and asked for the ambulance. I'm holding her steady and monitoring her. You just stay where you are for now. You've got a nasty cut above your eye."

Hunter pushed himself up further and pressed a hand to his head. He felt a stickiness and pulled it away to get a look. His hand was covered in blood, and now his head was beginning to hurt like hell. He looked back at Fiona. Beth had turned her onto her side. "Has she had a heart attack?"

"I don't know. I don't think so. I've checked her pulse, and she's got a regular beat. The ambulance shouldn't be long now."

As she finished speaking, Hunter heard what sounded like a tractor coming closer. The next minute, the garden gate crashed open and Budgie appeared with another man who was carrying a large backpack.

"What happened?" Budgie asked. He flicked his head at the man beside him, slim, with dark thinning hair, who looked to be in his early forties. "This is the doctor," he announced.

"Someone whacked me," Hunter snapped back. "But will you see to my mum first? She's collapsed."

The doctor left his side and stepped inside the cottage. He heard Beth say, "This is Fiona, she's sixty. She collapsed approximately fifteen minutes ago. Her breathing is steady, her pulse is ninety-six and regular." After a pause, she added, "I'm a nurse."

"Okay, Fiona," the doctor said loudly, bending down, "I'm Doctor Grayson, Ian. I'm here to help you."

Hunter struggled to answer Budgie's questions — no, he didn't know what had happened. He hadn't seen anyone, and he didn't know what he had been hit with — this was the form of questioning he normally undertook, when he was dealing with someone who had been attacked. While he answered the questions, he had one ear and eye on what was happening with his mother.

Fiona had come around, and although groggy, was responding to the medical questions Doctor Grayson was asking. Hunter watched him checking her heart and blood pressure before turning to Beth. "I don't think it's a heart attack, but I'm going to take her back to the Medical Centre and check her out." Then, turning to Hunter, he continued, "And I want you to come with me as well, so I can check out that head of yours. It looks as though that wound might require a couple of stitches."

The Medical Centre was a converted bungalow, a stone's throw away from the village, and it was well equipped; the room they were ushered into served as a mini A&E as well as the doctor's consulting area. Following a quick examination, despite him having a pounding headache, Hunter was pleased to learn that he hadn't got concussion. He was even more pleased when the doctor told him that the cut above his eye didn't require suturing and that Steri-Strips would do just as good a job.

The diagnosis for Fiona was taking a lot longer. Her breathing had become shallow again, and although conscious, Hunter could see she wasn't all there. What was more worrying was seeing how anxious she had become. Laid back on a couch, she had become agitated, her legs thrashing at the sheet covering her. Beth was holding her hand, trying to calm her, telling her to take deep breaths.

Doctor Grayson trotted out of the room, but was only gone a few minutes. He wheeled in some equipment on a trolley. "Fiona, I'm going to check out your heart on this ECG machine," he said, pushing the trolley up against her bed and plugging it in. "It's nothing to worry about. It just shows me how your heart is working." He started sticking discs to her chest.

Hunter knew this was going to take some time and so slipped out of the centre to join Budgie, who was just finishing a call on his mobile.

Turning to Hunter, he said, "My Deputy is at your cottage with one of our Specials. They're just having a good look around the place to see if they can see anything. See if any evidence has been left behind. It's going to be difficult because of the darkness, but they're giving it a go. Now, are you sure you didn't see the person who hit you?"

Hunter shook his head. "No, it was too dark. They blindsided me. I don't even know what I was hit with. All I remember is hearing a noise outside and opening the door and then *whack*." He took in a deep breath. "I don't think it was Billy, though."

"Why do you say that?"

"I think if it had been Billy who'd attacked me, I wouldn't just have a cut above my eye, and he would have attacked my dad as well, while I was unconscious." Hunter told Budgie about the phone call, the video message Billy had sent hours earlier, and the discovery of the strangled cat. Then he told him about the straggly-haired man he'd seen at the Bel Air Inn and the barman at The Stocks.

"I know the manager of The Stocks. I'll check out the barman myself tomorrow. And the Bel Air has got a good CCTV system, which covers the courtyard, so we should be in luck. I'll give them a call first thing, and if you feel okay we'll pay it a visit and have a scan through yesterday's footage, and you can point out the guy you saw. I'll see if he's one of our residents. If not, I'll get his picture printed off and circulate it to my team. It shouldn't take us long to trace him if he's staying on the island. And for now, I've organised for extra locks to be fitted on your doors and windows. One of the

Specials runs the DIY shop on the island. He'll have it done in a couple of hours. It'll not stop anyone from getting in who's determined, but it will give you time to react. And you'll just happen to find a couple of baseball bats waiting for you when you get back. If anyone asks, they've been left there for your lads to play with — know what I mean?"

Eyeing the mischievous smile spreading across Budgie's mouth, Hunter nodded. The more he was getting to know Budgie, the more he was admiring him. This was coppering straight out Barry Newstead's book.

"And now, I'm going to get over to your cottage and see if anything's been found. I'll hang on there until you get back."

Hunter nodded again. "Thanks Budgie. I really appreciate this. I'm going to see how my mum is doing. As soon as I know she's okay, I'll join you."


When Hunter returned back inside the centre, Fiona was sitting up, the rosiness returned to her complexion. Beth and Jock were still at her bedside. There was no sign of Doctor Grayson.

"Where's the doctor?" Hunter asked.

"In the back," Beth replied. "He's just putting the ECG machine away."

"Is she okay?" He looked to Beth.

Beth brushed loose white hair away from Fiona's face. "Doc says it was a panic attack and nothing to do with her heart. No lasting damage. She's just got to take it easy for a day or two — " Beth turned to Hunter's mother, squeezing her hand — "haven't you, Fiona?"

Hunter switched his attention to his mum. "You gave me quite a scare there, Mum."

# CHAPTER TWENTY-SIX

Sitting in the back of Doctor Grayson's trailer, Hunter reflected on the events of the past few hours. Everything seemed so surreal, and yet the most surreal event of all was happening right now — the doctor giving them a lift back to the cottage in a trailer towed by a tractor. If things weren't so serious, he'd be laughing at the spectacle of it all. He was sure that in several weeks, when he shared the experience with his colleagues back at work, it would produce more than a few chuckles.

Dropping them off at the cottage gate, the doctor told them he'd see them at the centre tomorrow for a check-up and then bid them good morning. Turning his tractor around, he trundled back up the lane.

Although there was no sign of life outside the cottage, all the downstairs lights were on inside, and Hunter led the way up the path to the door, turning the handle slowly, calling out, "Hello," as he pushed it open. Suddenly, he was on edge.

Inside the cottage, Budgie was waiting for them, sitting in an armchair holding an empty mug. He had a startled look on his face, and Hunter guessed from the tired look in the cop's eyes that they had just woken him from a doze.

Pushing himself up straight, stretching out his back, Budgie said, "I made myself a brew while I was waiting. I hope you don't mind?"

Hunter held up a hand and shook his head.

"I've sent my Deputy and Special off home. They've had a good hunt round, but they've not found anything evidence-wise. It's not helped by how dark it is, so they're going to return around lunchtime and put in a good search. You can help if you want. It would be much appreciated, or I can ask for some support from CID across on Guernsey?"

"To be honest, Budgie, I don't know if they'd be able to do any more than what's already been done."

"That's a reassuring comment coming from a detective."

"I mean it, Budgie. They couldn't do any more."

"Well, I'll be putting in a report to the duty Inspector across on Guernsey tomorrow, and I'll see what response I get. And as for now, I'm done here. I'm going to disappear and leave you all in peace. After the night you've just had, I'm guessing all you all want is to get your heads down. When you get up and sorted, give me a call, and we'll go to the Bel Air and go through the CCTV. You can point out the man who you think was watching you. I'm going to speak with the manager of The Stocks Hotel later this morning about the barman."

"Thanks, Budgie, that's much appreciated."

The Constable glanced at his watch as he made for the door. "Ten past four. It's a long time since I've been up at this time. I haven't dealt with anything like this before. You'll be the talk of the island tomorrow."

"And there I was hoping to keep a low profile."

Budgie forced a laugh. "Not anymore, I'm afraid, but that might not be a bad thing. Everyone will be on alert now." Setting down his cup, he headed for the door, waiting for a second before pulling it open, as if unsure what he would be facing. It was still pitch-black outside, and he stood on the doorstep scouring the garden. After a few more seconds, he turned and skipped his gaze around. "Right, I'll catch up with you all later," he said, stepping into the night and closing the door after him.

Hunter turned the key in the lock and set the two newly fitted deadbolts, eyeing the craftsmanship. Budgie had done them proud. The professional manner in which the island cop had handled his attack made him mentally check himself to go that extra mile in future when a similar situation arose back on his own turf. He turned, switching his gaze between Fiona, Jock and Beth. They looked weary, and yet none of them were making any moves to go to bed.

"I don't know about you, but I could do with a drink after that," Hunter said.

They simply nodded their heads. Fiona pulled out a chair from the dining table and dropped down onto it, dispensing a weight-of-the-world sigh. Jock placed a reassuring hand on her shoulder and flashed Hunter a guilt-ridden, apologetic look. Hunter thought for a moment that his dad was going to burst into tears, and feeling embarrassed, he averted his eyes. For several seconds, a heavy silence descended. He didn't like to see his dad like this. He had never felt such a sense of powerlessness before. Normally, he would have a situation like this under control, and the fact that he didn't worried him.

# CHAPTER TWENTY-SEVEN

Hunter looked at himself in the bathroom mirror, running a hand over his unshaven jaw, while brushing his teeth. Dark rings rimmed his eyes. Not surprising. He hadn't slept, despite the two generous slugs of whisky he'd downed as a nightcap. Every slight noise, both inside and outside the cottage, had jerked him alert. He'd got up twice and looked out of the window, even when he wasn't sure if he had heard anything or not. Now he felt drained, and his head was a twisted mess. He couldn't wait to catch up with Budgie and view the CCTV footage from the Bel Air. Hopefully, the cop would be able to identify the man he thought was watching him and resolve at least one of his problems.

Finishing brushing his teeth, Hunter fixed his sight upon the Steri-Stripped cut above his eye, tapping the swollen area. He winced. Boy, that hurt. Right now, he wished he was in his father's gym. He could just go several rounds with a sparring partner to punch out the anger and frustration overwhelming him. Putting aside his toothbrush, he recalled the sad look his father had given him only a few hours earlier. He felt like shedding a tear himself.

Downstairs, everyone was up. Beth was on her mobile, and Hunter could make out she was talking with her mum and dad, making arrangements to pick up Jonathan and Daniel. Fiona was making a hot drink and Jock was in the conservatory.

Hunter sidled up to his mum. "You okay?"

Fiona nodded meekly. "Aye, son. Are you?" She looked at the cut over his eye.

"Sure. In a couple of weeks, you'll hardly notice anything."

She handed him two mugs of tea. "Take one through to your da; he's feeling sorry for himself. I'll make us all some breakfast before we pick up the boys."

"You sure you're okay?"

"Course. Stop fussing. I had a panic attack, that's all. You heard what the doctor said. Now away with you, and leave me be."

Manufacturing a grin, Hunter patted her hand, picked up the two steaming mugs of tea, and ambled through the lounge and into the conservatory. His dad was on one of the sofas, looking out over the garden. Hunter handed him a mug.

Jock looked over. "Do you think we should leave?"

"Why?" Hunter countered.

"Because of what happened last night."

"If you're thinking that was Billy, you're wrong. If it had been him, you and I wouldn't be having this conversation. That was someone else trying to scare us."

"But it was still someone capable of doing us harm."

Hunter studied his dad's face for a few fleeting seconds before replying. "Look, I'm onto this." He dropped his voice, glancing in the direction of Beth and Fiona before returning his gaze. "I didn't mention this to you, because I didn't want to worry anyone, but yesterday afternoon, when me and Beth were at the Bel Air, I think I saw a bloke watching me, and I'm going with Budgie later to look at the CCTV there and see if he knows who it is. If he knows him, Budgie and I are going to have words with him and see what he was up to. If he doesn't know him, he's going to plaster his face all over the island and track him down. Either way, it'll be sorted. And as for Billy, my boss is onto it. If he tries to leave the UK, then he'll be picked up at passport control. Things are covered, Dad. And think about this — where will we go if we do leave here? We can't go home; Billy knows where we live. We'd be in far greater danger if we went back. No, we just sit tight until Billy is caught. Hopefully, it won't be too long."

Nodding, Jock broke away his eyes and sipped his drink.

As Hunter watched his dad looking back over the garden, in his thoughts, he re-ran the words he had just spoken. The voice of reason inside his head was attempting to qualify that what he had just said was the right thing, and yet another part of his conscience was saying that while he might be trying to convince his dad, his experience told him he certainly wasn't convincing himself.

# CHAPTER TWENTY-EIGHT

Hunter, Budgie, and Mick Woods were sat in the back room of the Bel Air Inn, hunkered over a monitor and CCTV player, the landlord whizzing through feed from the previous day.

"What time was it roughly?" Mick said, his eyes not moving from the screen.

Zipping across the screen was footage from eight different cameras, inside and outside the pub, and Hunter was having difficulty monitoring every section, though in the bottom left-hand corner he saw that they were just coming up to the 2 p.m. mark. "It'd have been between quarter past and half past two when we got here. I first noticed him about ten minutes after I'd sat down with the drinks."

Thirty seconds later, Mick paused the footage and pointed at a segment of film in the top right-hand corner. "Well, that's you and your wife just arriving."

Hunter noted the time as 14:23. He had been spot-on with his timing.

The landlord let the footage run at its normal speed, and Hunter's eyes darted from one portion of footage to another, following the recorded image of himself and Beth choosing a bench in the courtyard, then him buying their drinks and chatting with Mick, to the point where he handed Beth her cider and took his seat. At this stage, Hunter noted that the bench where he had seen the straggly-haired man seated was empty.

Mick again speeded up the film, freezing the image less than a minute later and arrowing his finger at one of the sectors at the top of the screen. "This your guy?"

"That's him," Hunter replied, leaning in to get a close-up view of the man who he had been convinced had been watching Beth and himself. At the point where he had freeze-framed the image, the stranger had his chin tucked into his chest, looking down, but he recognised him from his hairstyle. He saw that the man was wearing a black, padded, weather-proof jacket, jeans and hiking boots.

Mick returned to playing the film at normal speed, and all three sets of eyes followed the straggly-haired man coming into the pub, ordering a pint of lager, and then moving outside and taking up the seat at the bench where Hunter had noticed him.

Hunter was now leaning in closer, gripped by the presence of the stranger seemingly hunched over his drink and focused only on that. The resolution of the footage was crisp and clear. *Perfect.* "Do you know him?" he asked, turning to Budgie.

Budgie shook his head. "He's definitely not one of the residents. I've never seen him before."

Mick responded, "Yesterday was the first time I've seen him as well. I just thought he'd come for drink before he got the ferry back to Guernsey. He only had the one lager and never came back into the pub. I assumed he had gone down to the harbour."

Hunter continued watching the fragment of CCTV showing the stranger. Most of the time the man had his head down, sipping occasionally at his lager. A couple of times he lifted his head, and although you couldn't tell on screen, Hunter knew the man's gaze was aimed in his and Beth's direction. On the third occasion he lifted his head, Hunter said, "Freeze it there."

The landlord did as he was asked, and the three of them centred on the man staring across the courtyard.

"Can you zoom in on that frame?"

Mick clicked on one of the buttons and the section with the recording of the straggly-haired stranger took up the entire screen. Everyone's eyes were glued to the image. The man's face was in profile, and Hunter got his first clear glimpse of him. He couldn't make out the colour of his eyes because they were in shadow, but he concentrated on the pinched features, long thin nose and his sharp jawline peppered with several days' worth of stubble. He reminded Hunter of someone who used drugs. He had seen so many of similar appearance from his Drug Squad days, and yet he didn't have that vacant look of a druggie. He seemed so much more alert, as if he was using his appearance as cover to fool. Hunter held that thought.

"Definitely don't know him. And never seen him before," announced Budgie. He took out his mobile and snapped a shot of the frozen image. Checking that the photo was good, he showed it to Hunter. "I'll send this to all my Specials, and I'll email it to all our hotels and B&B places, and the food-store. As you know, there's a lot of people on the island at the moment because of the festival, but I'd say he's the kind of guy who would stand out, wouldn't you? If he's staying here, I'll soon find out."

Hunter thanked him and said, "On another note, did you manage to speak with the manager of The Stocks?"

"I rang him just before I came here. Told me that the young man's name was Ian McDonald. He's twenty-one and comes from Musselburgh near Edinburgh."

"He told me that's where he was from when I chatted with him last night," interjected Hunter.

"The manager took Ian on five weeks ago, and he has no credentials as such, because he was hired just to do bar work. But, he says, Ian's a good worker and has given them no cause for concern. I've done a check on the details I've been given, and nothing comes back on the young man. The manager says he's staying in staff accommodation, so he's going to keep an eye on him for us."

Hunter acknowledged this with a nod.

Detective Superintendent Dawn Leggate was at her desk, scrolling through her emails, when her BlackBerry rang, making her jump. *That'll be Hunter*, she thought to herself, picking it up. He hadn't checked in yesterday when he should have done. *I'll give him a flea in his ear.* But when she viewed the screen, she saw it wasn't Hunter, it was Detective Sergeant John Reed. She answered.

"You wouldn't fucking believe it, Dawn. Bloody missed him again."

She was surprised at how raised and agitated John's voice sounded. He was normally so calm, even when under the most intense pressure. This could only mean one thing. "Billy?" she replied.

"Aye, fucking Billy. You won't believe how close we were. He has the fucking luck of the devil."

"Rewind, will you, John? I can obviously gather this call is about Billy Wallace."

"Sorry, Dawn, but that guy is as fucking slippery as a snake."

Pushing back her chair, Dawn lifted her eyes to the ceiling, switching her phone from one ear to the other. Down the line, in the background, she could hear raised voices. People were shouting to one another. "You're still not making sense, John. Just take a deep breath and tell me what's going on."

Following a long pause, John answered, "Last night, our Ops Room got a call from the manageress of a low-budget hotel on the outskirts of Edinburgh, telling us that she'd seen the news about the man we were after for the murders and that she had

147

someone fitting Billy's description staying there. She said he'd booked in for three nights, but she'd only seen him for one of those and that was when he'd first booked in. She said he'd asked for his room not be cleaned so no one had been in it, and she didn't know if he was in there or not. Late last night, I sent over two detectives to check things out, and sure enough they found the white Kia Sportage belonging to Alec Jefferies in the car park. The plates had been switched on it. So, I got my two guys to sit on the place, while I pulled together an armed team to bust it this morning. We did the raid an hour ago, and he wasn't there. Anyway, I've just seen the hotel CCTV and it shows him disappearing out the back, two days ago. He made his way down to the basement and slipped out by the laundry room wearing one of the staff overalls. He's been on the run for forty-eight hours, which ties in time-wise with what happened to the cop at Jock's house."

"So, we've no idea if he's still down here, or returned back up there, then?"

"Not at the moment, Dawn. I've got as many on it as I can muster."

"Bloody hell, John, we could really do with nailing this bastard. And quick."

"You're telling me. That's not all…"

"Hit me with it."

"He's changed his appearance."

"How?" Dawn paused and added, "I mean, what's he look like now?"

"In his room we've found a discarded bottle of men's hair-dye, and there was a load of hair in the sink. It looks as though he's trimmed and dyed his hair brown and cut off his beard. We also found a receipt in the bin. As well as the hair-dye, he bought a jar of camouflage make-up from the chemist. You know, the type people use when they've got a bad birthmark. I'm guessing it's to cover his scar."

"Do you have an image?"

"The CCTV in the hotel is crap, to be honest. It's black and white and probably the cheapest system you can get. I've got someone going through it, but I'm not hopeful that we can get anything good enough to circulate."

"That's a bummer. Okay. Fingers crossed you'll get him up there now he hasn't got transport."

"We could certainly do with a change of luck."

"Well, thank you for updating me, John. Keep me posted, won't you?"

Dawn was about to end the call, when John said, "Another thing. We believe Billy's armed. We've found a couple of bullets in his room. They match the type we found at Alec Jefferies' flat. The bullets are an unusual type — they're for a gun Russian Special Forces use for covert ops and assassination. It's known as a PSS silent pistol. It's one of the guns Alec smuggled back from Afghanistan."

"Fucking hell, John. Things were bad enough before. Billy Wallace was a headcase without a gun. Now he's an armed nutter."

"Tell me about it. We're pulling out all the stops up here."

Dawn took a deep breath, concern suddenly washing over her. "Okay, John, keep me up to date and let me know if I need to start getting worried about Hunter and his family." She hung up before he could answer, and for a moment she stared at her phone, biting down on her lip. *One step forward, two steps back.* What was she going to tell Hunter when he phoned? *The psycho who's after your dad has now got a gun. No, I don't think so. He's on the other side of The Channel, and he's got enough going on in his life without me adding to his burden.* Setting aside her phone, she returned to her emails.

# CHAPTER TWENTY-NINE

By the time Hunter left the Bel Air Inn with Budgie, a full search of the island was underway. Budgie had sent the image of the stranger to all his contacts, asking if his whereabouts were known, as well as requesting he be contacted the moment anyone spotted the man. He had also made a series of phone calls to all the Island Specials, pairing them up and allocating them a portion of the island to search, telling Hunter that his team were familiar with all the derelict places on the island as well as the usual campsites. The Constable had also put in calls to the island's fishermen asking them to carry out a sea patrol, especially requesting that they checked the caves once used by the island's smugglers. Hunter was not only amazed at how quickly the island cop had pulled this together but the resources he had available. This really was a case of the island community all working together for the greater good. Hunter knew of nothing like this in the UK and let him know how impressed he was.

Budgie thanked him, adding, "You won't be saying this in half an hour's time. We've got our own area to search, and I'm counting on your help."

"Looking forward to it. There's nothing I'd like more than to catch up with the guy I saw at the pub and quiz him."

Budgie led Hunter away from the pub, back in the direction of where they were staying, branching off by the cottage gate along a track that was signposted 'Hogsback', telling him that this overlooked one of the island's main beaches and was where Sark Henge was located.

Tramping down a muddy incline, turning a corner that headed into a small copse of trees, they were suddenly faced by a change in weather. Hunter had noted earlier that thick clouds had descended and that it was distinctly cooler, but now, as they followed the track that led them through the bank of trees into a field, fine rain met them at an angle, peppering their faces, forcing them to pull up the hoods of their waterproofs. It was uncomfortable going.

Five minutes later, they were approaching chest-high hedges of bramble that signalled the far edge of the field they were in, and as they negotiated an opening Hunter saw they were entering a wide expanse of land that overlooked the sea, though the view wasn't that good. The fine rain had turned to sea-fret, blurring everything beyond a few hundred metres, so all he could see beyond the headland was a narrow section of steep craggy cliffs disappearing into misty grey waters.

"This is Hogsback," Budgie announced, shielding his face. "Usually the view from here is stunning. Not today, I'm afraid." Pointing right, to where Hunter saw a huge pile of broken bracken, trees and bushes, he added, "This is where the Festival of Light ends next Friday. Everyone comes up here after the procession through the village to throw their torches onto the bonfire to light it." Then pointing left he said, "And that's Sark Henge."

Hunter followed the line of Budgie's outstretched arm; a hundred yards ahead, he could just make out a series of upright stones perched on the shoulder of the cliff overlooking the sea.

"Come on, I'll show you them." Looking around, he continued, "You can see that no one's camping up here, so I'll give you the tourist spiel and then we'll head back to your cottage. There's nothing here for us."

As Hunter tramped towards the Henge, he could feel his boots becoming sodden, and by the time they had reached the circle of stones, water had crept through the leather and his feet were starting to get damp. They halted at the edge of the circle and Hunter was surprised at just how small it was; the nine stones were roughly chest height, set around a circumference of no more than forty feet. He had expected it to be far larger and threw Budgie a questioning look.

Budgie smiled. "I know what you're thinking. Is this it? To be honest, it's not that ancient. It's made up of stone gateposts that are old, but the circle itself was built only recently to commemorate four hundred and fifty years since Queen Elizabeth I granted the Fief of Sark to the Seigneur." He let out a chuckle. "Anyway, we're proud of it and it makes for a good talking point." He took another look around him, straightening his face. "Well, there's certainly no sign of life up here, and the weather's not fit for man nor beast. Come on, we'll go back to yours and I'll check in with the others and see if they've come across anything." Dipping his chin into the collar of his waterproof, Budgie set off back towards the track.

Dawn Leggate took the call from Hunter driving home from work, ending their conversation on the driveway of her home. Storing everything to memory, she turned off the engine and sat for a good minute, staring out through the windscreen at the garage door, thinking things through. Given what John Reed had told her this morning, and this recent information from Hunter, the Billy Wallace investigation had suddenly cranked up a gear. Her first priority when she got into work tomorrow was to speak with her counterpart on Guernsey and discuss tactics, and the other thing on her mind was to send up a liaison team to Scotland to join her former colleague, so she had a constant overview. She was eternally grateful there were no other pressing matters at work at the moment. Happy with the decisions she had come to, she picked up her bag off the front seat and climbed out of the car.

Entering the house, she was greeted by the sound of Frank Sinatra singing 'You make me feel so young' and smiled to herself. Michael was playing swing music again. That could only mean one thing — he was cooking.

"I'm home," Dawn shouted along the hallway, closing the door behind her, planting her bag down on the hall table and unbuttoning her coat.

"I'm in the kitchen," Michael called back. "Just rustling up some food."

Slipping off her low heels, she stretched out her toes and made a detour into the lounge, turning down the volume of the music system, before making her way into the kitchen. He always had it on loud, and Michael's choice of music wasn't hers. She smelt spaghetti bolognese the second she entered. She had only grabbed a yoghurt for lunch, and suddenly she was hungry. Michael had his back towards her, stirring away at the stove, and she looked him up and down, setting her eyes on the metal cage wrapped around his right leg that held his smashed femur in place.

A lump emerged in her throat. Is this what survivor guilt felt like? For a moment, her thoughts spun away to the night that had happened. It was still as fresh in her mind as if it were yesterday. She had come home late from work to an empty home — Michael had gone out for a curry with his mates, leaving her a note saying he would make his own way home. She'd had a couple of glasses of wine, taken a long soak in the bath and turned in after the ten o'clock news. And then the loud rap on the front door had woken her, and thinking it was

Michael who had drunk too much, she'd tramped downstairs, flinging open the door, ready to blast him with some choice words. She had been so surprised to find a traffic cop standing on the doorstep, nervously trying to break the news to her that Michael had been involved in a hit and run, was in a bad way in hospital and he had come to drive her there. She had arrived to find Michael in ITU, machines beeping all around him. He had been in a bad way. He'd had a fractured pelvis, right femur and right arm, a serious head injury and was unconscious.

Dawn had learned that not only had the car mown Michael down, but it had also deliberately reversed back over him. It had been touch-and-go for 48 hours, but thankfully he had pulled through. Although now, weeks later, he was limping around and frustrated he could neither go to work nor to the gym, he was on the mend. And, thankfully, he couldn't remember anything about the accident, so suffered no flashbacks.

In the days following the accident, colleagues had kept Dawn up to date, and she had quickly learned that the chief suspect was her ex-husband, Jack. Thinking that a hit-and-run accident had seriously injured your partner — and could have killed him — was bad enough, but learning that the culprit was your ex was even worse. And the man had heaped even worse misery upon her. Not content with damaging Michael, Jack had gone on the run, targeting her, planning to kill her in similar circumstances, and he had almost succeeded; she had just left the pub with some of her team after celebrating the fruitful end of a case, and was making her way across the car park, when Jack had driven his car straight at her. Barry Newstead had seen it and pushed her away, taking the full impact, killing him instantly.

As that thought now entered her head-space, a vision of that night flashed inside her brain. Watching Barry fly over the roof of Jack's speeding car, being dumped like a rag-doll, was still fresh and raw as if it had happened yesterday. She had tried to dull it several times with wine, but it was still there when she had sobered up. The legacy her spiteful husband had left her with was not going to go away quickly, and seeing Michael like this was a constant reminder. Also, Jack was on remand for one count of murder and two of attempted murder, with a court case pending, and so her ordeal with him still wasn't over.

"How's it going with Billy Wallace?" Michael said, shaking her from her reverie. Setting aside his wooden spoon, Michael hobbled sideways to the fridge, poured a glass of Chardonnay, offered it to Dawn and returned to the bubbling bolognese, stirring it gently. "This should be another ten minutes."

Dawn took a slug of wine. The crisp refreshing flavours of pear and lemon sparked her taste buds, and surprisingly, immediately took the edge off her tension. Billy Wallace had been the cause of their coming together. Eighteen months earlier, while based in Scotland as a DCI, Dawn had been the Senior Investigating Officer overseeing the brutal murders of three retired detectives who had been murdered by Billy and his henchman Rab Geddes. Her team had discovered that the killings had been out of revenge — the three retired detectives had been responsible for getting Billy and Rab convicted and jailed for the murder of a young woman and her daughter back in 1970. The person who had given evidence against the pair of killers had been Hunter's dad, and after being freed, following 36 years in jail, they had targeted the retired detectives to find out the new identity and location of Jock Kerr to carry out their revenge against him.

Michael Robshaw had been Hunter's boss, and during the investigation to apprehend Billy and Rab, Dawn had liaised regularly with him on the joint operation for their capture. At that time, she had just separated from Jack, after discovering his affair with a girl he worked with. She had just instigated divorce proceedings and, although not planned, she and Michael's frequent meetings had been a refreshing series of moments and had resulted in a relationship forming between them.

After the arrests of Billy and Rab, Michael had told her he was getting promoted to Force Crime Manager and suggested she apply for his job at Barnwell. The pressure of her marriage breakdown, the wish for a fresh start and the offer of promotion had been a great lure, and she had grasped it. Moving in with Michael after securing the post of Detective Superintendent had been the icing on the cake.

Dawn took another swallow of wine before answering with, "It's taken a nasty turn." She told him about Hunter being attacked, his sighting of the stranger and how once again Billy had slipped the net up in Edinburgh. "He's obviously got someone across on the island, and that's worrying. Hunter assures me that he's working well with the island cop, and it does seem as though he's covered a lot of bases. Nevertheless, I would prefer it if a couple of my team were there as well to support him. The other thing I'm going to organise is sending up a couple of detectives to Scotland tomorrow to join forces with John."

Michael gazed over his shoulder. "Have you made a request to send a team across to Sark?"

Dawn shook her head. "It's not something I've done before. I didn't know the protocols. Do you?"

Michael shook his head. "Never had any involvement with any of the Channel Islands before. Tell you what, I'll put in a phone call tomorrow and find out what we need to do to send a team across. And if everything's okay, I'll sort the budget as well."

Dawn leaned in and planted a kiss on his cheek. His unshaven skin prickled her lips. "Having the Force Crime Manager for your partner does have its perks."

"So, it wasn't just my charm, charisma and leg-up for promotion you wanted me for, then?"

Dawn glared at Michael, faking snake-eyes, tipping the point of her glass in his direction. "Michael Robshaw, how could you? I got this promotion on my own merit, and you know that."

He let out a hearty laugh and simulated a fisherman with a rod and reel bringing in a catch.

"You're intolerable, Michael Robshaw." Dawn downed the remainder of her wine. Her day was ending on a high note.

# CHAPTER THIRTY

Dawn Leggate got in to work early to check all the documentation and travel tickets were in place and to brief the two detectives she had selected to send up to Scotland. She had chosen Hunter's working partner Grace Marshall, who was acting as temporary Sergeant in his absence, and Mike Sampson from his team. With regards to the contingent she wanted to send to Sark, she had two detectives in mind, but she was waiting to see if she had both authorisation and the budget before approaching them.

Dawn checked her watch as she finished the last of her lukewarm coffee, saw that it was just after 7.30 a.m. and rang John Reed's number. She knew he would be at work. John was a creature of habits. Like herself, when a job was running, his energy levels were at an all-time high and he practically lived at work until it concluded. She also knew that he was an ardent Rangers fan, and they had played last night, and the morning after a game he would always hold court in the office, providing his own analysis of the team's performance with his colleagues. She could just visualise him now with his feet up on the desk, nursing a mug of tea against his chest, re-living the highlights of the game with whoever was in the office, whether they wanted to listen or not. Her call was answered on the second ring.

"Morning, Dawn, shit the bed?"

She cracked a smile. They went so far back that John was the only Sergeant she allowed to call her by her first name. Everyone else referred to her as boss.

"To what do I owe this pleasure?"

"John, I'm sending you up two of my best officers this morning. They're on the eleven-twenty train and should be with you just after four. They're booked into the hotel near the railway station. They're fully up to speed with what's gone on, and I'll be doing a final briefing with them before they leave."

"Looking forward to meeting them."

Pausing, she said, "How have you gone on since we last talked?"

"It's not good news, I'm afraid, Dawn. We tracked Billy via CCTV to the railway station, where we believe he got the train to Doncaster, which, although no consolation, definitely nails him for the attack on your PC at Jock's place. We literally have no idea where he is at the moment."

"What about contacts?"

"Most of his old contacts have died. He has a sister who's in her sixties, but she's had nothing to do with him since he shot that mother and bairn. All his immediate family are no longer around." Taking a deep breath, he continued, "He obviously has someone he's in contact with, because how else would he have arranged his escape? But as far as that goes, we haven't found who that person or persons are yet."

"Have you checked with the prison to see who's visited him while he's been inside this past eighteen months?"

"That's one of the actions. We're speaking with the Governor today to get access to his records."

"Okay, John, you seem to have everything in hand."

"We're pulling out all the stops here, Dawn. Believe me. We want Billy back inside as much as you do. How's Hunter and his da, by the way?"

"So-so. Hunter's keeping himself busy helping out the island cops. I spoke with him last night, and they're currently doing a search of the island for whoever whacked him. He tells me it's a pretty tight-knit community, so he's hoping to have them locked up pretty sharpish. I'm making a request to send a couple of my team across there. I don't know how that's going to go down."

"Oh, okay. Well, I wish you well. And I'll keep you in the loop. Or rather, your spies will."

"Now, now, John, do I detect some sarcasm there? You know I'm not sending them up there to interfere."

He gave a quick burst of laughter. "I know, Dawn. Just teasing."

"Oh, and John…"

"Yes, Dawn?"

"No getting my officers pissed."

She caught another burst of laughter from John as she ended the call.

Hunter studied his face in the bathroom mirror. He looked shocking. It wasn't just the bruising around his head and eye, but how tired and pale he looked. He'd had yet another restless night. He had spent the early hours of the morning listening to the sounds around the house, getting out of bed on several occasions to gaze out through the window, over the garden, because he was unsure what the noise was. But he had seen nothing, and no matter how hard he had tried to convince himself it was his imagination running wild, he had still jerked upright with each fresh sound. He had eventually fallen asleep, but it had been well after 4 a.m. For the second night running. Now he was knackered. He ran a hand along his jawline, turning his head. The two-day stubble did nothing to help his appearance, and determined that he could at least try and look fresh, he lathered his face with shaving gel to start a wet shave.

Twenty-five minutes later, shaved, showered and dressed, Hunter made his way downstairs. Fiona was in the kitchen with Beth, making a pan of porridge. Beth was pouring hot water over teabags in four cups. He saw Jock in the conservatory, staring out over the garden. The weather still looked murky. There was a busyness about the cottage, and yet Hunter sensed an unease. The troubles of the last week, especially the last few days, were beginning to take their toll. Pasting on a false smile, he wished everyone a "Good morning," in high-spirited fashion, sidled up to Beth, gave her waist a hug and picked up one of the mugs of tea she had just added milk to. The same was returned, but again the smiles weren't genuine. No one was kidding anyone. The strain on everyone was there for all to see.

"What's happening with Jonathan and Daniel?" Hunter asked of Beth.

She finished stirring the cups and dropped the spoon into the sink. It went with a clatter. "I've asked Mum and Dad if they can stay with them for now. Apparently, they've done nothing but talk about what happened to you and Nannan Fiona. Mum said they seemed really nervous about having to come back to the cottage, so she's offered for them to stay there."

Hunter watched Beth's mouth tighten. Her bottom lip started to quiver. He held her eyes, adjusting his gaze, trying to pass on some reassurance. He stroked her arm. "I think it would be a good idea. I'm going to speak with Budgie and see if there's anywhere else we can stay. Somewhere where the boys might feel safer. I've already rang The Stocks Hotel, but they're full."

"Did you have any joy yesterday with your search?" Fiona asked.

Hunter shook his head. "I spoke with Budgie late last night. They've searched most of the island and checked all those that are camping, but no joy. The hotels and B&Bs have not got anyone staying there who looks like the guy we saw at the Bel Air, so he's now speaking with those who rent cottages and rooms. As he says, it's a lot harder because of all the people here for the Festival of Light. He's pretty confident, though, that the guy will turn up."

"What about the police from Guernsey? Are they coming across?"

Hunter was just about to respond when his mobile rang. He snatched it up off the side, seeing Budgie's name light up the screen. He held up his hand to Beth and his mum.

"Morning, Budgie."

"Morning, Hunter. What are you up to?"

"Just having breakfast, why?"

"Well, drop what you're doing and get over to the police station. I'm just on the way there. We think we've found your guy."

# CHAPTER THIRTY-ONE

The police station was in a two-storey building next to the Chief Pleas Office — the island's Parliament. It was a shared building, accommodating both Fire and Ambulance Service, with Budgie's office on the first floor. Hunter bounded up the stairs, knuckle-rapping the door, entering without waiting for an answer. The office was roughly twelve feet by twelve but filled with so many filing cabinets and desks that there was very little space to manoeuvre around. Budgie and four of his Special Constables were standing over one of the desks, poring over an Ordnance Survey map of Sark. They looked up as Hunter entered.

"We're just sorting out our approach and who's going to do what," Budgie said, placing a finger over the area of map they had been studying.

"What have you got?" asked Hunter, joining them, eyes hopping one from cop to another before turning them on the map.

Budgie lifted his finger and pointed. "I got a phone call this morning from one of our residents who rents out a couple of cottages she and her husband own. They're located in the woods in Dixcart Valley, and the lady who rang me believes one of them has been rented by our man. It was rented four days ago for a fortnight. The name it's been rented under is Mr T. H. Law. She met him when she handed the keys over, and having looked at the photo she's certain its him. What I'm doing now is just sorting out our best approach." Budgie stabbed his finger over an area of woodland. "It's not clear on this map, but there are a group of five cottages in the middle of these woods. I think our best approach is through the woods to the back of the cottages. Then we'll split up. Hunter, I want you and three others to cover the rear, just in case he does a runner, and one will come with me to the front. It's going to be a door-knocking exercise only, and I don't want him seeing you, Hunter." He paused, looking at Hunter, before continuing. "We can't prove he's the one who attacked you, so it's softly, softly. If it is the man from the Bel Air Inn, I'm going to tell him we're just carrying out checks of people on the island because we've had a number of break-ins. Then I'm going to get his details, if he'll give them."

Hunter acknowledged with a quick nod. "What about the name he's given? Have you checked him out?"

"I've run it through the computer and there are a number of hits for Law, but none of them with the initials T. H. That's why I'm going to see if he'll give me his full details."

Hunter nodded again. "You seem to have everything covered, Budgie."

Budgie folded his map and picked up his radio, glancing at them all. "Let's rock 'n' roll, then."

The six cops made their way through the village in the direction of Hunter's cottage, their number attracting several turned heads. As they stepped onto the track, beside the gate to the cottage, Hunter realised where they were heading; he and his family had taken this route, their first day, to the Dixcart Hotel. A brief image of the cottages they were heading to flashed inside his head and he tried to retain that vision, but all he could hold onto was a brief memory of them having a picture-postcard feel about them. He was eager to see them again. He especially couldn't wait to see if the man staying in one of them was the same guy he had seen at the Bel Air Inn.

More importantly, he was eager to get his identity so that he could check any connections to Billy Wallace. If that was flagged up, it would be a game-changer.

The trek through the woods was more hazardous than Hunter's last one; the wet and damp weather had made the narrow path sloppy and the fallen leaves slippery underfoot. There were times they all had to grab onto a tree each to stop themselves sliding onto their backsides. The last part of the journey was making the crossing over the stream. Hunter saw that it wasn't as tranquil as last time; the water had gained in volume, gushing against the banks and rocks, splashing up onto the wooden bridge they walked over. The liquid roar was deafening, and Hunter thought he wouldn't like to make this journey at night.

The backs of the five granite cottages sprang into view as they emerged from the woods. They were joined together in one long line, and the track led them past the gable end of the first cottage. The cottage rented by Mr. Law was at the opposite end. Hunter's eyes roamed along the row. His last memory of this setting had been of warm pink stone cottages set among beautiful cared-for gardens. That last fairy tale impression of them was now masked by a fine mist, which dismally subdued the colours.

"Hunter, you slip along to the end with my three. I'll take Kevin here and we'll do the knock. If I need you, I'll shout."

Hunter and three of the Special Constables nodded without saying a word and set off slowly along a flagstone path that ran the rear of the cottages. Budgie and Kevin slipped through a gate that took them past the shoulder-high garden wall of the first cottage.

It took Hunter and the three Specials no more than a minute to reach the end cottage. Their silent approach had ensured no one had come out. They pressed themselves back against the stonework of the last cottage, close to its back door, in case whoever was in there made an attempt to flee. Hunter felt his heartrate picking up and took a great gulp of air to steady his breathing. He turned an ear to the back door, trying to tune in to the sounds inside the cottage. Everything was quiet. Suddenly, the radio of the Constable standing beside him erupted, making them all jump. It was Budgie. His voice raised a notch, he was telling them to get around to the front.

At a fast jog, Hunter and the three Specials slipped around the side of the end cottage and joined Budgie and Kevin, who were standing by the front door. It was ajar a good foot, and Hunter immediately noticed a stain on the doorstep that flowed into the hallway. It was blood. Not a large swathe, but enough to be worried about. Someone, or something, had been badly hurt. Hunter could make out the imprint of a shoe tread within it. He met Budgie's concerned look. "You haven't been inside?" Hunter questioned.

"Called you as soon as I saw this," Budgie replied.

"Okay, I'll take a quick look. Everyone stay here, then if there's anything untoward, only I'll have contaminated the scene." Hunter received approving looks from everyone, and bunching his hand and slipping it inside his coat sleeve, so as not to leave fingerprints, he slowly pushed the door inwards with his forearm.

The doorway led straight into the lounge. He stepped inside, stopping next to the door, and instantly noticed further bloodstains in the form of splatter arcing across the lower half of the wall. Mr Law, or someone else, had taken a nasty whack. He peered around. The room was approximately twelve feet square and contained a mocha-coloured two-seater sofa and armchair, and a flat screen TV on a stand in one corner next to an open fireplace with a grate. It looked as if there had been a fire burning at some stage, but only ashes were left. There was a magazine open face-down on the floor beside the sofa. The floor was wooden floorboards, and he noticed some further splatter.

Hunter called back, "Someone's certainly taken a battering, but there's no one here, so far." Stepping further into the room, avoiding the blood marks he reached a staircase in the middle of the house. He noted the house was as cold inside as outside, and that told him the front door had been open for some time.

At the bottom of the stairs, he paused. Another doorway led to the kitchen. He poked his head inside. It was slightly smaller than the lounge, wooden units running around three sides with a small table and two chairs against the fourth wall. Hunter noted a couple of dirty plates and cups and an empty microwave meal-for-one container on the draining board next to the sink. Nothing else was out of place.

"I'm going to check upstairs," he called without looking back. The steep narrow staircase split to two rooms at the top. The bedroom to the front contained an unmade double bed, a wardrobe, a set of drawers and a bedside cabinet all matching in cream with wooden tops. At the back were two rooms — a much smaller bedroom, containing a single bed and a set of drawers, and at the end of a narrow hallway was the bathroom, a grouping of aftershave, deodorant, toothbrush and wash bag on the window sill. The house was empty of life.

Hunter carefully made his way back down the stairs, returning to the front door, hugging the wall all the way. Outside, Budgie and the four Specials were waiting, wearing expectant looks.

"There's no one in there, but I'm not happy with this one bit. The windows are all still latched, and the back door's locked." Pointing to the bloodstains, Hunter added, "Except for the blood, there's no sign of a struggle, or fight, or anything, but that looks reasonably fresh to me, probably only several hours old, and it's my guess that the victim answered the front door and was attacked on the doorstep. More than likely taken by surprise, like I was. No time to defend themselves. This certainly needs following up." Pausing, he said, "It might be a silly question, Budgie, but do you have anyone on the island trained in forensics?"

Budgie shook his head. "We don't have the call for anyone to be trained. If we need forensics, and it's very rare we do, we call on Guernsey. I can only remember them coming here a couple of times in the last ten years, once for a suicide, and once when we had a spate of burglaries committed by someone from Jersey employed by a hotel."

"Okay, I need you to make that call. In the meantime, we need to secure this scene and carry out a search of the surrounding area just in case someone is lying around injured. With regards to the house, we need to preserve those bloodstains and find something to put on the floor so we don't contaminate it while we carry out a search of the place and see if we can find anything which will tell us who exactly our guy is and where he's from."

They found some old boxes and sacks in an outbuilding, and Hunter, slipping into work-mode, covered the main stain by the front door with a large box, and laid the sacking inside the cottage, spacing them apart so that they could step from one sack to the other, enabling them to move from one room to the other without tainting the integrity of possible forensic evidence. One of the Specials ran back to the station and returned with a box of latex gloves and paper overshoes.

Hunter paired the Specials up, instructing two to conduct a search of the immediate surroundings, while he and Budgie and the other two Specials carried out a search of the cottage. He and Budgie took the upstairs, selecting the front bedroom as their starting point. Hunter took the wardrobe. There wasn't a lot of clothing hung up in there at all, just three T-shirts, a sweatshirt and a pair of jeans. The man certainly hadn't packed to stay here any length of time.

In the bottom of the wardrobe was a small suitcase. It wasn't locked, and Hunter unzipped it. Inside was a UK passport. He was elated. He took it out and opened it. He instantly saw that the photograph was that of the person he had seen at the Bel Air Inn, but after reading the name of who it belonged to, he attracted Budgie's attention. Holding it up, he said, "Well, according to this passport, our man is certainly not called T. H. Law."

# CHAPTER THIRTY-TWO

A search of the cottage gardens, and a narrow section of woodland backing onto the cottages, revealed no injured persons, and all they found inside the cottage of note, besides the passport, was an e-ticket for a return flight from Guernsey to Glasgow in the name of the passport holder, Nicholas Strachan. Hunter checked out the passport. It appeared genuine enough. He put it into a plastic bag with the e-ticket, put a note inside with time and date and pushed the bag into his coat pocket. Then, they secured the cottage and returned to the station.

Once there, Budgie checked out Nicholas Strachan on the computer, only to be disappointed when nothing came back, and Hunter scanned the passport, attaching it to an email, which he fired off to Dawn, providing her with an update and requesting follow-up checks of their mystery man. That done, Hunter helped Budgie compile his report for the Guernsey police and left him to make arrangements for CSI to forensically examine the cottage.

As Hunter bid goodbye, Budgie was preparing to organise an extended search of the area around the scene, calling on more of his island resources. Once again, Hunter was suitably impressed given Budgie's lack of experience in matters such as this and stored his thoughts of praise for when he next spoke with his boss.

On his way back to the cottage, Hunter rang Beth and found she was at her parents' with Jonathan and Daniel and that they were about to have lunch. Hunter checked his watch, surprised to see that the morning's work had taken up over three hours of his time, and told her he was joining them.

At Ray and Sandra's, it was just himself, Beth and the boys for lunch — Fiona and Jock had gone to the island's chocolate factory to sample the wares and have coffee. Out of earshot of the boys — they were watching TV — Hunter was quizzed about the morning's events, and in a low voice he told them what they had found.

"So, you don't know if this Strachan fellow is linked to this Billy Wallace guy you're after?" said Ray.

Hunter shook his head. "Might be just sheer coincidence, but then I ask myself why give a false name? What is disturbing, is not finding him at the cottage and finding those bloodstains. Once again, that might be just sheer coincidence. It might be completely innocent. Say, for instance, it could have come from an injured animal. But it's not just by the door; there's the splatter on the wall and floor."

"You think someone whacked him, then?" asked Beth.

Hunter shrugged his shoulders. "Or someone else has been attacked there by this Strachan fellow. Not sure at all. More questions than answers at the moment. Budgie's organising another search around the cottage this afternoon, just to make sure he's not lying around anywhere, or someone else is for that matter."

"You think he's on the run?" Beth asked.

"I wouldn't have thought so. Why leave your passport and return ticket? I think something's gone off, but I'm not sure what that is yet. Budgie says he'll give me a ring if he finds anything. So, for now, it's just a waiting game."

After lunch, Hunter, Beth and the boys went to the Visitor Centre, had a browse in the information room where there was display about the history of Sark, and then picked up and worked their way through a number of 'things to do' brochures. They soon found that many of the activities were seasonal or weather-dependant, so a boat trip around the island and kayaking, which they fancied, had ended until the following March. All they were left with was hiring a bike or going on the many walks, touring the island. The boys weren't interested in any of that and asked if they could go back to Beth's parents, where Grandad Ray had promised to take them to the fire station and show them around the adapted fire engines housed in the garage beneath where Budgie worked. Hunter and Beth acquiesced and took them back to Ray and Sandra's cottage, where they left them, and went up to the Seigneurie Gardens and strolled around the walled estate.

The afternoon with Beth was leisurely and enjoyable, and although Hunter found his thoughts straying at times onto that morning's event, it was only occasionally, and by the time they came out of the garden, Hunter's thoughts had switched to thinking about what they were going to eat for their evening meal. Grabbing a pot of tea at the Gardens' café, Hunter suggested he and Beth should go out again for food, and Beth eagerly agreed, saying she would ask her parents if they would mind if Jonathan and Daniel stayed over again.

Leaving the café, Beth put in a call to her mum, popping the question about the boys sleeping over. Sandra told her she was more than happy for them to stay, telling her they were still at the fire station with Ray. Thanking her and promising to pick them up first thing in the morning, Beth ended the call wearing a huge grin. She said, "You and I have a date night."

Hunter reserved a table at The Stocks Hotel, and in relative peace he and Beth got ready for their evening out. Fiona and

Jock were staying in with a bottle of wine, telling Hunter that they had found a couple of films among the DVDs that they hadn't seen before.

As Hunter was starting to dress, following a longer than normal soak in the bath, Budgie rang. He told him they had done a full search of all the cottage gardens, and had ventured a good way into the woods, but hadn't found anything. They had also spoken with each of the cottage residents, but no one had heard or seen anything and none of them could help with information as to who Nicholas Strachan was. Only the immediate neighbour had spoken with him, and that was to say 'Hello' and 'Good morning.' Hunter thanked him and told him he'd be in contact tomorrow and turned off his phone; his boss hadn't got back to him following the sending of his email, and he'd decided no phone call was going to disturb his night out with Beth.

As they left the cottage it was starting to rain, and Hunter grabbed one of the umbrellas by the door, testing it worked and had no holes before setting off. Their stroll through the village brought about a considerable amount of yawing, avoiding puddles that were starting to form on the uneven surface. Beth was cursing her choice of footwear — dainty ballet pumps — which were starting to get damp.

By the time they reached the hotel, both of them were beginning to feel cold, and the warmth of the interior was very welcoming. There were a lot more people in the bar than during their previous visit, and the sofa they had grabbed before was now taken by a couple, and so they took a tub chair each. Hunter ordered one of the local beers and a house white wine for Beth, noticing it was a different barman serving. He immediately asked after Ian McDonald, the name Budgie had given him, and was met with the reply that he was off sick.

Hunter instantly switched his thoughts to what had gone off at the stranger's cottage, visions of the bloodstained lounge washing around in his head, and he desperately wanted to ask more questions of the barman, but decided it was best not to say anything which might alert Ian McDonald, should he be involved. He would put in a call to Budgie once he was back at the cottage, requesting a check of him to be done in the morning.

Hunter returned to Beth with the drinks, plonked himself down beside her, took the top of his beer and picked up the menu.

Beth selected a Caesar salad, and Hunter chose the black pudding with poached egg for starters, and they both wanted the fillet steak again for their main. The restaurant was full and noisy, but that suited them both as neither could avoid talking about Billy Wallace, debating if Nicholas Strachan was linked or not. It was at this point Hunter told Beth about his suspicions of the Scottish barman, particularly given what had gone on at Strachan's cottage. He told her he was going to ring Budgie once they got back to the cottage. Beth had just responded that he should, when their meal arrived.

Both enjoyed their food, once more commenting on how wonderfully cooked the steak was. When it came to paying the bill, Hunter left a generous ten-pound tip. The stroll back to their cottage was better than the earlier journey; the rain had ended, and many of the clouds had parted, allowing them a great view of the stars.

Beth pulled Hunter close, resting her face against his shoulder. "Thank you for a lovely evening," she said, giving his arm a squeeze.

"And thank you," Hunter returned. "It was perfect, wasn't it?"

# CHAPTER THIRTY-THREE

Hunter jolted out from a deep sleep, flicking open his eyes, blearily darting them around the room. His heart began to race. For a moment he lay there, holding his breath, wondering why he had awoken with a start. Although he couldn't hear anything other than Beth's gentle breathing, he was certain something must have disturbed him. Still holding his breath, he listened.

Nothing.

He decided to get up and check things out. He gently slipped out from beneath the duvet and padded towards the window, where he stared outside. Like previously, it was so dark he could hardly see anything, and so made his way onto the landing where he stopped, ears straining downstairs.

Silence.

Still not comfortable with the situation, he decided he was only going to be satisfied when he'd checked out the whole of the house and so made his way down. The moment he stepped through the doorway into the kitchen, he felt a chill. A gentle breeze was coming from somewhere. Icy fingers ran down his spine. He quickly scanned the kitchen, then the lounge, where his gaze was immediately drawn to the sight of the curtains lifting.

*The window's open.*

Heartrate spiking, he felt his chest tighten, and clenching his hands into fists he took a few steps forward. His right foot splashed into something wet, and before he glanced down, a smell he recognised caught the back of his nose and throat.

Petrol.

A lengthy, shiny, black pool travelled from the lounge window, across the floorboards, a good ten feet into the room. He caught a sound outside the window, and it only took him a split-second to identify what it was.

A zippo lighter.

He spun sharply and bolted for the stairs. In a second, he was clambering up the flight, two steps at a time, screaming "FIRE!" to his family. As he reached the landing, he heard a loud whooshing noise below. Someone had lit the petrol.

Dressed in just their sleepwear, Hunter, Beth, Fiona and Jock stood huddled together outside in the doorway of the outbuilding, watching flames lick the frames of the dormer windows, listening to cracking and splitting woodwork as it succumbed to the raging fire and heat. The downstairs was well alight, and the lounge window had already exploded from its frame. Now the fire had reached upstairs and was beginning to take hold.

"All our stuff's in there," Fiona said softly, covering her mouth and looking on, horrified.

"The main thing is we're all safe. That's all that matters," Jock replied, pulling his wife close.

Hunter's eyes were locked on the burning cottage, almost in a hypnotic state. He shivered. Someone had just walked over his grave. If he hadn't have woken up and gone downstairs, none of them might be here. He leaned in closer to Beth, grateful nothing had happened to her.

That fucking Billy Wallace. He could fucking kill him.

The arrival of the fire engine halted his thoughts. It had seemed an eternity since he had dialled 999 on his mobile, though he guessed it was probably less than quarter of an hour ago. Given that it was manned by volunteers, and the engine was towed by a tractor, they hadn't done badly getting here. Though it didn't look as though they were going to be able to save much of the cottage. Hunter could now see flames coming through the roof slates.

Beth's father was among the firefighters. He ran up to them. "Everyone okay?" he enquired anxiously, his eyes set on his daughter.

"We're fine," Beth responded. "Hunter heard something and got up. It was a good job."

Ray tapped his daughter's arm. "Okay, good. Now, let's see if we can save anything." He trotted away to his team, who were already rolling out the hose.

"Is everyone okay?" It was Budgie. He was dressed in just a thin waterproof jacket over joggers and a T-shirt. He was out of breath. "I got here as fast as I could."

Hunter repeated what Beth had just said.

"What happened?"

Hunter told him about being woken up and then going downstairs and finding petrol poured over the floor.

"Bloody hell." Budgie looked to the burning cottage momentarily and then returned his gaze. "Did you see anyone?"

Hunter shook his head. "Whoever did this was outside. I didn't even see their shadow."

"I'm so sorry, guys, I should have posted someone here, but I used everyone who was available for yesterday's search."

"You weren't to know this was going to happen. No one was."

"But I feel responsible."

"Don't."

A sudden loud revving sound from the fire engine drowned out Hunter's voice. The water pump generator had kicked in, and Hunter watched two firefighters aim a jet of water at the roof of the cottage. Ray was beside them, pointing up to where fresh gouts of flame had just broken through another area of the roof. Within seconds, the blaze had disappeared and thick black smoke belched upwards.

"Listen, guys," Budgie shouted over the noise of the generator. "We need to get you somewhere warm and safe. I'm going to make a call. I'll get the Community Centre opened up. We use it for emergencies, though, except for exercises, this is the first time we've used it. We have some camp beds there, and sleeping bags, and we'll get you a warm drink. There's nothing anyone can do here tonight. Tomorrow, we'll see what we've managed to save in the cottage." Budgie checked their faces and they all nodded back.

Hunter had just stepped out from the doorway of the outbuilding when his mobile rang. He saw it was a number he didn't recognise, and quickly decided not to answer, ending the call. Following Budgie down the path, his phoned pinged. He had a text. Stopping by the gate, Hunter looked at the message and froze.

*Just warming up ha ha*

On the stroll through the village to the Community Centre, Hunter noticed Fiona's breathing was starting to get ragged.

Beth noticed it too. "Are you all right, Fiona?" she said, taking hold of her arm.

Even in the low light, Hunter could see his mother's face was pale. It had the look and texture of putty. He watched her drawing in a sharp breath, leaving open her mouth. She looked ready to faint.

"Fiona," Beth prompted.

Fiona put a hand to her chest. "It feels tight."

Beth guided her to a nearby low wall and helped her sit. "Take a deep breath, Fiona," she said.

Hunter thought his wife's voice sounded remarkably calm given the circumstances. He was starting to worry. His mum didn't look good at all.

Beth grabbed hold of Fiona's wrist, feeling for her pulse.

"Do I need to get the doctor?" said Budgie, reaching into his pocket for his phone.

Hunter searched out Beth's eyes, throwing her a questioning look.

She held up a finger, a sign for them to hold on a minute. "Just lower your head for me, Fiona, and take several deep breaths." Her voice exuded authority and still remained composed.

Fiona did as she was told, taking in great gulps of air, releasing it slowly. After thirty seconds, she lifted her face and everyone saw that her colour had returned.

"Fiona, you are fine," Beth said soothingly. "You're just having another anxiety attack. Just carry on taking deep breaths for a minute."

Hunter took a deep breath of his own. *Fucking Billy Wallace.*

On his bunk below the deck of the boat he had hired, Billy Wallace listened to the rain drumming the fibreglass roof with good thoughts in his head. He had managed to score some coke in the last pub he'd visited. Laying out two lines on the back of his mobile, he hoovered them up with a cut down straw. The hit came within seconds, and he half-closed his eyes, experiencing the rush cascading through his body. He had missed this in prison. The shit he managed to get his hands on in there gave him nothing like this.

Opening his eyes and taking back control, he swiped the residue from his phone with the side of his hand and turned it around, activating the screen to watch the video again that had been sent to him half an hour ago. Slightly grainy, he could just make out Jock and his wife steadily making their way down the garden path, their bodies backlit by the fire destroying their rented cottage. In the background, he could see that the firefighters were doing their level best to douse the blaze, but it looked as if they were fighting a losing battle. The clip lasted for a good thirty seconds and as it ended, he replayed it for the third time, a wicked grin slashed across his face. His accomplice had done well. *The Kerr family will be shitting themselves after this.*

The shipping forecast announced that there would be a temporary lull in the storm in the next few hours, and although it would be dark, the skipper he'd hired knew these waters like the back of his hand. Soon he would be on Sark, and the work his contact had done would mean he would be facing the grass who'd put him away.

The last time he and Jock had met, Jock had got lucky, and that's why he'd ended up in prison. *Not this time.* Though there was still one major obstacle in his way. Someone who could damage his plans — Jock's son. He had planned this so carefully over the last eighteen months, and the last thing he wanted was to fail. He had special plans for Hunter. Plans that would ensure there was only going to be one winner, even if it did mean him going back to prison where he would eventually die. At least he would have the pleasure of knowing he'd taken down Jock and that detective son of his.

# CHAPTER THIRTY-FOUR

Sleep had been out of the question for Hunter, even though he was drained and the camp-bed he had been given was surprisingly comfortable. He had tried, but failed, his brain on overdrive, repeatedly thinking what might have been had he not woken up. When he had closed his eyes, images had disturbed his inner vision; on rewind had been the horrified looks on Beth's and Fiona's faces as they watched the cottage burn. Jock's look had been no better. He had just stared, in shock. Hunter wanted to throttle the very life out of Billy Wallace for what he'd put his family through.

There had been one moment in the early hours when he had almost succumbed to sleep, but then the wind and rain had started, lashing and rattling the huge windows that spanned two sides, and that had put paid to any hope of getting any shut-eye. Now, as dawn was breaking, and the wind and rain easing, he lay with his hands tucked behind his head, staring up at the ceiling, thinking about what he would find when he visited the cottage later this morning; he hoped that there was something they could salvage, that they hadn't lost everything they had brought.

Thin shafts of light were beginning to stream through the gaps in the curtains, and Hunter drew back his gaze, fixing it upon his parents and Beth. Each of them looked snug in their sleeping bags and appeared to be fast asleep. He wished sleep would come to him.

He scanned their surroundings. The room was no doubt the hub of the centre. Its walls were adorned with wildlife and landscape photographs from the island, paintings done by children — Budgie had already told them to expect some noise early on because the school was attached — plus posters, advertising talks and presentations. Tables and chairs had been pushed against the walls to make room for their beds. It wasn't an ideal setting, but under the circumstances Hunter was extremely grateful once again for Budgie's help. *The guy deserves a medal*, he thought, and he was certainly going to recommend him for a commendation when he got back home. It was the least he could do.

Shortly after 8 a.m., Hunter, Beth, Jock and Fiona rose from their beds, disturbed by activity beyond the walls of their room; they could make out the sound of pots and pans being moved around. Ten minutes later, there was a gentle knock on the inter-connecting door; behind it, a woman's voice asked if everyone was decent. Beth shouted for her to come in, and the door opened to reveal a fair-haired, slim lady, wearing glasses, who looked to be in her mid-fifties. She had on an apron over a pair of jeans and woolly jumper. "I'm just cooking you all breakfast. Would you like tea or coffee?" Hunter looked to Beth and then his mum and dad. Each of them wore a smile. It was such a welcoming greeting, given their recent experience.

After breakfast, Hunter made a relatively quick phone call to Dawn Leggate to apprise her of the situation, and as he ended the call Budgie showed up with a Special Constable that Hunter recognised from the previous day. They each carried a black plastic sack, which they dumped on the floor.

Budgie opened his up. "This is not ideal, I know, and I hope you won't feel embarrassed, but we've brought you some clothes that should fit. They're from our charity shop. They're probably not to your taste, and not to your liking —" he let out a chuckle — "but they are clean and fresh and should sort you out until we see what's left of your things in the cottage."

Everyone looked at one another.

"Beggars can't be choosers," said Fiona. "Thank you, this is much appreciated."

"And just to let you know, the fire fighters have managed to save most of the upstairs. The bedroom above the lounge, and the bathroom, are a write-off. You'll not be able to get anything from those rooms, but they've saved the two bedrooms above the kitchen. There is smoke damage, but it doesn't look as if anything's been damaged by the fire. That's the best news I can give." Budgie looked to Hunter. "You'll have noticed the weather?"

Hunter nodded.

"Well, the sea's really rough, so there's no ferry service today. That means no forensic or CID support, I'm afraid. They're hoping to send across a team from Guernsey tomorrow."

Hunter acknowledged this with another nod.

"Oh, and I've some real good news for you all…" Budgie looked to each of them. "I've found you some accommodation. Again, it's not ideal, but the place is dry and warm and will be able to cater for you all." Pausing and checking their faces, he continued, "It's a chalet on one of our campsites. It's got two double bedrooms, fully furnished, with a kitchen and lounge with woodstove. It even comes with a free supply of logs." He finished the last sentence with an edge of wit.

"There's no end to your generosity, Budgie," Fiona responded.

"Not me you have to thank for that, it's the farmer who owns the campsite. He's one of the Special Constables here as well, by the way." Looking to everyone, tapping the nearest black sack with his foot, Budgie added, "And now if you want to choose some clothes, I'll take you to the cottage so you can see what you can retrieve."

Beth's dad was waiting for them when they all arrived at the cottage. He was dressed in uniform, acting as Lead Firefighter. He wrapped his arms around Beth, pulling her close, greeting her with a kiss on the cheek. Releasing her, he asked, "You okay?"

"I'm fine, Dad. Thank you. We all are. Shook up a bit, but we're okay, given what might have happened." She threw her gaze in the direction of the cottage.

Ray let out a relieved sigh. "It could have been worse, I'll grant you that."

"Budgie says you've managed to save our and Mum and Dad's rooms," interjected Hunter.

Ray turned his attention to Hunter. "Yes. We couldn't save Jonathan and Daniel's room, I'm afraid. Unfortunately, everything in there's been lost. That room was directly above the seat of the fire."

Ray's words triggered another dreadful thought for Hunter. Jonathan and Daniel. He was so grateful they hadn't been there. It didn't bear thinking about what might have been. He shuddered.

"Shall we go and see what we can recover?"

Ray's voice brought Hunter's thoughts back. He nodded.

"We've shored up the ceilings with props, and the stairs seen pretty safe, but just stay close to the wall when you go up them," Ray said, setting off up the path to the cottage.

The moment they entered the smouldering blackened kitchen, the stench of smoke got into the backs of everyone's throats, causing them to gag.

Hunter pinched his nose and covered his mouth. The smell he noticed most was woodsmoke. But then he wasn't surprised, given that each of the rooms had beamed ceilings. The next thing he noticed was the gaping hole between the beams in the lounge. Poking through from above, he recognised a couple of legs from Jonathan and Daniel's bunkbed. The beams had prevented the bed falling through. Another chill ran down his spine as he pulled away his gaze. Below his feet, the floor was swimming with filthy blackened water. For a moment, Hunter studied the destruction. It was going to take a lot of work to return this to a habitable state. *It might even have to be pulled down*, he thought.

"Come on, follow me," said Ray, "I'll take you up to your rooms."

Hunter did as Ray had told him, staying close to the wall as he followed him up the stairs. He could smell the scorched plaster and saw that most of the stairway wall was cracked as he climbed. Reaching the landing, a cold breeze greeted them, and Hunter saw all the doors to the bedrooms were wide open. He zipped up the fleece Budgie had given him and stepped into his and Beth's room. His parents peeled away to theirs. The moment he entered, the cloying smell of soot caught the back of his throat, making him cough. He hawked and spat on the floor. Beth tapped his shoulder as a rebuke. Although Ray had told them their bedroom had been saved, he had expected to see some damage. True, the room was a mess, puddles in places over the floor, and the bed soaked through, but the fire had thankfully not touched anything. Hunter flashed Beth a grateful grin and went to the wardrobe, pulling open the doors. All their clothes were still on hangers.

Beth reached past him, pulled out a pair of jeans and held them to her nose. "They smell of smoke, but a good wash will soon get rid of that." Then she reached down and pulled out a pair of heels. "My favourite Karen Millens, thank God."

Hunter burst out laughing. "Beth Kerr, what are you like? We could have all been burned to death in our beds, and all you're worried about is whether your favourite pair of heels are okay."

She gave him a dig in the ribs and put back her shoes. Pointing to their suitcase in the bottom of the wardrobe, she said, "Come on, let's get all our stuff out of here and go and see this chalet Budgie's found for us."

Hunter dragged out the case, suddenly feeling a lot better than he did a few hours ago.

# CHAPTER THIRTY-FIVE

The sun wasn't even up when Dawn Leggate swung her car into the MIT car park, and she wasn't the only one out and about early — Hunter was also up. She had already ignored two of his calls while driving to work. She made her way upstairs, bidding good morning to the cleaner who was hoovering the MIT office as she keyed in her password to enter her office. Setting down her bag, she unbuttoned and slipped off her coat, draped it around the back of her chair, booted up her computer and took out her phone. Speed-dialling Hunter, she set her mobile to speakerphone and listened to it ring out.

He answered on the second ring. "Boss." He sounded slightly out of breath, as if he were on the move.

"Can you talk?"

"Two secs, I'm just going somewhere quiet."

Dawn listened to the sound of footsteps on wood followed by a door opening and closing, and then he was back on the phone, telling her it was okay to speak. She replied, "I've missed a couple of your calls, sorry. I was driving, and my phone wasn't hands-free. Has something happened?"

"How long have you got?"

For the next ten minutes, she listened to Hunter explain the most recent incident. Pushing herself back in her chair, her thoughts were switching into investigative mode as he expanded on the detail. When he stopped talking, she left it a couple of seconds to ensure there was nothing else forthcoming, and then she said, "You said no one was hurt?"

"No, something woke me up. If I hadn't have done, I hate to think what might have been."

"It's not worth thinking about." After a short pause, she added, "And you've no idea who it might be?"

"Something tells me it wasn't Billy. Again, like when I was clobbered a couple of nights back, I think if it had been him who fired the place, he would have been waiting to see what happened to us. He would have wanted to see what happened to my dad, I'm certain about that. He sent a text, by the way, telling me he was 'just warming up', but that was almost a good hour after it happened. I think whoever set fire to the cottage did a runner the moment it went up and then phoned or texted Billy. At the moment, there are two suspects we're looking at: this Nicholas Strachan guy and a Scottish barman at one of the hotels here." He went on to tell her about his suspicions of the young man known as Ian McDonald. "He was supposedly off sick last night, so Budgie's doing some follow up checks this morning and checking his ID." Pausing, he added, "Have you managed to find out anything about Nicholas Strachan yet?"

"No, I forwarded everything you sent me to John, but he hasn't got back to me. I do know he's tied up with the murders of the three who helped Billy escape, and he's got everyone available out searching for him, so it won't be his priority at the moment. The second he gets back with anything, I'll ring you." Dawn let what she had just said sink in and then added, "I'm guessing by your request you haven't found Strachan yet?"

"No. We've done a thorough search of the cottage he was renting and a search of a big section of the woods at the back. Budgie and his team are extending it today to see if there's any sign of him."

"And anything from forensics?"

"Hit a snag there, boss. The weather's taken a turn for the worse, and the sea's too rough for the ferry, so the team from Guernsey can't get to us at the moment. Apparently, it's like this every so often. A day or so and it'll change, I'm told."

"Okay, and just for your info, I've made a request for a couple of the team to come out and join you as well, but I'm waiting for a response from Guernsey. I'm guessing they'll not be too happy with the thought of us interfering."

"To be fair, boss, things are pretty much tied up here. Strachan's not going to be able to get off the island without the ferry, and Budgie is doing a pretty good job given the circumstances. There are certainly enough bodies for him to call on. All that's lacking is experience, and they're certainly happy with me being involved to supply that."

"That's good. Well, let me know how you're getting on. Tell me the moment anything changes or happens, and I'll chase up John again regarding this Nicholas Strachan fellow."

"Okay, thanks boss. I'll probably give you a call this evening. Budgie's sorted us out some more accommodation, so I'm going to get us settled in there, and then I'm going to join him and his team and see if they've got anything."

"Well, it does sound as though you're on top of everything there. I'll wait for your call. And please send my regards to your family."

"Thanks, I will, boss."

Checking there was nothing else, Dawn ended the call and turned to her emails, firing off another to John Reed, updating him about the fire at Hunter's rented cottage, and how it was started with petrol, believing it was an attempt to kill him and his family. It was an urgent prompt for him to get back to her ASAP. Then, she began her daily routine.

# CHAPTER THIRTY-SIX

The new place wasn't a chalet at all but a Scandinavian style log cabin with a porch at the front, a high-pitch roof and lots of windows. Inside was highly polished pine — walls ceiling and floor. Heavy rugs covered the floor. The lounge-cum-dining room had a cathedral ceiling with roof lights, giving it a bright and airy feel despite the foul weather outside. The only thing that wasn't polished wood was a large stone fireplace in which sat an iron grate loaded with logs.

"Beautiful," said Beth, coming up behind Hunter, resting her chin on his shoulder.

It certainly was, Hunter thought, setting down their suitcases. "I'm going to light that fire and see if there's anything to make us a hot drink."

"That sounds like a good idea," Jock said, dragging his and Fiona's cases in.

Hunter could see that both his parents had flushed faces, his mum slightly out of breath, but she looked a damn sight better than last night, he told himself.

Beth grabbed hold of their cases and began wheeling them to one of the bedrooms. "While you stick the kettle on, I'm going to sort through our clothes and see what needs washing and what doesn't."

"And I'm going to do the same," Fiona responded, taking them from her husband's grasp and setting off after Beth. Jock followed her into the second bedroom.

Hunter found a box of matches on the mantel above the fireplace, started the fire, made sure it had taken hold and went through to the kitchen. More polished wood was in here, including the cupboards. He rooted in the cupboards for cups and found everything he needed to make tea and coffee. Now he just needed milk. The fridge was a large American style one, and he opened it to find not only had milk been put in there, but also orange juice, margarine, cuts of ham, a wedge of cheese and fresh salad. The farmer's generosity caused a lump to form in his throat. Swallowing, Hunter shouted through to the others, "They've left us some food as well," and pulled out the cuts of ham.

He was surprisingly hungry, even though his stomach was still turning — his thoughts still on what might have been, had he not woken up. He knew that thought was going to hang around for a good few days at least, but he was determined it wasn't going to let it overshadow everything. He had other things to focus on. Finding Nicholas Strachan, for one. And right now, he had something else just as important to think about — getting something to eat and drink. *I'm as hungry as a scabby horse.*

As Hunter searched for some bread — hoping the farmer's generosity had stretched to buying them a loaf — he was reminded of one of Barry's regular statements: 'An army doesn't march on an empty stomach', and he broke into a smile as he opened up a cupboard he hadn't yet searched. He struck lucky. Not only had the farmer left bread but breadcakes as well, and Hunter took them out and began making sandwiches with the ham and cheese. By the time he had made four cups of tea, Beth, Fiona and Jock were joining him in the kitchen.

"The clothes are not as bad as I thought," Beth said, eyeing the pile of sandwiches and picking out a ham one. "A good blow in this wind on the line and they should be good as new. The wardrobe and drawers have protected them."

Hunter picked up a cheese and tomato sandwich he had made especially for himself and was about to bite into it when his mobile rang. He put down the sandwich and dug his phone out from his pocket, looking at who was calling. "It's Budgie," he exclaimed and answered. "Afternoon, Budgie, this place you've got us is fantastic…"

Budgie cut into his sentence. "Sorry to disturb you so soon, Hunter, but a couple of my team have just rung me. They've found a body in Dixcart Bay, and the description they've given me sounds like our man Strachan. I'm just on my way down there, and I'd appreciate your help if you wouldn't mind."

# CHAPTER THIRTY-SEVEN

The nearer Hunter got to the bay, the more fiercely he could feel the wind growing in strength. By the time he reached the slope leading to the concrete stairwell to the beach, it had become a gale, the sea roaring in its vortex, and as he put down a foot on the top step, he found himself being buffeted so much that he had to grab the handrail to stop himself being blown over the side.

Steadying himself, he took his first look at the scene. Thanks to the high-vis jacket, he instantly spotted one of the Special Constables he had been with the previous day searching Nicholas Strachan's cottage. The officer was shielding himself against the rockface beside the entranceway of the natural arch, and Hunter guessed the body was the other side of the bay. He signalled to the officer and steadily began his descent, his eyes roaming along the beach. Vicious waves were exploding onto the sand, sending up a booming noise as they broke, and as he steered his gaze through the wicked swell behind, Hunter found it hard to believe that a week ago this had been such a different setting; the sea had been so calm, mirroring the colours of the Mediterranean.

Shaking his head, he lifted his eyes skyward. Beyond the horizon, fists of storm clouds, the colour of indigo, punched their way across the sky and bands of rain like umbilical cords connected sky to earth. The view was so visually dramatic, which as an artist he appreciated, and yet with an entirely different eye and reason for being here, he prayed the distant storm was going to remain out at sea.

Loose, well-worn pebbles and wet sand made the short trek to the natural arch difficult, and he found himself catching his breath as he asked the Constable, "Who's here?"

The Constable cupped an ear towards him, throwing him a questioning look, the gusts obviously impeding his hearing.

Shouting to make himself heard, Hunter added, "Has Budgie arrived?"

"Five minutes ago," the Constable answered. "We've sent for the doctor, but he hasn't arrived yet."

Hunter was just about to ask if CSI had been informed, when he remembered where they were, and as he once more looked out to sea, he knew there was no chance of them getting here today. This was a unique situation. It was time to improvise, he told himself.

He made his way through the archway into the other section of the bay. Here, the horseshoe beach met with a sheer face escarpment of dark rock, and the noise of the sea being whipped up echoed from it, making it sound even more thunderous. Up close to the cliff face, where he saw there had been a rockfall, Budgie and two other Constables were atop a huge boulder, looking behind it, their backs to him. He knew there was no point in shouting, so deafening was the sea, that he picked his way through the litter of large rocks and boulders to where the cops were gathered.

Budgie turned as Hunter started to clamber up the rock. It was wet and slippery, and Budgie reached down to give him a hand up. "The body's down behind here. The face is a bit of a mess, but it certainly looks like our man."

Hunter joined the trio, and on hands and knees, securing himself, he peered over the large stone. Four feet below was the corpse, pinned between the boulder and the shale from the rockfall. One arm was misshapen; it clearly looked as though it was broken in several places, and the head, as well as being badly bloodied and battered, was at an awkward angle to the body. And, although not all of his face could be seen, there was enough on display for Hunter to recognise the weaselly features of the man he'd seen at the Bel Air Inn. He was dressed in a black fleece jumper and jeans that clung to his wet body.

Hunter pointed to the loose shale and then up the escarpment. "Did he fall when the cliff gave way?"

Budgie shook his head. "The rock fall is not fresh. It happened last winter. And he's come down from the top all right, but my guess he's been thrown over. There's a sign up there warning of the landslide, and it's actually a fairly steep decline to the edge. It's quite dangerous, and it's more likely he was dragged so far and then rolled over the edge. We'll need to check that out."

"So, given what you've just said, the most likely scenario is that he was attacked after he answered the door at the cottage, and killed or at least rendered unconscious there, and then whoever did it got him up to the top of the cliffs above us and rolled him over the edge."

"That certainly sounds right," said Budgie, nodding. "And it's my guess they did this at night, when the tide was in. Probably hoping the body would be washed out to sea, but instead it got wedged behind this rock."

"What about the barman at The Stocks?"

"I spoke with the manager this morning. He was definitely sick yesterday. The manager called in personally to see him. He told me he was sweating and throwing up when he saw him and called the doctor. The doc told him it looks like some sort of infection and prescribed him antibiotics. I've confirmed that with the doc." Stroking the stubble on his chin, he eyed

Hunter studiously. "Given what the doc's said, I wouldn't have thought he'd be in any fit state to do this. But the only way we're going to be able to confirm that or not, is all down to CSI." Pulling back his gaze and looking up to the threatening sky, he added, "And they're certainly not going to be getting here today. There's no chance of any boats leaving Guernsey harbour in this weather."

Hunter replied, "We're going to have to move the body, though. As you pointed out, it's already been covered by the tide once, so some, maybe all forensics have already been compromised. We can't afford to leave it here until CSI arrive. It could be days if this weather persists."

Budgie acknowledged this with a sharp nod. "Absolutely. All we're waiting for is the doc to get here, and once he's done the official confirmation that he's dead, we'll get the body moved."

"I'm guessing you don't have a pathologist on the island?"

Budgie responded with a shake of his head. "If we need any post mortems done, and it's very rare we do, we have to ship the body over to Guernsey. The last time we had anything like this was eighteen months ago, when we found a body at the bottom of the La Coupée — you know, the road that connects with Little Sark. It was suspicious at the time, but then we found a suicide note in his room at the hotel where he was staying. His wife had just left him." Budgie shook his head again, a tinge of sadness in his face.

"Okay, well I think there's one thing for certain: we can rule out suicide in this case, and finding our mystery man dumped here like this, and given what you've said about our Scottish barman friend, it's certainly thrown a whole new light on what's going on. And also, who else is involved? And who killed him? Is it Billy Wallace?" Hunter shrugged his shoulders, displaying a look of concern. "If Billy's here, it's imperative we find him before he finds us."

Budgie levelled his eyes at Hunter. "I'll put in a call straight away to Steve. He's the farmer whose chalet you're in. I've told you he's also a Special on the island. I'll arrange for someone to join him, and they can keep an eye on you in shifts. Finding Nicholas Strachan's body means we can rule him out as the person who fired your cottage, so we need to be extra vigilant now."

"That'd be very much appreciated. I'm not going to tell the family. They've gone through enough already. Especially my mum."

Budgie nodded. "I agree. I'll tell Steve, and whoever joins him, to keep a low profile." As he pulled out his mobile, they heard the voice of someone shouting. Everyone turned to see the doctor making his way towards them.

By the time the doctor had completed his examination, and they had placed Nicholas Strachan's corpse into a body bag and carefully hauled him out from his resting place, it was nearing dusk, and the storm that had held off for the two hours they had been there had finally crept in. Heavy, dark clouds hung over them, shutting out most of the light, and the rain mixed with the wind was producing a squall that was pelting them all with a fury. As exposed as they were, there was no escaping the rain; Hunter's jacket, which had come from the charity bag Budgie had brought, was soaked through, and he could hardly feel his hands as he helped carry the body bag up the steps to the doctor's waiting tractor and trailer.

As Hunter watched the tractor lumber away, he shivered. He hadn't been as cold as this in a long while, and his thoughts were on one thing — getting back to the cabin, peeling off his wet clothes, taking a hot shower and lying in front of the log fire with a glass of whisky. Before that, though, he knew they had to check out this theory as to how Nicholas's body had got down to the bay.

Budgie sent the Specials back to the office, ensuring one of them went with the doctor, who was transporting Nicholas Strachan's body, while he and Hunter went up to Hogsback.

The going was heavy, the ground sodden and boggy, and the wind was even more fierce, but once up there, they found partial heel marks — the sign that someone had clearly dragged Nicholas's body — though the weather conditions were starting to erase the imprints. Hunter knew that after another twelve hours of this, there would be nothing left for forensics to examine. He studied the scene for a moment and saw that the cliffs fell away quite treacherously, just like Budgie had mentioned. He couldn't even make out the edge from where he was standing. He tried to visualise Nicholas being dragged and rolled over the edge. How the man's life had ended.

Wiping smears of rain from his face, Hunter gave the area one last look. Daylight was fading fast. He knew there was nothing they could do here today, and he turned to Budgie, mouth set tight. With a jerk of his head, he indicated they should go. As he set off back to the Emergency Station, a feeling of great frustration overcame him.

# CHAPTER THIRTY-EIGHT

In joggers and hoodie Hunter stood on the porch of the log cabin, a mug of tea cradled in his hands, watching the curtain of rain fall before him, listening to it hiss as it hit the ground. The heavy rainfall through the night had caused light flooding around them, and the solid bank of grey cloud dominating the sky told him that there was no sign of it stopping anytime soon. He wondered if Billy Wallace was out there somewhere. Watching. *Well, good luck to him. Hope he's piss-wet through.*

He knew that in the farmhouse fifty yards away two of the island cops were looking out for him and his family, and that reassured him. Nevertheless, once again, he hadn't slept. Though surprisingly, he didn't feel tired. The finding of Nicholas Strachan's dead body had been something he hadn't expected and had been the centre of his thoughts all night. This morning, when he turned up to meet with Budgie, the island would be conducting its first ever murder enquiry. And the island cop had already asked him to lead on it. Him, a DS, acting as Senior Investigating Officer. This would be unprecedented. He would need to call on all his training. Plus, he was going to have be resourceful, particularly given the lack of forensic or medical support available. At least for the time being.

He took a last swallow of his tea, slung the dregs to join the rain puddles and checked the time on his watch. He had to ring his boss and update her with yesterday's find.

Dawn Leggate ended her call with Hunter and looked at the notes she'd scribbled during their conversation. She needed to contact John Reed urgently. He still hadn't got back to her about the last two emails she had sent, and this latest information had taken matters up a notch.

Waiting for her computer to fire up, she thought about the advice she had just given Hunter, specifically regarding his new status as SIO. Had she been too condescending? She hoped not. She hadn't intended it to come over that way. She knew from working with him these past eighteen months he was more than capable of running an investigation. She shook the negative thoughts from her head. Course she hadn't. Hunter was professional enough to accept her words as guidance rather than questioning his skills. She was being too sensitive. This thing with her ex was still eating away at her. Making her feel vulnerable.

Her deliberations were interrupted by the appearance of her emails on the screen, and switching her train of thought she checked the status of the ones she had sent John. She saw he hadn't even opened them. She rang his mobile. It would be quicker and easier speaking with him on this subject rather than sending another email.

John answered on the third ring. "Morning, Dawn."

"Morning, John, sorry to disturb you. I'm guessing you're busy, but I sent you two emails you haven't responded to, and I've just been given some additional information that now makes them urgent."

"Sorry, Dawn, I've hardly been in the office. Things have ratcheted up a notch regarding Billy. We've just managed to get some CCTV footage of him getting off a train at Motherwell two days ago. It looks like he came back up here following what he did down your way. We put in a call to Glasgow

Airport an hour ago, and we now think that yesterday he got on a flight to Guernsey. We're following that up as we speak."

"How the hell has he managed that? I thought he was flagged?"

"That was my reaction as well when I heard. But first of all, we haven't had that confirmed. I'm going to get confirmation, one way or the other, once the supervisor at the airport comes on duty. As soon as I hear, I'll ring you."

Dawn could sense the frustration in his words. She knew that someone at Border Control was in for an ear-bashing from John. Before she had time to comment, he was back on the line.

"Can you tell me over the phone about the emails you've sent? I'll see if I can help. It's going to be lunchtime at least before I get back in the office."

Dawn relayed the content of the emails she had sent relating to Hunter's sighting of the mystery man at the pub on Sark, followed by him being assaulted, and then their rented cottage being fired, explaining how Hunter and island cops had traced the stranger, who had initially provided a pseudonym of T. H. Law, but they now knew him to be someone called Nicholas Strachan from his passport details. Finally, she told him about the latest incident where they had found his body dumped on Dixcart Bay on the island.

She had only just got the last sentence out of her mouth when John responded, "Say that name again!"

She could sense an air of anxiousness in his voice. She repeated his name.

"Fuck me, Dawn!"

What he said next came as a complete shock.

# CHAPTER THIRTY-NINE

Head down against the prevailing wind and rain, Hunter hurried along the road to the station. It was further than he'd thought, and he could already feel his chinos clinging wet to his legs. He hadn't brought a suit. Chinos and a shirt were the most suitable attire he had in his wardrobe for his newly acquired role. The only other choice of clothing he had was jeans, and although nothing would have been said by anyone if he had worn his jeans, he wanted to give the right impression.

He felt his mobile buzz in his trouser pocket, and he had to slow his pace to retrieve it. The wetness of his chinos wasn't helping. Tugging it free, he saw it was Dawn Leggate. "Morning, boss. To what do I owe this pleasure? Please give me good news. I could do with some. It's absolutely chucking it down here. It's worse than Yorkshire weather," he ended with mirth.

It wasn't good news she relayed. In fact, what she told him brought him to a standstill. His head went into a tail-spin as he ended the call, and for a moment he stood in a trance, trying to comprehend what his boss had just said.

Hunter was soaked by the time he entered the station. Even his expensive leather brogues had let in water, and he felt cold and bothered as he climbed the stairs up to the Constable's Office.

Budgie and six Constables were waiting for him, and he felt their buzz the moment he entered, instantly lifting his spirit. He took in every expression of expectancy and enthusiasm they greeted him with, returning it with his own. Budgie looked to be the most excited of them all. His face was lit up like a child in a toyshop. He was holding out a marker pen, pointing it over Hunter's shoulder, and Hunter turned his eyes to the whiteboard Budgie was targeting. He instantly spotted it had been wiped clean, recalling how on his previous visit here it had been littered with telephone numbers and contact details of individuals. Now there were six A5 size colour photographs. Four of them were of their victim, Nicholas Strachan. One of them was the head and shoulders image captured by CCTV at the Bel Air Inn, and the other three were different shots of his body at Dixcart Bay before it was recovered. Hunter had requested that Budgie take them on his mobile because of the absence of CSI. The remaining two were from the cottage Nicholas had rented. The first was a full front view, and the second a close up of the bloodstain with the footprint in it on the flooring beside the front door.

Hunter studied them a second before taking the pen from Budgie, scribing Nicholas Strachan's name below the head and shoulders photograph and facing his team. "Morning, everyone. Like you, this a first for me. Not my first murder investigation of course, but acting as SIO it is, and on that note, Budgie, have you contacted CID at Guernsey and filled them in?"

"I have. I spoke with a DS yesterday evening, and told him what we'd got, and just before eight last night a DI rang me to clarify everything. He knows the weather is an issue for getting across to us, and he rang me an hour ago to say the forecast was shocking for the next couple of days and asked if we could hold the fort until he could get his team across. I told him the resources we'd got here and I also told him about your background. He was more than happy with that. The one thing good thing about this is that if no one can get to us, then whoever killed Nicolas Strachan also isn't going to be able to get away. He told me they would be putting together a team this morning and that the moment there's a suitable break in the weather, they'll be setting off."

"Okay, that's good. But for now, this rests on our shoulders, and I don't know about you, but it would be nice to have this wrapped up and a prisoner in the cell before they get here."

"It'd certainly be a feather in our caps," Budgie responded.

Hunter saw the officers responding to Budgie's comments with an eager nod. "Right, and on that positive note we'll crack on with briefing." He took a deep breath and pursing his lips said, "I also got a phone call this morning from my boss. As you know, I'd already passed on the passport details of Nicholas Strachan and sent the CCTV photo to see if we had any record of him, and…" Pausing for a moment, Hunter studied the officers' faces, then continued, "It appears that Nicholas Strachan was an undercover cop." He halted again, noting the shock in all their faces. "Apparently, he was sent by Glasgow Police to covertly monitor things at this end, and report back with any intelligence or information. My boss reassures me it wasn't to undermine anything we were doing, but because the Scottish Police had put in an official request to send a team over to assist with capturing Billy Wallace, and Guernsey hadn't responded, so they decided to send over someone who was experienced in undercover work." Hunter paused again. "Now we know why he used a pseudonym — ironically T. H. Law, as in 'The Law.'" He saw a couple reveal a wan smile and returned his own — a light moment to a sad event. He continued, "It would appear that three days ago Nicholas made a telephone call to a DS, who I know, up in Scotland, telling him that he was monitoring someone on the island who he believed might be a link to Billy."

"He didn't say who that was?" asked Budgie eagerly.

"No, unfortunately. Nicholas told him he was going to get back to him, but he never made the call. And we know why."

"So, whoever it was sussed him out and got to him first."

"Looks like that."

Hunter penned a time and date on the board. It was the start of the timeline. He turned back to his team. "That call to the DS was at two-eighteen p.m." He wrote another time and date. "And we found the cottage Nicholas was renting empty, with the bloodstain by the front door, at just after ten-thirty-five a.m. two days ago. So that's roughly a twenty-hour window, where there's no sighting or contact with Nicholas."

Hunter quickly studied the faces of his team. He could see concentration etched on all of them. "In terms of the injuries, what we do know, from the doctor's examination, is that he had numerous head injuries, and a variety of fractures to both arms and legs. The doctor believes that the fractures to the arms and legs were caused post mortem, when he went over the cliff. The head injuries, though, are pre-mortem. The whole left-hand side of his skull has been caved in. The doc says that although he's no expert, his guess would be that the injuries were caused by a hammer or something similar. That sort of attack would certainly fit in with the scene at the cottage."

Hunter let his words sink in. "But we aren't going to know anything for definite without a post mortem and forensic examination of the cottage, and from the latest weather update, we know that could well be a couple of days from now. Until then, we have work to do." Pausing once more, he continued, "First task is house-to-house enquiries around Nicholas's cottage. I know that there was some initial house-to-house, but not many people were around. Was that followed up?"

One of the Constables half-raised his hand. Hunter thought his name was Trevor. He had been with him when they had gone to Nicholas's cottage. He pointed to him to speak.

"Me and George did that." The slim, faired-haired, clean-shaven cop gave a quick sideways glance to his colleague beside him, who was in complete contrast — burly, with thick dark hair and a beard. The officer continued. "When we first did our door-knocking, only Margaret Hotton, in the opposite end house, was in, and she told us she had seen Nicholas a few times, twice going down to the bay, and once coming back from the shops, laden up with food bags, but it was from her window and so she hadn't spoken with him. When we told her about the blood we'd found, she was really surprised, but said she hadn't heard any sound of a fight, or anything like that. Next door to Margaret is Ben and Gayle. They own the café on The Avenue. They're out at work most of the day and so hadn't seen or spoken with Nicholas. The same goes for Sylvia, who lives in the middle cottage. She works in the charity shop on The Avenue, and so she hadn't seen or spoken with him. The cottage next to Sylvia's is a rental one and that's currently occupied by a retired teacher, who's taken it on an extended rent. She told us she'd said 'hello' to Nicholas a couple of times and that he'd told her he'd come for the festival. That was it. We told her about the bloodstain and asked if she'd heard anything, and she said she's slightly deaf, and so she has to have the TV turned up, so she hadn't heard anything."

Hunter thanked them, realising that the last woman they were talking about was the retired teacher he had met on Dixcart Bay, when Jonathan and Daniel had done their disappearing act. Hazel something? He recalled how she had told him she was renting a cottage in the woods. He asked, "Anything else, anyone?"

He was met with a shake of heads all round.

"Okay, disappointing, but not surprising given that we now know who he was and what he was doing here. He'd have deliberately kept a low profile to avoid attracting attention." Gathering his thoughts, Hunter tapped the marker pen on the board. Seconds later, he said, "We've heard that he's used the shops, so let's visit The Avenue and see if we can get anything there. Finally, I know from Budgie that all of you know just about everyone who lives on this island, except the tourists, and I also know that this is such a rare event that it will be the talk of everyone, but I've a big favour to ask." He scoured the officers' faces, holding each of them with his gaze for a second. "As tempting as it is to discuss this, I'd like to keep the fact that Nicholas Strachan was an undercover cop in this room for now. If it got out, it could complicate our enquiry. By all means chat about the murder, but just keep it to yourselves regarding his identity. Is that understood?"

Hunter received a round of nods.

"Thank you, everyone. And the last thing I want to do today is give you all the task of trying to find out the names of all the tourists who are here. I know that's a mammoth task, especially with it being the Festival of Light, but you know the hotel managers, B&B owners and those who rent out cottages just about as well as your own family, so I'm sure you can deliver. More importantly, could you ask them if they're suspicious of anyone? If they are, ring me or Budgie straight away with the names so we can check them out." Putting down the marker pen, Hunter said, "We meet here at eight a.m. tomorrow morning, unless anything else happens, and then Budgie will contact you. Good hunting, everyone."

# CHAPTER FORTY

Football tucked beneath his arm, Jonathan stood in the doorway of the bedroom he was sharing with his brother at Grandad Ray's and Nannan Sandra's home. Daniel was on the bottom bunk, playing with his Marvel characters. Captain America was in one hand and The Incredible Hulk in the other. Daniel was making whooshing noises while acting out a fight scenario between the two figures. The TV on the wall was on low, and Jonathan saw that the Marvel Avengers Assemble animated TV series was playing. He watched it for a few seconds, recalling the time when that was all he watched, but he considered himself too old for that now. Superheroes were kid's stuff now that he was about to go up to comprehensive school.

"What you doing?" Jonathan asked.

Daniel stopped Captain America in mid-flight and half-turned. "Playing Avengers."

Jonathan removed the ball from beneath his arm and threw it up to head height, catching it in both hands. "Fancy playing footie?"

"It's too cold."

"No, it's not."

"'Tis."

"Come on, don't be a wuss."

"No, it's wet and too cold."

"I'll go in goal if you don't want to dive."

"No, I'm watching this and playing Avengers."

Jonathan huffed. "Baby," he mumbled and stomped back downstairs.

In the garden Jonathan played 'keepie-uppie', juggling the ball to chest height with his feet and knees without letting it fall onto the grass. After a couple of false starts, he was now up to seventy-eight taps. His record was a hundred-and-twenty-three, and he wanted to break it this holiday.

The sound of branches crunching followed by movement flashing into the top of his vision interrupted his concentration, and the ball bounced awkwardly off his toe-end towards the bank of trees at the bottom of the garden. "Shit," he cursed and glanced around quickly to make sure his grandparents weren't around. He looked at the ball with an edge of frustration and then into the copse where the fleeting action had caused him to make his error.

The sight of a thick shadow among the bushes caused him to start, the breath catching in his throat, and he took a step back. He felt his heart jolt as the shadow came into the light. Then he relaxed when he saw who it was, a friendly smile lighting up their face.

# CHAPTER FORTY-ONE

"Is Jonathan there?"

Beth took the call from Sandra, trapping her mobile between ear and shoulder. She was folding a T-shirt of Hunter's, one of the many items she'd had to wash because of smoke damage from the fire.

"Well, he went into the garden half an hour ago to play football, and when we've just gone out to call him, he's not there. His football's there, but not him. Daniel's playing up in his bedroom, but there's no sign of Jonathan, and I was just wondering if he'd come over to your new place?"

Beth felt her stomach empty. She stopped folding Hunter's T-shirt and grabbed her phone, fixing it tightly to her ear. "Have you checked?"

"We've looked all over, Beth. Your Dad's even been out onto the lanes and called him. We last saw him kicking his ball in the garden."

Beth put a hand to her mouth. "Oh, Jesus, Mum."

"I'm sure he's okay. You know what Jonathan's like. Your dad's walking over to your place to see if he can see him."

"I'm going to hang up, Mum, and call Hunter — he's with Budgie." As Beth ended the call, a terrible dread swept over her.

Hunter borrowed one of the Special Constable's bikes and he and Budgie chased up to the chalet where Beth, her dad and his parents were all waiting, concerned looks on all their faces. Ray had his arm wrapped around Beth, whose face was pale, a rime of tears masking her eyes.

Hunter tried to calm his racing heart. Taking a deep breath to steady the panic, deliberately slowing his voice, he said, "Has he turned up?"

Ray shook his head. "I've taken the road Jonathan would have taken to get here and no sign."

"And you've definitely checked the house and garden?"

"Twice."

"And you didn't hear or see anything untoward?"

Ray shook his head again. "One minute he was kicking the ball, and the next he was gone. We found his ball at the bottom of the garden."

Beth started to sob. "It's Billy Wallace, isn't it? He's got him?"

A knot formed in Hunter's throat. "We don't know that, Beth," he answered in an attempt to reassure her, but he knew she was only saying out loud what he was thinking.

Upstairs in the Emergency Services Building, Hunter, Budgie, and his full complement of Specials were present, though not everyone could get inside the Constable's office. Half a dozen stood outside in the corridor, hunkered around the doorway, while the majority squashed together overlooking a map of the island spread out over a desk.

"I'm truly sorry about this, Hunter. I put a couple of guards on your place, but I never thought about Ray and Sandra. I thought your boys would be okay with them."

"This is not your fault, Budgie. I also thought they'd be safe with Beth's parents. The main thing we need to do is find out where Billy's holed up. If it is Billy." Hunter took a deep breath. "How did you go on with checks around the island?"

"The hotels and B&B places have all come back to us. There's no one fitting the description of Billy at any of them, and none of them have reported anyone they're suspicious of. I've spoken with the manager at The Stocks and Ian McDonald is confined to his bed, so that rules him out. We've still got to do the rental places, and there's around a couple of dozen of those, that's all. Do you have a recent picture of Jonathan we can use to show people?"

Hunter fished out his mobile from his pocket, activated it and pulled up a photograph of Jonathan from his gallery. He'd taken it the first day they had arrived here, when they'd all gone to the Dixcart Bay Hotel. He enlarged the photo on the screen and placed it over the map so everyone could see. As he looked at the image, he felt sick.

"We'll upload this and get copies printed off."

"What about numbers, Budgie? I'm thinking if it is Billy who's got Jonathan, he's a handful. He's not going to come easy."

"I'm going to put everyone into threes and visit the places in as close proximity to one another as possible. It'll take a bit longer to do checks of the properties, but it'll mean everyone will be within a few minutes of one another should backup be needed."

Hunter acknowledged Budgie's tactics with a quick nod. He wanted to storm all the places as quickly as possible and get Jonathan back safely, but he knew that what Budgie had organised made sense. "What about help from Guernsey?"

"Frustratingly, we're still in the same position as the past couple of days. There was a lull in the weather for a few hours overnight, but this morning it's back to square one. The sea's far too rough to travel. The forecast is that there is a possibility of a break later tonight, but we'll have to wait and see. The moment there's a break, a team will be over. They've promised.

And there's a Superintendent on the end of a phone for advice."

Hunter nodded again. If this had happened back home, there would be Gold, Silver and Bronze Commanders, an operation room fully staffed, plus trained search teams, Intelligence staff and media support, but these were extraordinary circumstances, and he knew they had to manage with what they had, at least for the next twelve hours. He handed his mobile over to Budgie so that Jonathan's photo could be uploaded onto the computer for printing off. "I'd liked to be involved."

Budgie held his look for moment, studying him. "Under normal circumstances you know you shouldn't, but these are not normal circumstances, Hunter. I do need your help, but you stay with me, understand?"

Hunter responded with a curt nod. "Thank you," he said softly.

From the printer tray Budgie pulled out half a dozen duplicated sheets of addresses. "Okay, these are all the properties on the island that are rental. I'm splitting the team in half. Twelve of you will do these in four groups of three, and the remainder will do the derelict and empty buildings. We stay in touch with one another, and I want each team to radio in every half an hour with an update. Everyone got that?"

There was such an overwhelming response that Hunter felt himself welling up. It had been an hour and a half since Jonathan had last been seen, and he felt both hopeless and afraid. Billy Wallace was a psychopathic sadist, and he just hoped they could find him in time before anything bad happened to his son.

# CHAPTER FORTY-TWO

The conditions in which Hunter and Budgie tramped across Hogsback were thoroughly depressing. The sky was rain-sodden and it hung everywhere like a mist, dank and cold. The ground was drenched. On the way here, they had carefully checked out a farm and its outbuildings, the owner giving them a helping hand, but they had found nothing untoward. Now the pair were making their way across the headland in the general direction of La Coupée, where Budgie knew of a couple of derelict cottages, long since vacated by islanders, but which nevertheless still needed checking out.

Hearing the echoing boom of the ferocious waves exploding onto the shore below them and ignoring how wet he was getting as he trudged through damp gorse, Hunter had just one thought in his mind — finding Jonathan safe. He prayed that nothing had happened to him. The entire journey from the Emergency Station he had been thinking dark thoughts, and no matter how hard he had tried to dismiss them, he had failed. Searching the outbuildings had triggered thoughts of when his partner, Grace, had suffered the same fate three years ago; her fifteen-year-old daughter had been abducted by a serial killer they had been closing in on. His mood had lifted momentarily when he remembered they had got her back safely, but then darkened again when he recalled Grace's daughter was still undergoing counselling. The thought of what Jonathan might be going through filled him with dread.

"The weather's closing in again." Budgie's voice broke into his thoughts. "We'll check out these buildings then get back to the station and see if anyone's got anything."

Budgie picked up his pace, making his way back to a path that skirted around the headland towards Little Sark, and as Hunter increased his stride, he suddenly felt lightheaded and had to catch himself. *My blood sugar is low.* He hadn't eaten since breakfast. He needed a sugar hit. He took in a long, slow breath, steadied himself for a second and then set off after Budgie. He'd grab a sugar-laden cuppa once they got back to the station.

Back at the chalet, Hunter couldn't rest. None of them could. It was the early hours of the morning and everyone was still up. The searches had been called off for the night; the weather conditions and darkness made it nigh on impossible to conduct a thorough hunt, and everyone was meeting back at the station at 8 a.m. For Hunter that was torture, even though he knew the right decision had been made.

On his way back from the station, Hunter had rung Dawn Leggate and updated her; he hadn't wanted anyone at the chalet to hear how fruitless the day's exercise had been or catch the anxiousness in his voice as he explained. It was the first time he had heard his boss flap. She had been outraged that no help was coming from Guernsey and promised that she'd be bending the ear of the Commander the moment their call ended.

Hunter had done his best to reassure her that it wasn't the fault of anyone on Guernsey, reiterating what Budgie had told him late that afternoon, during their yomp over Hogsback, after he himself had emphasised the urgency of the situation, and criticised his perceived lack of support from the mother island. Budgie had explained that it wasn't just the prevailing bad weather conditions, but the rise and fall of the tide — at 36 feet, the second biggest in the world — which, together with the sea currents and underlying rock formations around Sark, made for such a treacherous venture, that only the most foolhardy would risk it. While Hunter had managed to placate Dawn with Budgie's explanation, he could tell from her voice she hadn't been happy with the situation. Before hanging up, she'd said she was still going to contact the Commander on Guernsey.

By the time Hunter walked into the chalet, it felt as if he was going into meltdown. His head was banging, and he had difficulty focusing on the questions thrown at him, especially from Beth, who had become agitated by his laboured response. Fiona went to Beth's aid, embracing her, telling her everything would be all right, and then she scuttled away to the kitchen to get them all something to eat and drink. As if that was going to resolve the crisis.

Fiona made them all a sandwich and put together a bowl of salad, but a lot of that went untouched. Hunter felt sick to the core, and every mouthful roiled his stomach. Putting aside his half-eaten food, he rested his head in a chair, closing his eyes, trying to force himself to switch off, but horrific scenes involving Jonathan visited him, every possible scenario he had heard about from police incidents involving child abduction invading his thoughts. It was a living nightmare, and he realised that unwinding anytime soon was out of the question.

Snapping open his eyes, he tried to look at Beth, but she wouldn't hold his gaze. As he looked to her again, she was on the sofa, her gaze fixed on the ceiling as if she was in a dreamlike trance. She was probably thinking similar things to him; as a nurse, he knew she would have been exposed to child-abuse stories of nightmare proportions, which wouldn't help alleviate her suffering.

Fiona and Jock were fairing no better. Jock was sharing the sofa with Beth, his shoulders slumped and his arms hanging limply. He looked washed out, his eyes and head somewhere else. Fiona was the only active one. She had been going backwards and forwards to the kitchen, continually asking everyone if they wanted a hot drink and tidying things up that didn't need tidying up. Hunter wanted to scream at her to sit down, but he knew from his own experience that everyone handled trauma differently.

Roll on 8 a.m. and he could start looking for Jonathan again.

# CHAPTER FORTY-THREE

Hunter awoke with a start. Weak light in the gaps in the curtains told him it was morning, and he could hear the faint shuffling sound of footsteps drifting up from the lounge. He was fully clothed, as was Beth beside him, who was still asleep, and he remembered that they had all decided just before 4 a.m. that it might be worth trying to get some sleep to prepare themselves for the day ahead. As he had rested his head in those early hours, he had thought he would never be able to get to sleep, such was the activity in his mind. Nevertheless, he obviously had. And it had definitely done him good, because he felt surprisingly refreshed.

He gently rolled over and picked up his phone. 7.18 a.m. and no calls or texts. He recalled that they were all meeting at eight to continue the search. *I need to get up.* He pushed himself up, disturbing Beth.

"You're awake," Beth mumbled, looking his way, rubbing bleary eyes.

"Just. Got to get up. Meeting with Budgie and the team in half an hour."

"I'll get you something to eat," she responded, propping herself up on an elbow.

"No, don't rush. I can hear someone else is up downstairs. I'm guessing it's Mum. I'll grab some toast and a brew and I'll bring you up a cuppa." Swinging his legs out of bed, Hunter sniffed an armpit. He needed to get out of his T-shirt and grab a shower.

Everyone was in by the time Hunter arrived at the station. He pulled off his sopping-wet waterproof and gave it a good shake. It was another horrible day. Not just the rain, but the wind had picked up as well. He knew no one was coming to the rescue today.

For the second day running, they started the briefing clustered around the Ordnance Survey map of Sark, Budgie drawing a ring around the properties and areas that had been searched, confirming with those who had carried them out that their examination had been thorough. Hunter was reassured by their responses.

After that, Budgie carved up the remaining locations for the day's exploration, allocating three to each site like the previous day. Hunter's eyes zoned in on each of the places Budgie was pointing to, which included the old silver mines on Little Sark, hoping one of them was going to reveal where Jonathan was being held. Sark was such a small island in comparison to the other Channel Islands, yet still a huge place to hide a child. A feeling of doom suddenly overcame him, and he responded by telling himself that Jonathan was okay — that he hadn't been harmed and he definitely wasn't dead. This was about Billy and Jock. Billy wanted Jock, not Jonathan. Jonathan was the bargaining chip. The conduit to get to Jock. Soon Billy would call. Hunter knew it.

Rain battered Hunter and Budgie as they made their way over the Gouliot headland, where Budgie had told him there were a number of old tunnels made by the Germans during their wartime occupation. He'd said they had all been sealed with steel plates, but he wanted to check them out for himself. It was something Hunter would have done.

By the time they had checked the last one, seeing that the covers were still welded in place, Hunter was soaked. His waterproof had managed to prevent his underneath fleece becoming wet, but his jeans were plastered to his legs and water had trickled into the tops of his boots. For a moment he stood looking out across to the Isle of Brecqhou, most of it shrouded in mist, listening to the crashing sea and the screams of the herring gulls around him. The freezing rain assaulted his face, making him feel thoroughly miserable, but his thoughts were firmly on two things — finding his son and finding Billy Wallace. He had so much anger inside him that if he confronted Billy right now, he would kill him.

*Where the fuck are you, Billy?* In the midst of his thoughts, he heard Budgie's mobile ring. Hunter snapped around his head as Budgie yanked it from his pocket, cupping a hand around it as he put it to his ear. "Hello, Constable Burgess." He had to shout above the wind.

For the next couple of minutes, Hunter studied Budgie's features as he listened to him answer the call with a series of clipped yeses and nos, frustrated that he couldn't hear the other side of the conversation. When he heard Budgie explaining in some detail the searches that he and his team had conducted, he knew it could only be one of the bosses across in Guernsey he was speaking with. Ending the call, Budgie momentarily looked out to sea before engaging with Hunter, a disturbed look on his face. "That was the Operations Superintendent on Guernsey. The Coastguard's just told him that there are storm force conditions predicted for the next twelve hours. There's no chance of anyone coming until at least tomorrow."

Hunter threw back his head, slinging the obsidian-coloured sky a hate-filled stare. "FUCK!" he yelled at the top his voice.

# CHAPTER FORTY-FOUR

"Where have you been? Don't you answer your calls?" Dawn knew she was sounding angry on the phone, but she couldn't help it. She had been trying DS John Reed's mobile all day, leaving him several voicemails, the last one two hours ago, reinforcing that it was urgent, but he hadn't had the decency to respond until now.

"Sorry, Dawn, I've been so busy…"

She broke into his reply. "I left you a message two hours ago saying that it was urgent."

"I know you did, and I apologise, but I've really been up to my neck in it. I got a lead on Billy that urgently needed following up." The inflection in his voice raised on the pronunciation of the word 'urgently.'

Dawn caught the agitated note in John's voice, which made her sit up, more so as he finished his sentence, and suddenly she felt guilty about her brusqueness. Swallowing the knot in her throat, she responded, "Billy! That's who I've been trying to get hold of you about. Hunter's son's gone missing on Sark. He thinks it's either Billy or someone who knows him. Have you managed to find out where he is?"

"Fucking hell, Dawn, I'm sorry I didn't answer your calls. I thought you were just after an update, but I couldn't give you one because our enquiries have been so fluid all day. We've never stopped. If you'd have said that in your message, I would have got back to you straight away. You know I would." John broke off for a second and continued, "The answer to your question 'have we found him?' is no, but in relation to where he is, we think we know."

"Well, don't keep me in suspense, John."

"What I can definitely say is he has gone to Guernsey. He caught a flight from Glasgow two days ago. It was an internal flight, so the border checks weren't done. I've given the supervisor involved a round of fucks, but that's too late now. The horse has bolted, so to speak."

"Shit, so he could be on Sark!"

"I thought you said yesterday that the weather was too bad for the ferry or anything."

"Too bad, health and safety-wise, maybe, but that wouldn't stop our Billy. He managed to escape from prison while being guarded, so a bit of bad weather's not going to stop him. I'm going to have to alert Guernsey and see if I can push them to get a team across on the island sharpish."

"Just before you do that, you made a comment about someone helping Billy. I think I've got the answer for you."

Dawn straightened up quickly. "Oh yes?"

"The fact that Billy only caught a flight two days ago makes the timing all wrong for Nicholas Strachan's murder. So, he has to have been killed by someone else on that island. And if you recall, I told you he'd texted me to say he was onto something, but never got back."

"I remember that. So, who's across on Sark helping Billy? What have you found out?"

"You know I told you that we'd tracked Billy across to Edinburgh but couldn't find a connection to anyone there?" John paused for a couple of seconds as if waiting for Dawn to ask a question. When she didn't, he continued, "Well, we have found a connection. The Governor at Barlinnie finally got back to me this morning with a list of people who've visited Billy. A couple of them are well-known villains from his past. They're old stages now. Lost their reputations at least a decade ago and well past doing anything themselves, so we quickly ruled them out. But there was also Alec Jefferies' name on that list. Remember him? He's the guy we found shot dead in the flat in Motherwell with two others. We believe he was the one who organised Billy's escape."

John paused again. "And there's one other. A woman. Her name crops up seven times on the list. The last time she visited Billy was five weeks ago, and surprise, surprise, the address she gave is in a small town just outside Edinburgh. Preston Pans. She's got a flat there, and that's where I've been all day. We got a warrant and busted the place this morning. Unfortunately, there was no one there and a check with neighbours revealed that no one's seen her for the best part of a week. But there is evidence that someone's stayed there recently. Certainly, just before Billy caught the flight from Glasgow, from shopping receipts we've recovered. We strongly believe it's Billy. In between coming down your neck of the woods to Jock's house, we're guessing that's where he put his head down while we were looking for him after the shootings.

"We've done a thorough search, and forensics are still in there as we speak, so we're hoping to turn something up. One of the things we have found is a receipt from a travel agent for a flight booking from Manchester to Guernsey, and it's not in Billy's name, it's in hers. And there was no sign of her passport, so I put in a call a couple of hours ago for a check. I've literally just got a phone call back from Border Control at Manchester Airport ten minutes ago; that's why I haven't rung you until now. They've confirmed she did get on a flight to Guernsey. And get this: the flight she got on was the same one as Hunter and his family."

"Jesus!" For a few seconds Dawn didn't respond. She thought about what John had just revealed. Coming back to the moment, she said, "And there was just her on that flight? She didn't travel with anybody?"

"As far as we know, she was alone. Neighbours have confirmed she lives on her own. We don't believe she has a partner or companion."

"Bloody hell, John, so as far as we know, for the past week this woman has been keeping tabs on Hunter and his family?"

"It would appear so, Dawn, yes."

"And more than likely she's the one, then, that whacked Hunter, burned down the cottage they were staying in and murdered Nicholas Strachan." Pausing, she added, "And she's now involved in Hunter's son's abduction."

"I think it would be a good bet. There is something else I've found out about her."

"Go on, surprise me."

"She's a fruit-loop."

"She's more than a fucking fruit-loop, John. I would say she's as bad a psycho as Billy, if she's responsible for all this."

"They're certainly well-matched, Dawn. And given what I've learned today, I think it was no accidental match. Certainly not on her part."

"What do you mean by that?"

"We've only just started on our enquiries, but we've not found anything in her background which would link her to Billy in the past. The Governor tells me she started writing to him within a fortnight of him being convicted and used to send two to three letters to him every week. He said they had monitored many of the letters she'd written, and their content would appear to show that she was just besotted with him, simple as that. Notoriety and all that." Pausing, John added, "It makes you wonder what turns these women on about sickos. But having said that, I've also found out about something she did a few years ago, and to me she seems just as bad."

"She obviously is. No ordinary person goes burning down a house, when everybody was in it, and then murders an undercover cop. Tell me what else she's done?"

"According to her convictions, harassment and grievous bodily harm. I haven't got the full SP on her, but there is a little bit about her in our Intelligence System. Apparently, five years ago she was a teacher and became infatuated with a younger male colleague and began stalking him. When he rebuffed her advances, she threw cleaning fluid, containing hydrochloric acid, in his face and also attacked his girlfriend with the stuff. She did two years in prison."

"Lovely woman. Well, that definitely confirms the fruit-loop. She and Billy do have a lot in common."

"I've got a photo of her from her flat. It looks to be a good few years old, but the neighbours tell me it's a good likeness, so I'll email it you as soon as we finish. But before you go, there's something else I need to tell you before you get off to warn Hunter and inform Guernsey Police."

"You mean, there's more good news?"

John gave a short laugh. "Not for her there isn't. The girl Alec Jefferies was living with. The girl who was shot beside him in bed, we think by Billy. Mary Brown."

"What about her?"

"She's this woman's daughter. She's the link with Alec Jefferies, who helped Billy escape."

"Billy's shot this woman's daughter?"

"Yes. And it's my guess she doesn't know. We haven't revealed Mary Brown's name to the press yet. I have no doubt that Billy's using this woman, and he'll more than likely kill her once he's got everything he wants from her."

"What's this woman's name, John? I need to get this and her photo to Hunter as soon as."

"Hazel Brown."

# CHAPTER FORTY-FIVE

Back in the Constable's Office, cold and wet once again, Hunter rubbed the tops of both arms, trying to return the warmth to his body. It had been a fruitless, frustrating day, and with daylight diminishing Budgie had reluctantly sent everyone home. Much to his frustration, they hadn't been able to locate Jonathan or find a clue as to his whereabouts. *Beth will be beside herself.* Hunter didn't want to go home with the news.

"I know it's no consolation, Hunter, but I believe Jonathan's safe. You've said yourself, it's your dad that Billy's after. My guess is you'll get a message from him soon."

Hunter was about to respond when he felt and heard his mobile ping. He had a message. A cold shiver ran down his spine. He caught Budgie's eye, pulling his phone from his pocket and switching his gaze as he activated it. He let out a breath when he saw the message was from Dawn, letting Budgie know everything was okay by lifting his eyes briefly and mouthing who it was.

Dawn had sent a long message. Three sentences in, Hunter stiffened and locked onto the screen, flicking through the message as quickly as possible, though not missing anything he read. Coming to the end, he thumbed up the photo and feasted his eyes on it. The woman staring back at him took him completely by surprise. He knew her. Or at least he'd met her and knew her first name, because she'd told him that when they'd bumped into her.

Hunter spun his mobile around, allowing Budgie and four of the Constables who'd come back with them to view the image. "This is what my boss has just sent me. This is a woman called

Hazel Brown, and my boss believes it's the person who assaulted me, set fire to the cottage and who killed Nicholas Strachan. The text she's just sent me indicates she's the one who's been keeping tabs on me for Billy. That has to be right. I met her on Dixcart Bay a couple of days after we'd been here. She told me she was a retired teacher who was renting a cottage on the island."

One of the Constables jabbed a finger towards the screen. "I spoke with her when we were doing house-to-house. She's renting the cottage next to Nicholas Strachan's."

Everyone's eyes darted between one another.

"That's our answer. I bet that's where Jonathan is," exclaimed Budgie.

Everyone started picking up their gear and putting their coats back on. Budgie passed Hunter a torch and they quickly made for the door.

"There is a possibility Billy could be there. The boss says he caught a flight to Guernsey two days ago."

"In this weather?" yelled back the lead Constable, who was almost at the bottom of the stairs. "I don't think so. Anyway, there's enough of us."

Hunter sucked in air almost in unison with each stride, his throat aching, as he raced towards the cottages where Hazel Brown and possibly Billy Wallace were holed up. Behind him, he could hear the crunch of his comrades' boots as they chased after him, Budgie shouting for him to slow down. He only had one thing on his mind as the biting wind snapped at his face and cheeks, and that wasn't slowing down.

As Hunter rounded the bend that brought the row of five cottages into view, though in the fast fading light he could only make out their outline, he took in a deep slug of air, slowed briefly to steady his ragged breathing, and then bolted up the path towards the door of cottage number four. He turned the handle swiftly, smashing his shoulder against solid oak, and had he not held onto the handle he would have gone face-first into a heap, as he quickly discovered it wasn't locked.

Stumbling into a well-lit front lounge, where a roaring fire was burning in the grate, the warmth hit him with the same fierceness as the icy wind a second ago. He let go of the handle and steadied himself against the wall. He was fired up by adrenalin, and everything around was sharp in focus and sound. Behind, he could hear Budgie and the others a short way off, and in front Hazel Brown was launching herself from an armchair. The television was on.

"Where's Jonathan? Where's Billy?" Hunter screamed.

Hazel stared at him for a second, and then the corners of her mouth curled up and she released a maniacal laugh.

Hunter took a step towards her. "Where the fuck is Jonathan, you bitch?"

She ceased laughing and her face changed, rage burning in her eyes.

The way Hazel attacked was totally unexpected. She launched herself at Hunter, screaming as she came flying at his face with clawing hands. He threw up his arms instinctively to ward her off, but she hit him full on, throwing him backwards against a wall unit. He could hear things crashing around him as the bottom of his spine hit the edge of the cupboard, jarring him, sending a shooting pain down his legs. The impact knocked the wind out of him and he twisted and tried to push himself away, but her hands flew at him again, clawing his face, trying to gouge his eyes.

Snapping shut his eyelids to protect himself, Hunter swung a punch blindly and felt it connect, hearing Hazel yelp. He flashed open his eyes, pushed himself sideways and moved into boxing stance. His face stung like hell, and the base of his back felt like it had been thumped by a hammer.

Hazel had covered her face with her hands, moaning, and as she spread her fingers he saw blood beginning to flow. She glanced at her hands and then looked his way. She gave him such a demonic stare that for a moment he actually felt afraid, and as she removed her hands he saw her mouth was bleeding. With another scream, she tore at him again. This time, Hunter was ready. He ducked away and threw in another punch. It caught the side of her head and her legs folded beneath her, dropping her to the floor like a sack of potatoes. That was when everyone piled into the cottage, pushing their way past Hunter to get to Hazel. She tried to get up, rolling onto her knees, but Budgie and another were on her, spinning her over, pulling at her arms. They had the cuffs on her within seconds.

Hunter was shaking, trying to catch his breath. He looked down at Hazel. Dark make-up was running down from her eyes, and a gash of blood smeared her face, and in that moment, she reminded him of the Joker in *The Dark Knight*. "Where's Jonathan?" he yelled.

Hazel just looked at him and laughed, blood bubbling between her teeth.

He took a step towards her, and Budgie pushed himself up, placing himself as a barrier between Hazel and Hunter. "Don't, Hunter," he said, through stern lips.

Hunter was about to speak when his phone started ringing, startling everyone, causing them to focus on him. Frowning, he dragged it from his pocket. Only a number flashed on the screen. He answered, "Hello?"

"Is that Detective Kerr?"

"Billy."

"Listen, if you want your kid to live, do as I say."

Enraged and yet scared, Hunter listened as Billy Wallace issued instructions.

# CHAPTER FORTY-SIX

Hurriedly retracing their steps back to the village, Hunter and Budgie followed the road that took them past the Seigneurie Gardens and on to the track that led to Port du Moulin. The wind and driving rain were coming from the north, buffeting them, and many times they had to brace themselves to avoid being blown sideways. By the time they had reached the beginning of the path leading to the cliffs at Port du Moulin, Hunter's calves were burning, he was lathered in sweat and gasping for breath. Budgie was in no better state. Slowing his pace to a slog, Hunter swept the way ahead with the torch Budgie had loaned him. As they approached the track to the coastal path, the beam picked out Jock, who was waiting by a fence.

Hunter came to a stop, bending in the middle, resting his hands on his knees, as he drew in air.

"What's happened?" cried Jock. "Have you not found Jonathan? Has something happened to him?"

Hunter lifted his head. "We know where he is. Billy has him. We're going for him now." He forced the words out in between grabbing lungfuls of air.

"Where is he? If that bastard's done anything…"

Hunter stopped Jock mid-sentence, throwing up his hand. "He says he hasn't yet, but he's threatened to. That's why I rang you. He's told me to meet him just down here." Hunter pointed along the path, where it disappeared into darkness. "And he's ordered that you be there as well."

"That fucking suits me." Jock brought up his hands. They were bunched into fists. "Let's go and get the bastard."

As Jock turned to steal a march, Hunter planted a hand on his shoulder, stopping him mid-stride. "There's every reason to believe Billy's armed, Dad. We can't go running in gung-ho. We have to do this my way."

The look Hunter received from his dad told him the magnitude of the problem had registered. "It's you he wants, Dad, you know that."

Jock nodded.

"But I'm coming as well. In my book that's two against one, but we're going to have to box clever if we're to get Jonathan back."

Jock dipped his head towards Budgie. "What about your lot?"

"I've got some of them on the way, but I'm afraid we aren't going to be of much help to you. I don't know if you've realised, Jock, but this road leads down to the Window in the Rock. That's where he's told Hunter he wants you come. This path is one road in and one road back. That's it. There's no other way to get there. He's been quite clever in selecting this place. He knows the set-up, and he's told Hunter that if anyone other than you two turn up, Jonathan will be killed, so I daren't risk coming."

"Fuck," Jock cursed.

"It's a problem, Jock, but not a massive one. I can come with you some of the way, but then I'm going to have to hang back. When my other lads join me, it's going to mean we're a couple of hundred yards away. Less than a minute to get to you."

"Is there no other way at all you can get to this Window in the Rock place?"

Budgie shook his head. "It's just a hole cut into the rock face. It leads through to a hundred-and-fifty-foot sheer drop to the sea. We can get above it, but the cliffs are too high for us to get down. This path is the only way in."

"Well, son, it looks like we're buggered. Billy's outsmarted us for once." Rubbing his chin, his face taking on a thoughtful look, Jock said, "What about just me going? It is me he wants."

"This is my fight as well, Dad. It's my son he's got. The bastard's not getting away with this. I don't trust him one bit."

Jock accepted with a sharp nod. "Well, shall we do this, then?" He patted Hunter on the arm twice then held his hand there, squeezing his bicep.

Hunter held his dad's eyes. For the first time since this had started, he caught strength burning within them. He could see Jock was ready for the fight. "Let's do it," he responded, setting off.

The three of them started at a jog, Hunter leading the way, the beam of light from his torch bouncing ahead, picking out their path.

"There's a bend just up ahead which goes past an old cottage," announced Budgie between breaths. Once we get to that, I'm going to have to drop back and wait for the others. If I go any further, there's a likelihood Billy will see me, and we can't afford for that to happen. After the cottage, the path goes on for a couple of hundred yards, then you'll come to the Window. Be careful there; the path drops away quite sharply on the left-hand side. The Window is to your right, cut into the rock."

"Got that," said Hunter, and he picked up his pace again. By the time they got to the cottage Budgie had mentioned, Hunter's legs felt heavy as lead; he'd run almost three miles since they had left Hazel Brown's cottage and all at a fair lick.

Budgie eased his pace. "This is where I stop. Be careful, you two. All I can say is I wish you luck."

Hunter bid Budgie a silent goodbye with a quick wave, and he and Jock jogged on. Hunter needed to conserve himself; his energy levels were dropping fast, and he needed to be on top of his game when he confronted Billy.

Sweeping the way ahead with a bright light, Hunter realised they had entered a line of trees. Although he could pick out individual branches as they passed, everything outside the beam was pitch dark, and Hunter realised he needed to be careful. The last thing he wanted was for Billy to take them by surprise, and so he dipped the torch so that the stream of light was only picking out the path ahead.

Thirty seconds later, Hunter and Jock were met by a ferocious gust of wind that took them by surprise. That was quickly followed by a loud roar and a series of crashing noises that Hunter recognised as the sound of the storm-ridden sea. He knew they had now entered the coast path where very soon they would be facing Billy. Recalling what Budgie had warned, Hunter swung the torch left and right, picking out where the path fell away into darkness at his left, and where, to his right, a wall of wet granite made up the steep cliff face that would lead them to the Window in the Rock.

With a degree of trepidation, Hunter pressed forward, ignoring the wind and rain that battered him. He was taking in everything around him, trying his best to pick out any noise above that of the storm. It was eerie.

Suddenly, the torchlight caught the edge of a dark fissure set into the rock and Hunter knew they had found the Window. Taking as wide a berth as possible, he and Jock edged to face it full on, and even though Hunter knew it would leave them exposed, at least this way it put some space between them and the entrance. He swung the beam into the entranceway, but all it met was a black wall. They had no option but to get closer.

As Hunter took a step forward, he held his breath. This is where he wished he had the backup of an armed response unit, but there was no chance of that.

"Come in, you two."

Hunter recognised Billy's voice coming from inside the Window, but he couldn't see him. He lowered the torch to the base of the entrance and peered into the dark hole.

Nothing.

"I said come in. That is, if you want to see your son."

Billy's voice was even more threatening, and Hunter threw a quick glance at Jock and walked towards the dark doorway, stopping at the entrance.

"Dad!"

Hunter heard his son's cry before he saw him. He flashed his torch, and five yards ahead was his son, Billy's hunched body ensnaring Jonathan, one arm curved in front of his neck and the other holding a gun to his head. Both of them pinched their eyes as the powerful beam hit their faces.

"Lower the fucking light, or I shoot him," snarled Billy.

Hunter could see that the pair were perilously close to the back edge of the Window and so instantly dipped the torch, focusing its light below their chests. For a moment he stood transfixed, his head awash with so many things, trying his best to recall everything from his training and experience. For a second his brain was mush, and then hearing Jonathan begin to cry dragged back his thoughts. Just hearing him, even though it was a cry, told him he was alive. He wanted to rush forward, sweep his son up and give him a big hug. His voice quavering, he said, "Let him go, Billy. He's done you know harm. It's us you want."

"Do you think I fucking wanted this? You've caused this! This is about me and your da. I told you not to get involved. This is both your fault."

Hunter lifted the torch slightly to catch a glimpse of Billy's face. The first thing he picked out was the scar that snaked from the bridge of his nose and across his cheek. The other thing Hunter noticed was that Billy's hair was darker, plastered wet to his head, and that he'd shaved off his beard. One thing that hadn't changed was that menacing stare he had. *Total fucking evil.* Hunter judged how many strides it was to him, trying to calculate if he could get to the gun before Billy could pull the trigger. He slowly edged his right foot forward.

Billy pressed the gun harder into Jonathan's head, causing him to yelp. "Stay where you are."

"Dad!" Jonathan called again.

Hunter put up one hand in surrender, leaving the other where it was, so that the torchlight was still covering Billy and his son. "Easy, Billy. Don't do anything silly. I'm staying where I am."

"It's me you want," Jock shouted behind him. "Let my son and grandson go, and then it's just you and me, what do you say?"

A crazed laugh burst from Billy's mouth. "You're fucking dead anyway. Stop cowering behind your son or I'll fucking shoot him before you."

Despite the threat, Hunter saw that the gun was still pressed firmly to his son's head. He needed that to change if Jonathan wasn't to die. Steadying his delivery as best he could, he said, "Billy, it doesn't need to end this way. This is something we can sort out. You know there's no way you're going to get off this island, no matter what plans you think you've made. The entire police force in the UK is looking for you, and the

238

Guernsey Police are already on their way. Just drop the gun, Billy, and I'll put in a good word for you when you go back to prison."

Billy released another burst of demented laughter. "Go back to prison! Course I know I'm going back to prison. I'm not fucking stupid! But I'll also go back to prison knowing the grass that caused me all this grief in the first place will be fucking dead. I've nothing to fucking lose!" His tongue lashed over his bottom lip. "Now, step out from behind your son, Jock, and let me get a good look at you before I kill you!"

Hunter couldn't miss the change that was happening in Billy's face. He had seen the signs a few times in his career. Nothing any of them could say was going to stop Billy from firing that gun. He had to think and move quickly for any of them to get out of this alive.

Suddenly, Billy pulled the gun from Jonathan's head, and although his aim was in Hunter's direction, his eyes went right past him, fixing on Jock. "Do as I say, Jock. Step out where I can see you."

This was Hunter's chance. As calmly as possible, he said, "Jonathan, don't be scared. Remember what I told you about stranger, danger." As he finished his sentence, he sensed movement behind him.

"Let my grandson go, Billy. If you want to kill me, I'm here."

Hunter realised Jock was moving into the firing line, and he saw that Billy had shifted the gun to somewhere beyond his shoulder. Without warning, Hunter yelled, "NOW!" while at the same time throwing up the beam of his powerful Maglite, hitting Billy full in the face, dazzling him.

As Billy fired off a wild shot, everything seemed to unfold in slow motion. Hunter saw Jonathan pull sharply forward and down, exactly as he'd taught him. That caused Billy to lose his balance, releasing his grip around his son's neck. Then, dragging up a leg, Jonathan snapped it back fiercely, ramming Billy on the right shin. Billy yelped as Jonathan half-spun and pushed away with both hands. Jonathan's blow caught Billy full on the chest and he staggered back, firing off another shot that hit the roof, ricocheting away in a shower of sparks. And then, as he fought to gain his balance, his heels caught a lump of granite, and suddenly he was falling backwards, hands clawing at air. A second later, he was tumbling through the opposite gap of the Window, letting out a bloodcurdling scream of panic, and a split-second after that, Billy had dropped out of view, only his terror-stricken call telling them he was still alive. Two seconds later, there was silence.

For a moment Hunter froze, a cluster of stars exploding and dancing at the back of his eyes, and he could hear the roar of blood shooting from one side of his skull to the other. It was only brief; Jonathan's call snapped him out of his trance. Jonathan was running towards him, and he scooped him up in both arms, pulling him into his chest, embracing him. He could feel a flush of tears wash over his eyes as relief overcame him.

"Grandad!"

At first, Hunter thought Jonathan's call was for a hug, but then just as quickly he caught an edge of concern in the tone, and he snapped his look backwards to where he'd last seen Jock. What he saw pulled him up sharply. Jock was lying in a crumpled heap, an arm flung across his chest, blood seeping through his jacket.

# CHAPTER FORTY-SEVEN

Sat in an armchair beside a fire that was down to glowing embers, Hunter cradled a tumbler of whisky, trying his best to unwind but failing miserably. The images from that evening were replaying themselves over and over, refusing to stop, and he was on his second whisky, hoping to dull his jangled nerves.

He looked across to the sofa where Beth and Jonathan lay. They were cuddled together in a throw, Jonathan's head resting in her lap, eyes closed, Beth weaving her fingers through his tumble of dark hair. Hunter studied his son's peaceful look and wondered how he was going to be affected by what had happened. It would be something in the ensuing days, even weeks, that he and Beth would have to monitor and deal with. Beth was better equipped than him to cope — with her skills as a nurse — but he knew he would have to be there for Jonathan as well and give every bit of support he could, no matter how small. He certainly was going to be there when he was interviewed; the police from Guernsey would want to speak to him, that was unavoidable, and that was where he could help best — by ensuring that Jonathan wasn't going to made to feel as if he was to blame for what happened to Billy. He was going to protect him at all costs.

Hunter took another slug of whisky, saw it was almost gone and emptied the glass with another swallow. "Shall we go up?"

Beth lifted her head and offered him a weak smile. "I'm ready if you are. I think Jonathan is."

"I'm not surprised, with what he's been through." Hunter pushed himself up. "I'll just give this glass a quick rinse, put the fireguard up, then I'll be up."

241

Beth nodded, rousing Jonathan with a firm ruffle of his hair. He blearily opened his eyes. "Come on, young man, bedtime," she said.

Jonathan gave a gentle moan and stretched.

Beth pulled the throw off them and began folding it. "Do you mind if I sleep with him tonight?"

"Not at all. It might be best, to be honest."

She approved with a nod. "I'll stick my head round your mum and dad's door and see your dad's all right before I go get my head down."

"Okay." As Hunter headed into the kitchen, an image of Jock lying bleeding in the tunnel of the Window in the Rock burst into his brain, dragging back the awful memories from earlier. When he had rushed and grabbed hold of Jonathan, after Billy had fallen, and then turned and seen Jock lying there, believing him to be dead — that Billy had shot him — he had initially panicked, blood rushing to his head, fighting for breath. But then, after what had seemed like an eternity, Jock had stirred, flashing open his eyes and crying out in pain. Hunter had been so thankful that his quick prayer had been answered.

By the time Budgie and two others had got to them, Jock was sitting up, holding his arm, and a quick examination revealed that although he had a nasty wound to his arm, it wasn't life-threatening or life-changing. He was quickly transported by ambulance to the medical centre, where the doctor discovered that one of the bullets, most probably the one that had ricocheted from the roof, had nicked the top of his left arm. He had been extremely lucky, and seven stitches later, although visibly shaken, he was as almost good as new. Dosed up with painkillers, he was now tucked up in bed.

Billy wasn't, though. They had only been able to do a cursory search because of the conditions and darkness, aiming their torches down the way he'd gone, but there had been no sign of him. They had all come to the conclusion, after he had not answered their calls, that the likelihood was that Billy had met his fate on the rocks at the bottom of the 150-foot drop. No one had displayed any sorrow as they'd decided to call off the search until daybreak. The only thing Hunter had felt sorry about, as he had trooped away, was how all of it was going to affect Jonathan. From the second when he had gathered Jonathan up in his arms and felt his fragile frame trembling as they'd walked away from The Window in the Rock, he hadn't been able to shake off that feeling of utter despair.

Rinsing his glass, staring out through the kitchen window into darkness, Hunter recalled what Beth had said earlier about how kids could be more resilient than adults. In Jonathan's case, he certainly hoped so.

Hunter was awoken by the ring of his mobile. Rolling over, he snatched it up from the bedside table. He looked at the screen before answering. It was Budgie. He answered.

"The cavalry are on their way," he said excitedly.

"What?"

"The storm broke early this morning. I've just taken a call from the Ops Room Inspector on Guernsey. They've commandeered the Lifeboat and one of the ferries and half of Guernsey's police force are on the way over here. Should be with us in forty minutes."

"Too bloody late now," Hunter replied sleepily.

Budgie chuckled. "We don't want to be telling them that. They think they're coming to our rescue."

Tutting loudly, Hunter said, "Talking about rescue, anything about Billy?"

"Nope. Not so far, anyway. I'm at The Window now. A couple of us got down here at first light and started looking for him. We used the old winch that's here. Fastened a rope to it, and one of the lads went down right to the bottom, but there's no sign of him. The tide would have been in last night, so it looks like he's drowned and been washed out to sea. We're going to have to wait for the Lifeboat to get here so we can do a proper search, but with the currents round here, and how rough the sea was last night, he could have been dragged for miles. We might never find his body."

"Well, I have to say, I'll not be shedding a tear at his passing."

"Neither will I, mate."

"With everyone coming from Guernsey, do you need me to come and join you?"

"I wouldn't. You just stay put. You've got enough on your hands. They're going to want to speak with you, obviously, but they're going to be tied up at the Window for a good few hours. And they've got to deal with Hazel Brown."

"Crikey, I'd forgotten about her."

"She's been in a cell in the old prison since we locked her up. I'm told she's not a happy bunny this morning. The place is freezing. Oh, and by the way we found a hammer covered in blood secreted among the woodpile at the back of the cottage she's renting. It looks as though we can nail her for killing Nicholas Strachan."

"Great. That's good news. It's nice to know she'll soon be in a nice warm cell across in Guernsey."

"Certainly will. So, as I say, the team have got enough to be going on with for now. It's my guess they'll not have enough time to speak with any of you today. It'll give you some breathing space at least. I'll give the briefing to whichever gaffer comes with them and help with things down here."

"Thanks, Budgie, that's great." Following a short pause, Hunter said, "I'm concerned about Jonathan."

"I know what you're saying. Look, leave it with me. I'll tell them he's too shook up, given the circumstances, and he's probably going to need at least a couple of days. There's you and your dad they can talk to for now to get what happened."

"That'd be great. I'll make myself available for them, just in case they do have time today, and I'll have a word with Dad when he wakes up. I'm going to send Jonathan and Beth across to her mum and dad's place, just to keep him out of the way for now."

"I understand. Leave it with me to sort. I'll keep you up to date."

"Cheers."

"And I'll see you all tonight."

"Tonight?"

"The Festival of Light. Had you forgotten? They're not going to cancel that, no matter what's gone off. It's one of the highlights of the island. There's a couple of hundred guests paid good money to be part of it. We'll have a riot on our hands if we cancel it." Pausing, Budgie added, "Saying that, if we did cancel it, there's enough cops here now to deal with a riot." Following a short burst of laughter, Budgie ended the call.

Later that day, as the sun started to set, Hunter, Beth, the boys, and both sets of parents joined the large gathering in the square at the end of the village, where the horse and carriage rides normally parked. Hunter guessed, from the numbers squashed together, that most of the islanders were here. He kept looking round for Budgie, or for any of the other Constables, but he couldn't see any of them. He guessed they were still by the Window in the Rock, searching for any sign of Billy. During the day he'd heard the drumming rotors of a police helicopter and seen a glimpse of it flying overhead, but since that early morning call from Budgie he had not heard anything else about what was happening.

Hunter's thoughts were suddenly extinguished when a series of "Oohs" and "Aahs" went up, and then he found himself being forced to one side by the momentum of the crowd around him. As the crowd parted, he got his first picture of what the Festival of Light was all about as he caught sight of a procession of about fifty people marching towards them along the street. Each of the group held aloft a flaming torch, casting a warm orange glow all around. They turned left in unison onto the track to Hogsback, and everyone started to shuffle and press forward, and Hunter soon found himself being dragged along by the crowd, following the torch-bearers. Ten minutes later, tramping along a familiar route, this time in better circumstances, Hunter and his family entered the wide expanse of Hogsback. The majority were heading to where the huge bonfire had been constructed, but a small group of a dozen or so branched away to where the stones of Sark Henge overlooked the sea.

The next minute, Hunter found himself forced back as the crowd reacted to a loud whooshing noise, and a wall of heat reached him through the throng, as gouts of yellow and orange flame shot above them, sending sparks into the night sky. The bonfire had been lit, the spectacle greeted by shouts of delight. Breaking into a smile, Hunter turned to Beth beside him. The radiance from the fire was lighting up her face, and for the first time he saw relief and contentment etched on her features. Seeing that made him feel so much better.

A hand on his shoulder startled him, and he spun around. It was Budgie.

"Made it, then?" Budgie said, pointing towards the bonfire. "Good, isn't it?"

Over Budgie's shoulder, Hunter spotted the group of people who had earlier made their way towards Sark Henge. They were now inside the circle of stones, thrusting hands to the sky in worship. "They're certainly enjoying themselves," Hunter replied, dipping his head.

Budgie glanced around to the Henge. "It's what a lot come for. Same with Stonehenge, I guess."

Hunter nodded thoughtfully. As Budgie returned his gaze, they locked eyes. "How many of the islanders know what's gone off?"

"Everyone, I would have thought. You're quite the celebrities, you know. This will be a conversation piece for years." Budgie let out a chuckle. "But just setting aside all the horrors you've experienced this last ten days, this is still a beautiful island, don't you think?"

Hunter thought for a moment and then had to agree.

# A NOTE TO THE READER

Dear Reader,

It was only a matter of time before the island of Sark featured as a setting in one of my novels. The idea has been inside my head since the Autumn of 1973 when I first heard about it. Back then, as a fifteen-year-old with a dream to be a writer, I frequently visited my Uncle Gordon who was a lover of books with a wonderful imagination for writing, and in front of a blazing coal fire, with only a side light on, we discussed plots, characters and the drafting of a story. One of those discussions centred upon a book I had just read - Agatha Christie's 'And then there were none' (different title back then) especially its setting on a remote island. It was on that note he brought up Sark, filling me in on its history, and how it had no recognised roads, with only horse and cart for transport and no street lamps. At the time, although it was fascinating information, I can remember thinking he was stretching his imagination a little too far. I revisited the thought of using the island 40 years later when I began writing after retirement, and to my surprise I discovered that with the exception that it now had street lamps in its main street the rest of what he had told me was true. However, the opportunity to use it as a location didn't come until the writing of this book; what better location to have Hunter and his family flee to in fear of their lives from a psychopath on the run. I tried to get a feel for the place using Google Earth but somehow it just didn't work, and so in September 2018 I paid the island a visit, whizzing off a couple of emails prior to going there, enquiring through the island's Information Centre if there was anyone I could speak with to aid my research. I got several replies including one from the island's only cop 'Budgie' Burgess, who not only answered my queries on police procedure but volunteered to show me around and introduce me to some of the islanders. I had a wonderful five days there, visited almost every part of the island and came back home with the story firmly cemented in my thoughts. Without doubt, once this pandemic is over, I will be visiting the island again.

Before I close, I would like to express my gratitude to 'Budgie' who gave me a great insight into the policing of the island, how its Parliament works, and for his tour of the Emergency Services HQ. The joined-up practices of the Police, Fire and Ambulance Service there is something our Government should be looking at.

I also thank Beta-readers Claire Knight and Lesley Merrin for their comments.

Note: The Festival of Light does not exist. I created it for the sole purpose of this story.

This is now the sixth book in the series and I hope you have embraced Hunter Kerr and his casework enough to want read more. The next investigation is *Unsolved.* One of the ways you can let me know is by placing a review on **Amazon** or **Goodreads**. And, if you want to contact me, or want me to appear and give a talk about my writing journey at one of the groups you belong to, then please do so through **my website**. It has recently been updated and there are some interesting blogs about writing and Hunter Kerr.

Thank you for reading.

Michael Fowler

**www.mjfowler.co.uk**

**Sapere Books** is an exciting new publisher of brilliant fiction and popular history.

To find out more about our latest releases and our monthly bargain books visit our website:
**saperebooks.com**

Printed in Great Britain
by Amazon

55613848R00142